To Melanie,

GENESIS

Hope you enjoy it!

Colin Barrett

28.4.11

GENESIS

Colin Pallett

Book Guild Publishing
Sussex, England

First published in Great Britain in 2010 by
The Book Guild Ltd
Pavilion View
19 New Road
Brighton, BN1 1UF

Typesetting in Baskerville by
Nat-Type, Cheshire

Printed in Great Britain by
CPI Antony Rowe

A catalogue record for this book is available from
The British Library.

ISBN 978 1 84624 553 4

TO CLAIRE

PROLOGUE

The man in the black suit stood silently, watching the house. Inside, a new life had just been conceived, the life that the stranger had been awaiting for so many years. He smiled to himself in the darkness: the Seals on his prison would soon be broken and he could finally return to the world.

Leaning back, he exhaled deeply, the breath continuing for far longer than seemed possible. An inky black cloud rolled from his lungs, swirling shapelessly around him. It was huge, a shade of pure darkness the size of a small town.

'Watch over him,' commanded the stranger quietly. 'Make sure nothing too unpleasant happens to him.'

At these words, the dark shifted. It covered the small cottage, turning and twisting before rising slowly into the air to become a patch of black against the night sky.

The stranger reached up and removed the glasses he always wore. Looking down, he absently cleaned them with a corner of his suit jacket. Raising his head, he stared unblinkingly at the house, blood-red eyes burning brightly in the sockets as if lit by an internal fire. In one smooth motion, he replaced the glasses, shielding the world from those eyes.

'They'll hate you, boy,' he whispered. 'You will be a man apart and you will grow all the stronger because of it. Of that, I promise you.'

Inside the building, the woman got out of bed to fetch a cup of water from the pitcher on the window sill. There was no need for light as she poured herself a small drink.

Movement caught her eye and she peered into the night, expecting to see a fox. A man was watching her from a matter of yards away, lit only by the stars and the moon. It was impossible to tell anything about him but she shivered all the same at some nameless dread.

As she leaned further forward, the man lifted his hand and touched a finger to his brow in greeting. Despite everything she found herself repeating the gesture. But the stranger was already gone.

1

The midwife stood up. She was covered in blood, a single drop of which ran down the length of her forearm to hang momentarily from her elbow until it dripped unseen to the bare earth floor.

'I have done all I can, you'd better send one of the girls to fetch Chara.'

The father-to-be sought out the woman's eyes. She glanced at him before shaking her head and wiping the worst of the blood from her hands. His expression darkened as he digested her words but he knew that the point was well made. The blood loss meant that without the aid of the witch, she and the baby would die.

'Time is short, Varinas,' said the midwife, a middle-aged woman of nearly forty winters who had delivered over eighty babies and lost only six, a figure of which she was rightly proud. 'I would rather this child did not die, but the decision is yours to make.'

'That's right!' he snapped. His dark eyes seemed almost black in the candlelight and Shruna shrugged, indifferent to his anger. Varinas' gaze swung around his one-roomed house, barely seeing the familiar scene of poverty in which he and his family existed: the fire pit in the centre of the room with the open chimney above, along with the scattered belongings of six people living in cramped conditions. Eventually his stare fell on his four daughters who were all trying to hide behind one another with the result that the eldest, a nine-year-old called Esra, was pushed to the front.

The silence began to stretch out as Varinas contemplated his decision. A soft moan of pain from his barely conscious wife made him glance her way. He suppressed a cry of despair as he saw her condition. The whitening skin glistened with crimson and her cheeks were hollow through blood loss and malnutrition. The lines of her face seemed extenuated in the light from the fire, made harsh by her pain and the daily toil of survival.

'Esra!' he hissed angrily. 'Go to the witch and tell her we need her. Do it now!'

The girl nodded and scampered off to do as she was told. Without her, the three younger siblings tried to lose themselves in the shadows of the house to escape the glare of their father.

'She is not welcome in my home,' rumbled Varinas ominously as Shruna wiped the perspiration from the mother's forehead with a tattered rag soaked with the woman's blood. When the midwife made no reply, Varinas repeated his assertion more loudly and accompanied his words with an angry thump of his fist into the flat of his other hand.

'I heard you the first time,' said Shruna wearily. 'You are no different from all the others; you hate her and yet at the first sign of trouble you all go running to her, begging for her aid. And afterwards, words of thanks? No, just more bitterness and resentment that you had to ask at all.'

'I will not be so spoken in my own home and by a woman at that! Leave now!'

'Oh, Varinas,' said a voice from the doorway. 'Must you be this way all the time?'

Varinas and Shruna both turned to see Chara stood at the threshold, blocking what light remained to the day. Her age was unknown to any in the village, for the elders claimed that when their grandparents were small Chara had been there and that when they were gone, she would remain. The witch inspired a mix of terror and hatred in the people she lived amongst but seemed totally oblivious to the tension which always accompanied her presence. Despite her evident age, she carried herself with great dignity, for her back was still straight and her eyes burned with an almost feral intelligence. Many strong men over the years had shrunk back from her gaze and Varinas was by no means the toughest. He dutifully muttered something and averted his stare.

'I pray entreat into thine home, Varinas,' said the witch, giving the formal greeting which was required for a guest to enter another's house. To refuse to acknowledge or deny entry was considered ill manners of the worst kind and violence had been known to occur when visitors had been treated discourteously. Even so, for a split second it looked as if Varinas would refuse her, but a sob from his wife reminded him of his troubles.

'Entreat no more,' said Varinas, every word drawn from him with an almost physical effort. He tried once more to meet the witch's eyes but could not hold them and completed the sentence with a barely audible, 'friend.' He drew in a deep breath. 'And I pray you enter.'

The witch nodded at Varinas and walked inside, Esra slipping in unnoticed behind her.

As she passed Shruna, the midwife bowed slightly in a display of respect which Chara returned with a smile. The witch stroked the back of her hand along Shruna's cheek. 'Dear child, even as a youngster you were one of my favourites, a willingness to help others that many would do well to learn from.'

'My wife is dying,' interrupted Varinas angrily. 'Will you do nothing for her?'

'I will do more for her this day than you have ever done in your entire miserable life, Varinas. You were always a small man and your wife would have done a lot better without you. Get out of my way and let me see if I can save her and the child.'

Varinas was brushed aside and Chara approached the unconscious woman who was wedged on the high-backed birthing stool. Her legs were slightly apart and were heavily stained with blood, as was the ragged dress which had been pushed up to her waist. Chara placed one hand on the pregnant woman's distended stomach and put the other to her temple. Turning inwards, the witch gathered her will before guiding it into the woman for whose life she was now responsible. The other sights and sounds in the house faded into the background as she concentrated until it was as if she were floating free and alone.

There! The life force of the mother was weakening rapidly but there was an inner strength Chara found which was so strong she almost recoiled from it. This went far further than the usual self-preservation and desire for life that all living things had within them, it was almost palpable and yet ... Chara gave a sudden yelp of pain and snatched her hands back, her eyes coming open to focus on whatever damage had been wreaked on her fingers. The skin was already blistering and Chara stared at them in wonder, the pain merely highlighting the strangeness of the situation.

Shruna was at her side, a protective arm draped around the witch's shoulder.

'Mistress! Are you all right? Are you hurt?'

'Hush child,' replied Chara easily. 'I had a funny turn, it is of no consequence.' Shaking her head a little, Chara removed Shruna's hand and returned her attention to the patient.

With her face averted, none of the others saw the look which had settled on the witch's face. Never in all her considerable years had she felt such a power contained within a body. The essence which was sustaining the woman's life, however, was not coming from her but from the unborn child. Undoubtedly the child had the Power but even with this great gift if he was not born he would soon die.

Standing upright with vigour, Chara began unpacking a selection of herbs from small hessian bags tied to her belt.

'I need a mixing pot,' she said shortly, and instantly Shruna searched for one and handed the witch a grimy wooden bowl that Chara barely glanced at. Instead, she poured several coloured powders into it and stirred them with her hand. Opening her own water flask, she poured a few drops in until she had a dark red salve which she smeared across her fingers, all the time murmuring an incantation under her breath.

'Hurry damn you!' shouted Varinas from behind the witch.

'Your wife is dead,' replied Chara abruptly. 'All that matters is the boy.'

'Dead?' muttered Varinas, who took a step back as if he'd been struck. 'But she's my …' The words trailed off and he buried his face in his hands.

'Grief is a luxury we cannot afford just yet, Varinas, we still have a chance to save your son.'

The father looked up and wiped his face. 'What use is a son to me now?' he asked, and walked from the house.

'Should I go after him?' asked Shruna quietly as she followed the man with her eyes.

'Forget Varinas. Come here and hold her steady for me.'

Shruna frowned. 'I thought you said she was dead.'

'She is. Just not yet.' Catching the look Shruna shot her she added, 'The blood loss is terminal, there is nothing I can so, all we have is a chance to save the child.'

She drew in a deep breath and inserted her lotion-covered hands gently into the mother's vagina. The mixture coated the birth canal and with the merest hint of magic, the muscles stretched back revealing the legs of the breech birth.

Chara took a hold of the baby and pulled, slowly at first and then harder until over half the child was free of its mother.

'Damn!' she hissed suddenly. Her fingers probed deeper inside and an expression of consternation overtook her.

'What is it?' asked Shruna, the fear evident in her tone. Seeing the witch so obviously on edge was a new experience for the midwife and not one for which she cared.

'The cord is around his neck.' The witch withdrew her hands and, ignoring the residue on them, pulled out a small knife which she kept in a hidden sheath along her forearm. Without pause, she cut the woman's pelvic floor from the opening of the vagina to the anus. The mother gave no more than a soft sigh at this intrusion and her spirit left her body, as not even the great will of the baby could chain her to the mortal world any longer.

Casting the knife aside, Chara pulled the baby from its mother and quickly, yet with a tenderness which belied her gruff exterior, unwound the umbilical cord from around its neck. Holding the child, she struck it on the rear sharply and at once its cries echoed loudly in the home, a joyous sound which carried to the ears of Varinas outside, who appeared at the doorway but did not enter.

'It is a wonder he survived,' said Shruna cautiously. 'I have lost several when they become so entangled.'

The witch did not reply immediately but held the infant to her chest and wrapped her shawl around him. His face was screwed up tightly and he grabbed at Chara's finger, his small fist wrapping itself around it. His eyes were closed and his sobs had subsided, but still Chara held him.

'Come here, girls,' said the witch. 'Come and see your baby brother.'

At once the four girls scrambled to Chara's side, their normal hesitancy in her presence abandoned in their desire to be the first to hold the child.

'I'm the eldest,' said Esra primly. 'I should hold him first,' and she held her arms open to receive the baby.

'No, my dear,' said Chara. 'I think your father should be first.'

Varinas walked inside and approached the witch. He stared blankly at her for a second before passing her and taking a hold of his dead wife's hand. Kneeling down, he adjusted her clothing to hide the damage that the birth had caused and then buried his face in her unresisting shoulder.

'What's the matter with mother?' asked Fride, the youngest of the girls.

Shruna stepped past Chara and swept the child up into her arms. 'You've got to be brave now Fride, and more grown up than you've ever been before. Do you think you can do that for me?' The girl nodded and the woman continued, 'Your mother is at peace now, she rests with God who has called her back to His side. But this is not just a time to be sad, for now you have a brother who needs your help and your love.'

The children had gathered around both women, torn between their need to see their mother and their new sibling.

'No!' roared Varinas, surging to his feet and baring down angrily on the midwife. 'I will not have that … thing in my house! Take the devil child and go, he has robbed me of the only thing I had which made life worth living!'

'What of your children, Varinas?' said Shruna levelly. 'Do they mean so little to you?'

Varinas glanced at the girls who had shied away from the sudden outburst of anger. 'No, that's not what I meant. None of them killed my wife, I …' he stammered to a halt and turned his back.

'Your son needs you, Varinas, do not lose him this day as well as your wife.'

Varinas did not look at Chara when he replied, his voice even and devoid of any emotion. 'I have no son. Now the pair of you will leave while the girls and I say our goodbyes.'

Chara said nothing and walked from the house still clutching the child to her breast. Shruna gathered the few things to herself which she had brought with her and then made to leave. As she reached the door she said, 'Think on this choice you have made, Varinas, and pray it is the right one.'

'I thank you for your help, Shruna, although it seems I shall need it no more.'

Shruna nodded slowly, then left to catch up with Chara.

The two women walked together in silence, covering the distance to the witch's house quickly. She lived in the village, although there was an obvious gap between where the rest of the people built their houses and where Chara had hers, but this did not seem to overly concern her. When they reached her path she nodded to Shruna to go ahead and open the door, which the midwife duly did. Inside, the witch lowered herself into her favourite chair in front of the hearth and continued to stare at the babe she held in her arms. Shruna was closer to the witch than any, but even she had never witnessed such a profound alteration in her behaviour as she was seeing now. The harsh lines on her face were softer and she looked younger as she nursed the child.

'What is it you see, my dear?' asked Chara without turning her head.

Shruna laughed gently. 'How is it that you knew I was watching you?'

'What else is there to look at? You have been inside my home before and nothing much has changed since your last visit except that now we have this boy to keep us company.'

Shruna walked around so that she was directly before the witch and crouched down, touching the baby tenderly as she did so.

'Do you think Varinas will change his mind?'

'Who?' asked Chara distractedly.

Shruna frowned but pressed on regardless. 'I mean, it was obvious that he was distressed at his wife's death and that he is placing the blame onto the child, but with time he will see that punishing his son is only making the situation worse. We both know that the boy will be much better off with his family.'

'Do we?' said Chara vaguely. 'Varinas is a truly unpleasant man, even for these parts, and I have no doubt that the best thing, given the circumstances, is for us to find a suitable home for this child away from him. Perhaps even away from the village.'

Shruna recoiled with horror. 'Mistress! Have you any idea of what you are saying? If Varinas finds out that you have sent his son away without his permission he will pursue the matter with the Council and you know how much Headman Forme hates you! It would make his day if he could make proper charges stick against you and he would push for your exile.'

Chara chuckled. 'You get so far ahead of yourself sometimes my dear Shruna. Have no fear for me, I was looking after myself before your grandparents had learnt to walk. Forme has no power over me.'

'But he could see to it that you were driven from the village. Do you not remember what happened to the witch from Grissford last autumn! They say she screamed most awfully when they burnt her and all because a couple of cows got sick! Imagine what they might do if they thought you had put a child in danger.'

Fixing Shruna in a steely gaze, Chara spoke slowly and evenly and yet with an undercurrent of power that was one of the many reasons she had prospered over the years despite those who feared and despised her.

'Listen to me. The world does not begin and end with this village; it is a vast place with sights and sounds that you could not even begin to imagine. If I must go to safeguard this boy then that is what I will do, for have no doubts, this boy is special. I do not know how exactly, but I feel it and I have never been so sure of anything in my life when I say that this child will leave a mark on history that will live on through the ages. Men will one day speak of him with awe and I will not allow him to live out his days here with people like Varinas or Forme stopping him from reaching his potential.'

Shruna was stunned by the intensity of the words and could make no reply for several seconds. Eventually she said, 'He has the male gift then, is that what you are saying?'

'Aye that he has,' replied Chara, returning her attention to the baby on her lap. 'And it runs stronger in him than I have ever felt. He practically glows with magic and despite my tough words, Shruna, it will be him, not me, who forges his way regardless of how others try to hold him back.'

'There are always those who would exploit a magic user of any level, let alone one who is as strong as you are suggesting.'

'True enough, which is why he must be kept safe until he has come of age and is ready to make his own way.' She gestured at the fireplace and the stack of wood. 'Get the flames going, my dear, I feel the cold of the night ever more as I grow older.'

Over the next hour, Shruna lit the fire and prepared a light meal for herself and Chara out of what the witch had to hand in her larder. The baby was still asleep on the witch's lap and showed no signs of opening his eyes just yet. The moon was casting its light down on the world by the time Shruna had finished eating and the softer sounds of the night were filtering through. Away to the south, there was the hooting of an owl and close to the cottage's rear wall Shruna heard the noise of animals moving in the undergrowth as she closed the window and drew the curtains.

'The sky is clear, it will be a chilly night,' she said to Chara.

The witch nodded slowly in agreement. 'There is plenty of

wood, it will last us.' For the first time in nearly an hour she looked up and glanced at the bread and cheese Shruna had prepared for her and that she hadn't eaten. 'That was kind of you, my dear, but I think we should conserve our food.'

Shruna sat down in the only other chair and faced the witch. Both women's expressions were neutral and Shruna mentally prepared herself for some verbal jousting.

'Do I take it from that you have come to a decision?'

'I have.'

'And I can tell I'm not going to like it.'

'Life is unrewarding without challenges, Shruna. Without adversity we do not grow either as people or as a society. Only by facing difficult problems do we learn how to overcome them.'

'That may be true mistress, but it does not mean that we should go looking for obstacles merely so as we can think ourselves better for getting over them,' pressed Shruna.

Chara sighed. 'Perhaps, but if we turn from them all then one day we may discover that we have nowhere to go and that we are hemmed in on all sides by difficulties we shirked rather than faced.'

'So, what is this challenge which you have set out for us?'

'We are going to take this child from the village before dawn tomorrow and disappear into the world. He will grow up far from Varinas and this village and shall concentrate on learning to use his talents as befits a magi. We shall look after him until the day comes when he is strong enough to do it for himself, and after that? Who can say.'

'You know I would follow where you lead mistress but have you really thought this through?'

'I have done nothing but think about it ever since I laid my hands on his mother's belly.'

'How long has it been since you looked after a baby, mistress? Ten years, twenty, a hundred? How will we feed him and keep news of our departure a secret from Varinas?

Where will we go?' The questions tumbled out of Shruna as she thought of a new life away from the only home she had ever known.

'I have visited many other towns and villages over the years, Shruna. We will find refuge, have no fear of that. As for pursuers, I don't think we really need worry about things like that. No one will care that I have gone and Varinas will not miss a son he doesn't even take as his own.'

'You may be being over-confident, mistress. Varinas is still the child's father regardless of what he says now, and when he hears that we have taken his only male heir he may well decide that we tricked him and that he does want him after all.'

'We can ford that stream when we come to it. For now we have other concerns. You mentioned feeding the baby and that must be our next concern. Go to the front room and open my herbal cupboard. On the third shelf down you will see seven bags tied with string. The bag second from the right; bring it to me,' ordered Chara.

Shruna inclined her head and went to do as she was bid. Moments later she returned, clutching the small herb bag in her left hand.

'Pour it into the water on the table.'

Shruna smiled thinly as she saw the cup of freshly boiled water sat on the table. It hadn't been there when she had left the room and Chara gave no indication that she had moved and the baby was still asleep. But Shruna had seen the witch produce far larger shows of power than this and let it go. She stirred the white powder into the water and took the cup over to Chara.

'It's not for me, it's for you.'

Shruna eyed the steaming mixture and then looked at Chara. 'What is it?'

'It will do something inside your body that normally requires you to have given birth.'

'What, exactly?'

'Drink that and by the morning you body will have begun lactating and we can feed the boy. I'm afraid I cannot do it, my body is ...' she paused. 'Different to yours.'

When Shruna made no move to drink the potion Chara added, 'Of course I cannot make you do it and I realise what it is I am asking. You will be making yourself a part of this baby's life, and once that is done, it will be difficult to reverse it.'

Shruna did not reply and instead drank the fluid as quickly as its temperature would allow. 'Tastes like milk,' she said eventually.

'Well it would, wouldn't it? Now you should get some sleep, you can use my bed.'

'What will you do?'

'I'll make the preparations for our little trip and keep an eye on the boy here.'

Shruna nodded and turned to go, but then stopped. 'There was something else I think we should sort out today.'

'And what is that?'

'The child's name. I have given it some thought and now that we have decided to make ourselves his family we have a duty to name him. Since I shall be his surrogate mother, perhaps I should do it.' The witch made no response and Shruna pressed onwards. 'I would like to call him after you.'

'You don't think that it would be confusing to have the two of us run to you when you call?' she replied lightly.

'I meant for him to take the male form of your name,' replied Shruna, the merest hint of exasperation to her tone.

'Is that your wish, mother?'

Shruna did not flinch as she heard the title and accepted her future with strength and dignity. 'It is.'

The witch turned her gaze once more to the infant. 'Then so be it. The world shall hear and know this boy's name in the years to come.' She gently rubbed the sleeping child with her hands. 'My beautiful little Chard, rest, for tomorrow is a big day.'

After a poor night's sleep, plagued by thoughts of what the morning would bring, Shruna emerged from Chara's bedroom looking tired. The witch on the other hand did not appear to be any the worse for missing an entire night's rest and had packed what she believed to be the necessary provisions for their trip, abandoning most of her possessions in the process.

'It never ceases to amaze me just how much clutter one seems to collect over the years.' She picked up a clay flower vase and showed it to Shruna. 'This was made for me about sixty years ago by a potter whose son I cured of smallpox. He was very grateful.' Sighing, she placed it on the table. 'So very few of them are, and now I have to abandon it, which just seems such a waste.'

'Was the potter a good man?'

'Oh yes, one of the nicest I have ever known. He used to invite me to his house to share meals on more occasions than I can care to recall, which I believe his wife was less than happy about. I didn't always go but I did sometimes, and those moments hold a place in my memories.'

'If he was a kind man, then he would have understood.'

Chara turned from the table and the vase. 'You're probably right, my dear. Now let's have a look at you!' She ran her eyes over the woman, a process Shruna found embarrassing.

'What are you looking at?' she asked.

'Your shoulders. I've made this sling for the baby to hang it around you and I just wanted to know how much slack to put on it. It's more than likely fine, but when we rest tonight you must tell me if it is rubbing or uncomfortable in any way and I'll see what I can do.'

Shruna looked towards the baby, who was propped up in the witch's chair, hardly making a sound or a move.

'Chard seems quiet.'

'I put a small charm on him so that the hunger wasn't too bad for him, but the little wizard has waited long enough and now you must feed him.'

'Has it been long enough for me?'

'Ample time,' said Chara brightly. 'You're his mother now, Shruna, go to your son and nurse him.'

Shruna looked at Chara who, after only the tiniest of eye contact, averted her gaze. For the witch to do such a thing was unheard of and the importance of what they were doing suddenly and abruptly came crashing down on Shruna's shoulders – so much so that she almost lost her balance.

Drawing a breath and crossing the few feet that separated her from the baby, she scooped him up in her arms. The child opened his eyes and looked at her before the effort became too great and he closed them once more.

'He's beautiful,' said Shruna, tears flowing freely down her face. 'I have delivered many and seen the joy they bring but I never thought that I ...' she broke off.

'Beautiful and hungry, Shruna, do not forget that,' said Chara, some of the old edge returning to her voice.

Smiling, Shruna unbuttoned her blouse and held the child to her breast where he proceeded to suckle noisily. 'You're right,' she said happily, and sat down slowly in the now empty seat so as not to disturb the baby.

'I'll just check on a few things,' said Chara quietly, but Shruna gave no indication that she had heard and the witch slipped noiselessly from the room. At the door which led to the kitchen she paused and glanced back. She had no doubt that once Varinas was aware that they had left the village, he would want his son back, but right now all was well and the baby was safe.

Outside, the pre-dawn chill made her draw her shawl

tighter. She knew she was getting too old for this and that she should probably have put her feet up by now, but then she hadn't reckoned on finding this child. Her gaze took in her small cottage with its run-down appearance and she gave a rueful smile. Well, this certainly wasn't the place she'd pictured herself dying when she was younger but then, was anywhere? There were people she would genuinely miss, but then the flipside of that was that she was allowing herself the chance to make new friends in a new area where perhaps people were slightly more understanding. That thought made her laugh quietly as she realised it made her sound like a maiden who knew nothing of the world rather than the hard-bitten old so-and-so she actually was, but just for that second it was pleasant to suppose it was possible.

'No,' she said softly. 'The time has come to move on. Memories are not linked to houses of wood and stone but locked inside the heart, and I am lucky to be able to look back on experiences both good and bad, for it is that which makes us whole.'

By the time she returned to Shruna, the midwife had finished feeding the baby and was nursing him back to sleep.

'He was very hungry,' she said, without looking up.

'I daresay he was. Would you like anything before we go, you're eating for two now after all.'

'No, we mustn't waste time. Who knows how quickly word of what has happened will spread around the village. Best to put some distance between us and them before they realise we've gone.'

The witch nodded. 'I thought so too, so I hadn't made you anything.' Shruna glanced up and the two women chuckled at the joke.

Gathering together what they could comfortably carry, they left the house.

With her breath steaming in the air Shruna asked, 'Are you sad to leave so much behind mistress?'

Chara shook her head. 'No, not really. I am sadder that this boy has to start out this way but it is better he come with us than die a little every day here with men like Varinas who would see his talent as reason to despise him.'

'You believe his powers would show themselves regardless of what we do?'

The witch shrugged. 'Nothing is ever absolute, and male magic is not my strong point, but I think it highly likely. God had a reason for putting so much potential into one boy; I can't see Him forgetting about Chard, even if men would do so.'

'What about all of your herbs and spell components? They may fall into the wrong hands.'

'I have taken a few of the rarer mixes, but mostly the plants I need are to hand. Anyone who could find a purpose for most of my herbs would be helping, not hurting, but I can't see people voluntarily entering the home of a wicked old witch no matter if they thought she wasn't there.'

'That's probably even worse than sneaking in when you're at home. Never know what you might stumble across or into.'

Chara still had her hand resting on the door handle and slowly released it. She held her hand out to Shruna and the two women turned their backs on the cottage and walked silently through the shadows towards Shruna's own abode.

They made their way without seeing a soul, although a few lights were beginning to flare in some of the houses as the dawn approached. When they reached the midwife's home they entered like thieves and this time it was Shruna who gathered the minimum of essentials and Chara who looked after the boy. Like most people, Shruna had not acquired much in the way of material possessions, and apart from a couple of blankets and some warm clothes there was little that was needed.

Less than ten minutes later they stole their way from the house and walked from the village. Neither woman looked back.

2

Varinas made his way towards the building which sat in the centre of the village. Sometime around midday he had heard the news but had allowed the implications to stir around in his mind for several hours before coming to a decision. At first he had been relieved that the child was now physically apart from him as well as emotionally, but as the hours dragged by his relief turned to anger that he had been denied the chance to raise his son as he saw fit. Worst of all, it was the woman Chara that had stolen him away in the night like some kind of fugitive, for a life of God alone knew what. His wife was barely cold in the ground and now he had suffered a double blow by losing his only chance for an heir. Well, he'd see about that! He certainly wasn't going to spend the rest of his days a subject of ridicule around the village just because of a damn witch.

Stepping inside the hall, Varinas slowed his pace as he approached the door which opened onto the main chamber where village gatherings were held. He took a breath and mentally prepared what he was going to say to Headman Forme. Opening the door, he marched in, his chin up and eyes ready to meet any that looked at him.

At the far end of the hall sat Headman Forme, an old man with a balding head and deep lines across his face. Aged over fifty, his shoulders were large and his arms still strong, for there was no soft work for him; the farms beckoned every day and other duties only overtook them when the sun had gone down.

Flanking him on either side were two other men, both younger than him but with the same look of men who had worked the land their entire lives. There was no slacking in the brutal world of subsistence farming and any infringement on the time of the headman and his advisers had better be worthwhile.

'Ah, Varinas,' said Forme, his tone neutral. 'We've been expecting you.'

'Headman,' replied Varinas, giving a small nod in recognition. 'Shrinen, Henth,' he added to each of the advisers who nodded back.

'I think we have a fair idea of what it is you have to say, Varinas, but nonetheless I believe we should still hear it from you in your own words.'

'Thank you, sir.' Varinas paused, unsure of how to proceed, and decided to launch headlong into it. 'My newborn son has been taken from me by that bitch Chara and I want him back.'

Forme gave a slight laugh. 'To the point anyway,' he said to the men either side of him. 'How do you know this to be so?' he asked Varinas.

'Because I saw her carry him from my house last evening when he was only minutes old.'

'So why didn't you stop her?' cut in Shrinen, a tough man who's attitude to Chara was well known.

'My mind was …' He paused, trying to find a way of saying what needed to be said without it reflecting too badly on him. 'Confused. My wife was newly dead and I blamed the child for my loss which today I can see was wrong. It was Chara and Shruna who could not save her and now they have taken from me my only son.'

'Did you name him?' asked Henth, leaning forward slightly.

Varinas hesitated and when he saw the look that the men opposite shared, he realised that he had delayed too long and that lying was out of the question.

'I did not,' he said eventually, and stared at his feet.

Henth let out his breath through clenched teeth. 'For God's sake, Varinas, what were you thinking? Throwing a baby to a witch is one thing, not naming him is another!'

Varinas knew the law well enough: it was every man's duty to name his son before the day of his birth was ended and to fail to do so was a serious crime. By allowing another to fulfil this task he had made himself less of a man and less of a parent in the eyes of the men seated in front of him as well as the law.

'Then I don't really see what it is that we can do for you, Varinas,' said the headman. 'You should have come to us last night and then perhaps we could have done something, but now …' Forme allowed the sentence to trail off.

Varinas glanced from one dispassionate face to the next and realised that he was in danger of being dismissed, so he gambled. 'I am willing to go after them myself if needs must,' he said defiantly.

'Out of the question,' said Forme abruptly. 'There is no one available to see to your land or your girls.'

'Remember your duty to the village, Varinas,' put in Shrinen.

'All I am asking …'

'We are aware of what it is you are asking and the answer is no,' interrupted Forme. He stood up, signalling an end to the conversation. Then he sighed and said in a somewhat kinder voice, 'You are still quite young, Varinas, there is no reason why you cannot re-marry and have more sons. Wait until the grieving period is over and then we shall see what we can do. I can do no more, no matter what I might personally think about the situation. I have to put the good of the village first and we need you here.'

'Thank you for your time, headman,' said Varinas, and nodded to each of the advisers before walking from the room, his anger building with every step.

When he had gone, Henth turned to Forme. 'Think he'll do anything stupid?'

Forme stared at the space Varinas had recently occupied and slowly shook his head. 'He'll rant and rave at any who will listen but he'll do as he's told. He doesn't really have the intelligence for anything else. Soon as possible, we'd better find him another wife and then he can put this ridiculous episode behind him.'

'Pity really,' said Shrinen. 'If he'd done things properly we would have finally had a reason to be rid of Chara once and for all.'

'Well she's gone anyway,' replied Forme. 'Although I must say I think it's odd that she left so suddenly just because of a child.'

'Who knows what goes on in the mind of a witch?' said Shrinen dismissively.

Forme nodded again but did not reply.

The first day, Chara and Shruna travelled south through the vast flatlands of Northern Rostike, eager to put as much distance as they could between them and the village as soon as possible. They had to stop every now and again for rest and food but it was Shruna who noted just how out of breath she was, whereas Chara seemed fairly dismissive of the hardships they faced. The child suckled regularly and slept well, almost sensing the urgency of their situation and endeavouring to do all he could to aid them.

Days turned into weeks and still they walked, keeping from the main roads and shunning human contact whenever they did happen upon a village. Shruna began to question the wisdom of this for she was deeply weary and longed to rest, but could not find the words to voice her concerns – and so they walked.

One evening they made camp amongst some trees and

had lain down beside the fire when Chara stood and began to pace slowly along the edge of the flames. Shruna watched her, holding the sleeping baby to her chest, keeping him warm and rocking him gently when she felt him stir. Seeing Chara anything but serene despite troubles which would reduce most to self-pity was an unusual sight and she opened her mouth to speak.

'Something troubles you, mistress,' she said matter of factly. 'That much is clear and yet I can see no reason for us to be downhearted, for our circumstances have not changed this day from the last. To see you so uncomfortable distresses me and Chard. Will you not share your misgivings?'

Chara stopped and gave a half-hearted smile. 'You are right as ever, my dear, I awoke this morning after a poor night's sleep and dreams that even in the daylight hours still make me shiver when I dwell on them.'

'Premonitions mistress? I thought you put little faith in such things?'

'Indeed I do not, they're for the mad who think they see God when they've been drinking or priests who want to control their flocks, and have little relevance to true witchcraft. Yet they were so real, so exact in their details and repeated whenever my eyes closed. I tried to stay awake a couple of hours before the dawn but every time I closed my eyes, there they were, always there.'

'*What* were there?' asked Shruna quietly.

There was a pause before the reply, Chara's stare somewhere in the distance, her face totally masking her feelings. 'Not anything of substance, not flesh and blood but more like emotions made visible. I could almost taste what hate would be had it a shape. I could feel what terror must be like and I was sure I could see evil.' The witch shook her head slightly and sighed deeply. 'I must be getting sentimental in my old age; such things would never have bothered me in my youth.'

'These things, you believe they are a threat to us, to the child?'

'I don't know, my dear, I really don't. I can hardly imagine what they mean in general let alone to us in particular but I cannot help but wonder if they are not somehow linked to the boy, for I was never plagued by these dreams until he came.'

Shruna sought out the witch's eyes with her own. 'You mean this has been going on for some time?'

'Since the night he was born, but never this strong. I have dismissed it for longer than I should and may have put us all in danger for my foolishness.'

'But how can you say that, mistress? What have we to fear from dreams?'

Chara sat back down on her blankets and stirred the fire with a stick. Sparks and ash rose in the air as the witch stared into the flames, her gaze following errant wisps of smoke as they wavered in the still night air.

'More than there is to know, and then again perhaps nothing. I do not know, but for the first time in my whole life, I fear sleep.' With that the old woman turned her back and settled down for the night.

Chara awoke feeling restless; it was as if she hadn't slept, such was the tension across her back and shoulders. She sighed quietly. Perhaps she really was getting too old for all of this. Reaching out for the stick to stir the ashes, she saw it wasn't there. Pausing, the witch looked up at her surroundings and noticed the subtle differences which had been screaming at her since she awoke but she had somehow ignored. The world was grey and still, no sounds came from the dark undergrowth and no light shone in the grey sky. Standing, the witch was not surprised to see that her body lay in the same position she had fallen asleep in and that her ethereal form was lit with a curious red glow. Had it been possible, her soul would have sighed, but air was for mortals, not eternal life forces driven by magic. How many years since she had freed her soul from the confines of the flesh and soared the solar winds, marvelling at all she saw? She had given it up not because she no longer found it as enjoyable but because her magic was waning and it taxed her more than she cared to recover from and left her weak for days. Yet this was different; she had not voluntarily drifted from her body but rather had been pulled to this netherworld by a force she could not recognise but could feel all around her.

Stretching muscles that did not exist to ease tension she couldn't feel, Chara let her spirit go and instantly rose hundreds of feet into the night sky, leaving her small camp far below her. It was decades since she'd felt this much magic and she literally shone with it! Red sparks crackled across her body, randomly earthing into the grey soil far below. It was like being young again and Chara could feel herself becoming swept away in the euphoria of the moment.

She pulled up suddenly and mentally berated herself – this was not her doing, there was male magic afoot and she knew that it was not a part of her and could never be so. Searching with her spirit eyes she saw what she had dreamed these many long weeks but could not pinpoint, the shapeless mass of emotions always just on the periphery of her sight. A tangled mass of blackness, which stood out vividly against the grey of the sky, seemed to almost surround her. It burned with magic of such a magnitude that Chara tried to retreat from it lest it draw power from her own spirit, but wherever she flew it was always there, hungry yet waiting.

Looking down, Chara could just about make out the land but it was shrouded in mist and even as she watched it wavered out of focus and vanished. The blackness was everywhere: above, below, all around, and Chara shuddered in sudden fear. Many were the stories of junior magi losing their bodies and forgetting the world of the flesh when they first learnt how to fly. Bodies just left by their owners to wither and die, for without the soul, what is the body? She gathered her will and faced the nameless dark.

'I will return to my body for witchcraft has no reason to mix with wizardry.'

The silence remained and seemed to echo in her ears, it was as if the blackness of the night could hear her but merely chose not to answer. A shift in the pattern of the dark appeared to indicate some form of movement and Chara peered deeply into it but could see nothing. Shaking her head slightly the witch turned her back and flew toward where she thought her body to be.

Behind her retreating spirit the dark could almost be said to have a shape, but whatever it may have been it made no attempt to follow.

Chara awoke to see the worried face of Shruna above her. The midwife was holding a cloth to the witch's forehead and wiping away beads of sweat that had formed there. The suddenness of Chara's return to consciousness took the younger woman by surprise and she pulled back as the witch sat up.

'Praise God!' she said as she clutched at her chest, the shock setting her pulse racing.

Chara sat up and gently took the damp rag from Shruna's unresisting fingers and wiped away the last of the night from her face. 'I'm sorry if I startled you, my dear, I had a most disagreeable evening's sleep.'

Shruna smiled weakly. 'A disagreeable day's sleep I think you mean, mistress.'

'What do you …' Chara stopped as she saw the position of the sun. 'It is gone noon,' she said, mainly to herself. 'Yet I hardly closed my eyes.'

'Mistress?' said Shruna softly.

At the sound of the baby Chara stood up and walked to where he lay, protected from the wet earth by a thick blanket. He stopped his crying as he saw Chara leaning over him and gurgled happily.

'Just seeking attention, my little one, were you?' Chara sighed heavily and turned to see Shruna's worried face. 'There is a village called Grecha in a valley not far from here I once knew. If it is still there we shall set up home, the boy has travelled far enough to be safe from his father and those who would pursue us.'

'That sounds most pleasant, mistress,' replied Shruna happily. 'I must admit my feet tire from the long journey and I ache for a proper bed.'

'That appeals to me as well. Come, gather our things and let us continue.'

As the two women packed away their meagre possessions the witch cast another glance at the autumn sun, as if daring it to move so rapidly again, but it remained resolutely in place and Chara once more felt the weight of her years pressing down on her. It wasn't much further and she steeled herself for the final physical effort that would take her there.

It was just four days later when the three of them reached the village. Initially it was hard to tell the differences from the one that they had left behind all those long weeks before, but nevertheless there were subtle changes which gave witness to just how far they had travelled. Strictly speaking, they were still within the borders of Rostike but the country was relatively new and land boundaries were subject to almost yearly alterations. Chara dismissed such notions from her concerns: where men far away put lines on a map had nothing to do with her. What was of far more importance was what kind of man ran the village, for in an age of far-off lords, local politics could make all the difference. It would become abundantly clear very quickly that Chara was a witch. What mattered was how the headman viewed such people of power.

Their arrival had been noted long before they actually reached the main part of the village and when the two women and baby reached the road cutting the settlement in half, there was already a reception committee waiting to greet them.

Chara glanced at the four men blocking the thoroughfare with an experienced eye. Two hung back a little and were considerably younger than the two in front of them. The witch dismissed them from her thoughts; bully boys all looked the same and had ceased to intimidate her decades ago. However, the man at the front had the bearing of a leader and his blessing would be required.

Chara glanced at the sun, noting its position. 'Good noontime to you, headman. May God bless you.'

The man to whom this remark was addressed nodded, recognising the shrewd look in her eyes. He scratched his beard, which was streaked with grey, and did not reply at once. Casting a look to the man next to him he stepped forward and directed his comments to the witch.

'Thank you for the blessing, elderly mother, but I can't help but think that words coated in sugar often taste sour when swallowed.'

Chara very nearly smiled. Clearly this was a man of some discernment who would need swaying to their side of the argument. Inwardly she readied herself for the challenge. 'A perceptive point and one that needs to be brought out into the open sooner rather than later.'

The second man had walked around the witch and was looking at Shruna and the baby, the beginnings of a frown upon his face. He was perhaps forty, lean and wiry, and his expression showed quite clearly his annoyance at being there instead of taking his midday meal.

'We need this sorted quickly, Welcrar,' he said to the headman. 'I've got to get back to the east field.'

The headman shook his head. 'Always in a hurry is Deris,' he said conversationally to Chara. 'Never takes time out to just *look* and see what is right before him.' With these words his eyes narrowed and he studied the witch's face with such intensity that Shruna felt that he must burn holes in the skin.

If Chara was bothered by such scrutiny it failed to register on her face. At the sound of the two names her mind had gone into a race, trying to place them. Although the last time she had been in this village was years before either of these men were born, she knew that it was common practice for names to remain in a family and that it was likely that she may have met their parents or grandparents.

'Tell me,' she said suddenly, the corners of her mouth twitching just a fraction, 'wasn't your father the blacksmith here?'

Welcrar's eyebrows rose in surprise and then knitted together as he drank in the words. 'Possibly,' he replied, his eyes once more going to his companion, who had abandoned his study of the child at Chara's words.

'I recall how his shoulder used to trouble him during cold spells and that he feared he may have to give up the work which he loved and which provided for his family. I gave him the recipe for a balm that I believe soothed his pain and changed his life. His own words I seem to remember as I left the village. Yes, it is all coming back to me now. The family resemblance is there in the tilt of the nose and across the eyes; I don't know why I didn't see it before. How is your father?'

'He died eight winters back, heart gave out, but then he was old.'

'I am sorry to hear that, he was a good man, and I doubt he would have let women and babies stand out in the sun when they have endured a long journey to be here.'

Welcrar smiled thinly. 'I daresay you're right about that, but then my father was a very trusting man and these days trust is a luxury that not many of us can afford.'

'Indeed, trust has to be earned like anything else, no one can deny that, but to completely close your heart to it can be even more destructive than opening it too wide.'

'What skills can you offer us, elderly mother? We do not have the food or shelter to carry those who do no benefit for the village.'

Chara cocked her head to one side. 'You already know the answer to that, your father must have told you.'

Welcrar nodded. 'He spoke of the witch who cured his aches, but then he liked to talk.' The headman's face cracked into a grin. 'Could barely shut him up most days.'

'Aye, a kind man, your father.' The witch closed her mouth and stared at Welcrar, giving just the mildest of hints towards boredom.

'But talk of days gone by should be saved for when the sun goes down, rather than wasted while there is work to be done. Deris!' Welcrar called, 'take them to the tavern and have them settled in there.' He looked at Chara. 'I know that Fonner has the room but you realise that such things do not come cheap?'

Chara nodded but made no reply.

Shruna moved forward with the baby. 'Thank you, headman, you will not regret this.'

Welcrar glanced at her and the child as if seeing them for the first time. His gaze took in the infant, cradled gently in her arms. Something about the child bothered him. It was almost as if he had taken an instant dislike to it, even though he quite liked children as a rule. 'You best get the babe out of the sun, my lady, it may not feel that strong but those of us in the fields know how it can affect a man.'

'You are a kind man; the world needs more like you. My name …'

The headman held up his hand. 'Plenty of time for all that later, friend. Deris here will see you to your room and then at the end of the day perhaps you would all do me the pleasure of sharing a meal with myself and my family. Once we're all settled I can introduce you to the village. Probably best to wait for the morrow.' With a final nod to the women he began the walk back to the fields.

Deris dismissed the two other men who had remained silent throughout the discussion and gestured for the three newcomers to follow him to the village's only tavern.

'Is there anyone whose heart you cannot burrow into, mistress?' whispered Shruna to Chara as they walked to their temporary home.

The witch gave a sigh that suddenly made her look very old. 'If only that were true, my friend, if only that were true.'

In the third century before what would become known as the modern era, there began a series of changes which swept across the continent of Eurasia, forever altering the land and the peoples who inhabited it. Borders that had changed as often as the wind were suddenly being drawn onto maps with an air of finality and with armies who were prepared to defend them all year round and not just when their work in the fields would allow. The growth of the professional army was one of the most significant changes, for when there are men to be fed and paid for doing nothing when there is no war, taxes must be gathered from the population to support them. A taxation system requires a new type of man, the administrator, which itself leads to the creation of a more bureaucratic system of government. For taxation to make its way to the coffers of the lords and kings who order it, there must be roads for their officials to travel along, and these roads must themselves be built and serviced.

With change comes uncertainty, but also the opportunity

for wealth. Merchants and traders now had the beginnings of an infrastructure and could take their goods to a wider market. Those who only a generation or two earlier had thought trading with the next village risky and not worth the expenditure of effort, now thought little of trading with different nations. Humans and arrogols had always had this desire to forge alliances and to barter, although the elves and dwarves maintained that it was only so they could betray one another. But as the human and arrogol merchants grew rich, there were those in the more self-contained world of the dwarf and the elf who rubbed their chins and began to wonder if they were missing out on something. For their part, the human traders looked longingly at the beautifully crafted dwarf weapons with edges that gleamed razor sharp in the sunlight and the elf jewellery that had craftsmanship the rest of the continent could only marvel at and never hope to copy. It was as a result of this mutual realisation that there were a lot of benefits to be had from trade that a great deal of the old antagonisms were overcome during these years. Elf made goods for dwarf, dwarf made goods for human and humans traded with everyone, the lynchpin of the whole operation. That is not to say that things always went smoothly. Although there were those who could overlook history and accept old hatreds as merely that, there were plenty who did not see the new arrangement as a gift, rather as a curse.

Many were the incidents of small details causing disproportionate amounts of violence. The human custom of shaking hands over a deal had many elves wrinkling their noses in disgust. As if a race most beloved of the Creator would sully themselves by actual physical contact with humans; the mere notion was absurd and distasteful. One trader who had had his hand refused by an elf had dishonoured the contract and the whole incident had led to two deaths and a great deal of disruption to trade in that area. Such occurrences made certain that the transition to a more integrated world was never going to be a quick, or an easy, process.

The growth of the nation state at the same time almost seemed to exacerbate the tensions rather than serving as a way of defusing them. Curinlas was the oldest human country in the West and had strongly opposed Holayew formerly declaring itself a kingdom, since it regarded the southern peninsular as its own backyard, not an independent state. The elf stronghold of Bulair merely shrugged its shoulders at the vagaries of humanity. It saw the current state of affairs as purely temporary, given the human outlook on life, and whether or not one group decided to band together or not was largely irrelevant to the long-lived elves. For themselves they had no territorial ambitions beyond their present boundaries, but viewed the encroaching mass of humanity on all sides as a threat. Deaths of humans venturing into the forest were considered a form of suicide by the elves, who were quick to point out that those invited into their homeland never came to any harm and that trespassers got what they deserved. Most humans accepted this but there were those who saw something more sinister in what the elves were doing, who built up stories of fabulous wealth hidden deep within the forest kingdom. Such stories did little except stir up more trouble and disrupt the trade that had taken so long to build with the reclusive elves.

When the two warring states of Rostike and Rostian were finally able to put their differences to one side and draw up a peace treaty, those more resentful of human interference in elven affairs took it as further evidence of duplicity. For when humans stopped fighting one another, they would surely turn greedy eyes to the lands of the elf.

To the south, the great breakout of dwarf-kind was still taking place, with hundreds of dwarves abandoning their previous cave-dwelling existence for the fertile plains of the land they now called Lish-Kar or 'gift of heaven', but which the humans who still lived there called West Slavia. The explosion of dwarves from beneath the mountains on the southern edge of Bulair had caught the people living there totally off guard and they had found themselves retreating ever further southwards, away from the warrior dwarves. Cries for help to their compatriots in East Slavia went largely ignored except for offers to ferry them across the Slavian Sea for resettlement away from the dwarves. More and more, Slavia was viewed by the rest of the continent as the sick man of Eurasia and many leaders looked hungrily at those lands.

The elves had no reason to care that dwarves were replacing one group of humans, it was all pretty much the same to them, but a glance at a map of the new Eurasia being created by these changes was beginning to worry more than one noble elf. With the human seizure of the jutting peninsular to the north of the forest, the elves now found themselves totally surrounded by races who were historically elven enemies. The occasional buying and selling of manufactured goods did little do dispel the elf feeling of unease at what was happening throughout the continent.

One elf in particular was feeling less at ease than he had done for a long time, and although the constant stream of information from those elves who implored him to do something about humanity was irritating, it was not the cause of his frown today. Denegtacus picked up yet another sheaf of paper reporting yet another minor infraction of some trading agreement by a human merchant. The letter ran to some nine pages and, as far as he could see, the elf who had written it wanted his help in bringing the man to justice. The old elf smiled in a distracted kind of way, casually balled the letter up in his hands and tossed it into the corner of the room where it fell among many others of its kind. What did these fools expect? As if he didn't have enough to do, he had to read this drivel from whining elves who got what they deserved if they dealt with humans in any case. Quite how he had become the figurehead for the merchants he wasn't sure about either. Although he had encouraged trading with humans, he had never taken an active role in any of the treaties, and yet now he was getting dozens of letters a day *demanding* action! It was laughable and yet he still found himself reading the letters each day and occasionally picking out the odd one for further investigation if it seemed that the elf had a genuine grievance. Intimidating humans was, after all, easy.

No matter how hard he tried to immerse himself in the banal work which now swamped his desk, the real cause of his distraction kept coming to the surface. He had worked his magic for centuries, longer than he cared to remember in fact, but he could not recall a time when he had felt such a pull on the magic all around him as he had felt over the last few weeks. It was as if a powerful wizard was drawing magic into himself, affecting the balance that magic maintained to such an extent that he could feel it even here, buried deep within the leafy forest of Bulair. Denegtacus frowned deeply. Such thoughts did little good for he knew he was suggesting that there was sorcery at work and he was certain that this was not the case, for other wizards would have felt it and as yet none had come to him to express their concern. If not sorcery, then what? It was an itch he couldn't reach and it was a feeling the old elf had never had to endure in all his long years.

Standing up, he stretched his back and viewed his cluttered desk with distaste. Glancing over his shoulder to check he was still alone in his cottage he returned his gaze to the papers which ate into his time so much. With a wave of his hand the letters and reports vanished, leaving the polished wooden surface of the desk visible for the first time in months. He grinned mischievously. It was nice to have the chance to take back his day and use it for more important things, such as the tracking down of this mystery magician.

3

The witch watched Shruna nurse the child as she had done every day for the four months of the babe's life. It was a good feeling that coursed through her body as she saw the bond between mother and child forming through the simple act of feeding. It was something that she herself had never known, could never know, for when she had chosen the path of her life so many years earlier, she had forever turned her back on such worldly considerations.

Chara wiped a hand across her eyes, trying desperately to ease the fatigue she felt. How long had it been since she had slept properly? A month? Two? She smiled inwardly. She knew exactly how long it had been, for it was the same as the babe's age. The darkness that encroached on her sleep was always there, watching and waiting and yet never visible. Since that night when her spirit had been dragged from her body she had not truly recovered and she found herself suffering from bouts of fatigue the likes of which she had not known before. More and more she realised that she was becoming reliant upon the midwife who shared her home and that without her it was doubtful that the villagers would allow her to stay within the relative safety of their settlement.

Shruna noticed the look upon the weathered face of her teacher, how could she not? For it was a look that she had become increasingly familiar with over the last months and one that filled her with a primal dread. One of the truisms of the world was that Chara had always been there and always would be: staring into the lined face of the witch, who now simply looked like an old woman not long for this world, screamed that this truth was so much fairy dust.

Although the witch did her best to hide her weariness, Shruna had spotted the signs a while back but tried to avoid mentioning it, since the only time she had, Chara had reacted angrily. Now she felt she must speak but Chara beat her to it.

'I do not feel so good tonight, Shruna, I think perhaps I shall go to bed early.' Chara clasped her hands tightly together on her lap but made no move to go to her bedchamber.

Shruna did not look up but continued to rock the infant in her arms. 'Perhaps that is for the best, mistress, these last weeks have been tiring for you.'

Chara tried not to take the bait, but after a life such as hers resisting such things was all but impossible. 'I've had harder times young lady, have no doubts about that! I could keep going a while yet but we've got the babe to think of.'

'The babe,' repeated Shruna still not looking up. 'Of course.'

'Damn but you can be irritating, girl,' said Chara ruefully, a smile creeping across her face despite herself. 'Am I that obvious?'

'You have not been yourself recently, mistress, even Chard could tell you that. You try to hide behind your strength but, sometimes, admitting our weaknesses can itself be a strength.' With the child asleep, the mother turned her gaze to the witch. 'You should try to sleep; perhaps I could prepare a sleeping draft for you so that you might get an uninterrupted rest.'

Chara shook her head. 'No. I think tonight I should try something else.'

* * *

The preparations to fly involved a lot of pacing in the bedroom with the witch muttering to herself under her breath. She was too weak for this and she knew it. The risks were great but she knew that unless she got some answers she would never sleep properly again. The boy was special and it irked her a great deal that she had no way of knowing why or what the future had in store for him.

Coming to a decision, she lay on the bed, staring at the roof beams but not really seeing them. Her breathing became even and shallow as she turned the magic inwards, attempting to release the bonds that hold the soul to the body. A process that is never easy was made all the more difficult by her age and condition. Consequently, it was some time before her soul wrenched itself clear of the confines of flesh and soared into the heavens.

But pain is for mortals and her soul leaped high, soaring ever upwards. Enjoying the freedom, she allowed herself the luxury of indulging her whim and cut this way and that, watching the land race by beneath her. However, she was no apprentice wizard who forgot who they were and what they were supposed to be doing when they flew; she knew that she had work to do.

Even as she flew she was aware of the darkness and now, as she paused and turned, it was there, before her, still and silent. She watched as it pulsed and then tilted her head to glance down at the earth a long way beneath her feet. Her house was clearly visible and the darkness was directly over it, as if it was waiting for something or someone. The thought came to her suddenly and she inclined her head as if coming to a decision. The boy was central to whatever this presence was and although it was darkly prepossessing, it did not appear actively hostile.

'At least I have faced the darkness,' said Chara to herself, for she did not expect any reply from the shadows that confronted her. But a voice from behind did answer.

'Because you feared for yourself or because you feared for the child?'

Chara swung round, a defensive spell coming to mind, but the words drained away as she saw the elderly elf stood on the air, his arms folded deep within his white robes. Meeting another when flying wasn't unheard of but it usually only happened when you were directly seeking contact. This was the first time Chara could recall that someone had managed to sneak up on her while in this state of being, but as she faced the elf she could feel the waves of power emanating from him and realised that it was quite possible that he could have been there the whole time and simply not allowed her to see him. This was disconcerting to the witch who liked to remain in control of a situation, although it was nothing compared to the shock that hit her when she realised that this was no spirit that stood calmly before her, but a flesh and blood elf!

She peered carefully at him, her mind in shock at the impossibility.

'What is it that you see?' asked Denegtacus, tilting his head, the ghost of a smile passing across his lips.

'If it wasn't such an asinine comment, I'd say that what I'm seeing can't be true.'

'And why is that?'

'I've heard there are wizards who have the ability to actually lift their physical bodies clear of the ground, but the effort is enormous, and yet I sense that for you this is as natural as taking a stroll through the forest. Strong magic indeed.'

Denegtacus nodded. 'What you say has merit but then I am not a wizard but an enchanter.'

Chara would have jumped had she been in her body but instead her soul eyes merely narrowed as the meaning behind the words came to her. 'It seems I am in honoured company.'

'You know of me then?'

The witch gave an exaggerated bow. 'Who has not heard of the fabled L'tusian? I reckon my instincts about the boy must have been close to the mark since I find you hanging around above his crib.'

Denegtacus glanced down at the humble home some thousand feet below them. 'What have your instincts told you?' he asked, trying unsuccessfully to keep the interest from his tone.

'I helped to deliver the child but frankly I think he'd have crawled out on his own if I hadn't been there.'

'A witch at a birth? Is that normal human practice?'

Chara looked thoughtful as she weighed up how much to tell the elf, but even as the idea came to mind she realised that if this elf was who he said he was, he could pluck the information from her brain if he thought she was lying to him. She had heard of the wizards who had such spells and knew that it was unlikely to be a pleasant experience. The hardness behind the apparent easy-going exterior was clear and she had no doubt that he would do it if he believed he had to.

'Not really, although over the years I've done more birthing than I can remember. Most of them were the hard ones, mind, but I managed to save more than I lost.'

'So it was a difficult birth?'

Chara looked at the elf who stared back with practised ease. 'Just how much of this do you already know?'

The elf shrugged. 'I suspect a lot and I have put together some for myself. But know? Not a great deal and that is why I am here.'

'The birth was a breech, a bad one at that. I could feel the male magic coming from the child and it was only his will that kept the mother chained to this world. As soon as he felt he was ready to come out he released his hold on the mother and she died. The father rejected the boy, blaming him for the death, and so myself and a friend brought him to this village where he could grow up in safety.'

'You are leaving a lot out of your story, your whole role in it for a start.'

The witch made an indifferent gesture with her hands. 'Does it matter? The only thing that is of any real consequence is the boy and what will become of him.'

The enchanter walked slowly up to the witch, their eyes never leaving one another's. He stepped past her and stared at the darkness beyond.

'I feel something about this child. I have lived long and I have been a student of magic for all of that time, but the power is disturbed and I believe that this boy is the centre of it.'

'And what about that?' she asked jerking a thumb toward the dark that was always there, silent.

Denegtacus stared at it, a frown creasing his forehead. 'I don't know and I don't like not knowing. I have a sense for most things but ...' and he trailed off.

'The boy may be in danger from this?'

Denegtacus glanced at Chara before returning to stare at the darkness and did not reply to the question. 'When he is of age, I shall come for him to train him in the ways of magic.'

'You think he'll last that long?'

'We shall have to make sure that he does,' replied Denegtacus, his eyes locking to hers.

The next day Chara was confined to her bed, exhaustion keeping her there until late in the day. When she got up and made her way to the table, Shruna had prepared a light meal of bread, cheese and honey and it was all she could do to stop herself from falling into the chair. The concern was clear on the younger woman's face and Chara knew that she obviously looked every bit as bad as she felt.

'Mistress, I ...' But she couldn't find the words to complete the sentence and simply stared into the face of her mentor.

'You'll give me a complex looking at me like that,' said Chara with forced gaiety.

Shruna did not reply but instead went into the bedchamber she shared with the baby and retrieved a fragment of a hand mirror she had been given as a young woman many years earlier. Without another word she handed the object to the witch and took a step back, the worry etched into her features. Chara held the eyes of her friend, the unusual sensation of fear eating away at her insides. More than anything in the world she wanted to lay this mirror face down on the table, she did not want to see whatever it was that Shruna could see.

Foolishness! Her voice echoed in her mind and she turned her gaze to the mirror. A lesser person might have dropped it in shock or sobbed in self-pity but Chara's expression did not waver as she stared at the stranger reflected back at her. Her grey hair was now a brilliant white and the lines which before had been soft were now gouged into her face as if done with a knife. Her skin had sagged, giving her a haggard look, and her eyes had lost most of their lustre. Where yesterday Chara could have passed for a woman in her mid-sixties, she now looked over ninety.

'Now who will live that long?' she whispered under her breath.

'I don't like it and I tell you this, Ancient One, no good will come of any of it!'

Denegtacus eyed the Elf king across the magnificent table which was clear except for a crystal decanter of red wine and three glasses. The enchanter had listened to a lot of this sort of talk over the years and in a lot of ways he agreed with the king, but change is often painful. Whether or not it was change for the better would have to be seen, but once started, change was impossible to rein back.

The previous week had seen the first state organised exodus of citizens from Bulair, giving official sanction to a procedure which had been going on now for several years. The king's sons were some of the keenest supporters of greater interaction with the other races who inhabited the continent and it was his second son who had personally led the procession from the wooded homeland into east Curinlas. Many of the older elves, the king included, foresaw nothing but trouble but had bowed to pressure from the youngsters who saw only the chance for profit and excitement in a larger world.

Although there had been a great crowd who watched the several hundred strong elven caravan leave, the only real noise had come from sobbing mothers and the muttered warnings from the elders. A direct order from the king could possibly have halted it all but, as his son had cautioned him, that was by no means certain. Imagine the situation if the king forbade it and the elves still left, taking with them his second son? The king had scowled deeply at the impertinence of his offspring but had seen that short of having them put in chains there was little he could do to stop those who wanted to leave. Perhaps a few years ago he might have taken the chance, but wiser words from his wife had prevailed and he had reluctantly appeared in public to bid goodbye to his son.

'Perhaps not, Theaspida, but I believe more harm would have come from stopping them.'

The third and final occupant of the room leaned forward and rested her hand on the king's arm. His wife was one of the most beautiful elves who had ever lived, so gossip said, and even in her later years that beauty still shone through. More important had been her steadying influence on the sometimes wilful king, restraining his more impetuous impulses.

'Listen to L'tusian, husband; you know he speaks the truth.'

King Theaspida turned to his wife and smiled lovingly, his own hand closing over that of his wife. 'I know he does, I know you do and I know that there are probably servants in this palace who could tell me so, but I am still losing a son.'

'And I also, but an elf must make his own way in the world, even those whose father others call king.'

'I just feel that my ancestors would never have allowed this to happen and that the fault for all of this must be laid at my feet.'

Denegtacus sighed and swallowed some of the wine. It was a wonderful vintage and the glass itself had taken some crafts elf a great deal of time to make. The carved picture on the side gave the impression of a dragon wrapped around the rim. Denegtacus smiled at the image; all the dragons were long gone now.

'There is no blame, my liege, times change and you have proved yourself as good a king as any that have gone before you by having the sense to change with them rather than clinging to what you knew. The future is not to be feared but grasped. Better to have a say in what your people do outside the forest than allow them to go sneaking out against your will.'

'Some of them were doing that anyway,' said the queen lightly, her eyebrows arched just a little.

The enchanter smiled broadly and inclined his head to her. 'But I am different, my lady, I sometimes have to leave on short notice and it was after all one of your husband's predecessors who signed the law exempting me from royal control.'

'As I recall the story, dear L'tusian, you threatened to turn him into a human if he didn't.' Queen Amaril enjoyed these verbal games and Denegtacus always knew when it was time to back off and save at least some face.

'Perhaps we could prevail upon you to do that to Count Meralis,' said the king with a chuckle. 'He's been going on and on in council meetings about this issue and frankly if he carries on much more I might send him out into that big nasty world he fears so much.'

'You wouldn't!' said his wife in mock horror. 'You only have to put up with the count, I have to listen to his wife!'

The king turned back to the enchanter. 'Where are they now? We haven't received word this last day.'

'They are safe, do not fret,' replied Denegtacus. 'There are ships waiting in port to take them to Rittan where most of them will make their homes. The rest have the humans' permission to reside in Curinlas.'

'Permission! The word eats away at me. Elves taking orders from humans!'

'Hush, husband, you'll do yourself a mischief.' Amaril turned to the enchanter. 'Denegtacus, old friend, if you could get word to our son in your own special way, we would be grateful.'

Denegtacus stood up and bowed deeply, 'As ever you ask for gifts that I would beg to give as if you were asking for my life! It would be an honour. And now I must ...'

'Of course, please go with our blessing,' said the queen.

'And as you do, just check I haven't lost any more children to foolish ventures,' said Theaspida as Denegtacus walked from their presence.

'A good elf, that one,' said Amaril once he had gone. 'We need elves such as he.'

'There are none better, but he grows old. He promised me not to speak of it but I don't suppose he included you when he said it, but he has found an individual who he believes has the strength to take over from him, once he has completed the training of course.'

'Another L'tusian? The world would be a safer place if nothing else.'

'I don't know about another, I think he meant a replacement. He wants his work to go on, he sees it as a continuation of a line.'

The queen nodded thoughtfully. 'He is old, there are none who are old enough to know anything of his early years and we elves live for centuries. I must admit, I have often wondered just how old Denegtacus is. I even asked him directly once but he just smiled that smile of his and didn't answer, probably can't even remember himself.'

The king took a small sip of wine, enjoying the taste on his lips. 'You're most likely right, you normally are, but he said something else which has concerned me for a while now.'

'And what is that?'

'The child will only be sixteen when the training begins.'

Amaril looked sideways at her husband. 'That makes no sense, no elf has ever shown magical ability in childhood, the schools of wizardry don't even take pupils until they are fifty and come of age.'

'Exactly my thoughts, my dear, and it is an issue that I have had some difficulty putting from my mind. I simply cannot imagine a time when Denegtacus will not be there beside me, helping me to see the right path. As for replacing him with a child, the mere notion is drivel!'

The queen stared at the door that had recently shut behind the closest adviser any elf king had ever had and tapped at her chin in thought. She pondered the possibilities of what the words she had just heard meant. Her husband was both a good elf and a good king but he did find it hard to look at information from different viewpoints; that was her talent and she came to a conclusion that fitted with the facts quite quickly.

'Perhaps it is not a child that the ancient one will be training.'

'Come, come, my dear!' snapped the king. 'At sixteen they're barely out of short pants!'

'*Elf* children may not be, but human children reach adulthood at sixteen.'

The king's face looked almost comical as he heard these words, but that soon changed to a look of anger. 'Impossible! As if any human mage could replace an elf such as Denegtacus! And who would take orders from him? How could I sit in my council rooms listening to a human? The people would hang me from the royal tree!'

'It would explain his words, my lord.'

The king bristled as he continued to think through his wife's idea. 'Nonsense,' he finally muttered, but his eyes darted to the door as if he could drag the answers he wanted from the space Denegtacus had last occupied.

Outside, Denegtacus wandered down the corridor staring at the rich tapestries, some of which his magic had helped to weave. He stopped before one which showed the first elf king laying the foundation stone of the citadel where the royal family prayed to the Creator. Extremely old and kept behind protective glass which itself was sealed with spells of warding, it had been finished only seventy years after the ceremony and as such was a valuable primary source of history. Elven tapestries were not only works of art but depicted scenes from the past in some detail. From a really good cloth it would be possible to interpret many years and events of their heritage.

It was a hobby of Denegtacus to mull over the messages that were contained within the rich silks and delicate stitching. For most of those made in the last fifteen hundred years it was easy since he was the one who had put them there, but the early ones often taxed his mind. The depth of detail was extraordinary and there were many touches that he couldn't get his mind around. For example, in this first tapestry, the king was in the foreground but behind him to the right was the figure of a human wearing the robes of a magi. Fashion had obviously not changed a great deal over the centuries because he was dressed in such a way that even today he could have blended in with human wizards and not caused a stir. But in elven society his robes would have raised more than the odd eyebrow, for not only was he human but his robes were black when all elf magic users wore white. To dress as to blend with the night may encourage a mage to walk the paths of darkness.

Over the decades, Denegtacus had become something of an obsessive about this human and had constructed many theories to explain his presence in such an important tapestry at a time when human and elf relations were practically non-existent. There were boundless possibilities but most of them seemed absolutely farcical with little basis in reality. However, there was one that he kept coming back to time and time again: what if this human was something more than a wizard, what if he knew the power of enchantment?

It was this line of thought that had led Denegtacus to study the past using his vast powers to open viewing portals of times which had been. Through centuries of history and multitudes of locations he had searched for another reference to this black-garbed human and had come up short. But rather than dealing a blow to his theory, this had only served to strengthen it. He recalled the one time he had successfully opened a window to the very ceremony that the tapestry depicted, he had watched for less than a few seconds when he had felt the eyes of the human turn from what had previously occupied his attention, to lock with his own. They had stared at one another across several thousand years of history until a surge of magic had disrupted the elf's concentration and the portal had closed. It was practically impossible to cross the boundaries of time with any degree of accuracy and Denegtacus had never again found that particular moment in his studies.

Perhaps he had imagined their shared glance because he so much wanted the answers that eluded him, but somehow he didn't think so. It had been a moment when something in Denegtacus' mind had clicked and a piece of the puzzle had fallen into place. If this human was an enchanter, and the old elf was practically certain that he was, then it stood to reason that after Denegtacus was gone there would be another to take his place. This had made the elf remember the long centuries of training he had endured alone as he struggled with the gifts he had been blessed with and how he had yearned to be able to share them and to talk with a tutor about how to use them. That instant of clarity had sent Denegtacus down another, uncharted, course as he temporarily put aside his search for the first enchanter, the first L'tusian, to look for the third instead – his own successor.

How he was to go about this he had long mulled over but eventually he had used the portals to try to peer into the future to discover what he must do. However, looking into the future is far harder than searching the past, for every decision made can send the future spiralling off into a variety of different directions, all of which have the potential to be true. The elf began wading through these images, looking for the person who would replace him. Unlike the king, he had not made the error of thinking that the next L'tusian would necessarily be an elf and so had widened his search to the lesser races with whom they shared the continent.

Then, only nine years ago, he had been in his cottage working as he normally did when he had felt the change in the magic like an animal senses the changes of the seasons. It was instinctive and he would have been hard pushed to put it into words, yet he knew what it was and what it meant. That night he travelled the world seeking what he knew he should find and had watched the two women nurse the freshly born human baby who had caused such a disturbance. Often he had journeyed to the child and watched him grow and he smiled as he recalled the meeting with Chara floating high above where the child slept. He had told her that they had to keep him safe from the darkness that was there, threatening to engulf the child as he had grown through the early stages of childhood. Despite his words, he knew he had done nothing to help or support his development, relying instead on the witch doing it for him. Why? If this boy was as central as he believed then why hadn't he wrapped him in wool until such time as the training could begin? As always the answer came unbidden: the boy had to have knowledge of the world around him and grow in strength for himself. He would achieve nothing if the power was laid before him on a silver plate; much better that he fight for it and cherish what he then had.

The more the old elf stared at the tapestry the deeper he slipped into thought. Were these notions truly his own, or were they a way of washing his hands of the boy because he didn't really believe his own theory? No previous enchanter had come searching for him, he had learned his craft the hard way, so why was his relationship with Chard so important? What if he was wrong and he was considering handing over the powers of L'tusian to a man never meant to have them? The elf shuddered despite the fact the corridor was not cold.

Dismissing such negative and pointless speculation from his mind, he continued down through the palace towards the exit. Everything he had felt about this child led him to believe that he truly was the next L'tusian. Doubt had to be left aside if the training was to be successful and Chard was to accept his role in history. As the elf rounded a corner and disappeared from view, the sightless eyes on the tapestry continued to stare blankly into the corridor.

4

Chard made his way through the trees, gathering the herbs and roots that were always needed in order to make the balms and potions his family relied upon to maintain their status in the village. He had trodden these paths for as long as he had been able to walk, for Chara had begun his instruction in the ways of witchcraft before he had turned four. He recalled his first memories as those of sitting around the table, answering questions as to the ingredients that went to make up the various mixes that Chara used to cure the aliments that afflicted the villagers. Mixtures just seemed to stick in his memory and as the years drifted by the witch had introduced more and more complicated and dangerous medicines for the boy to learn. As always, he took them in his stride, consigning them to the recesses of his mind, ready to bring them forward when needed.

At the age of nine, Chara had begun the second part of his training, the magic that the witch worked using the power of the land itself. Witch magic relied on being in tune with the world, and according to human wizards this was the reason that only females could do it, for like the earth, they were the mothers, always responsive to the needs they felt around them. Elf magi derided such a view, believing that what humans called male and female magic was in fact merely a part of the same thing. But perhaps this was because all elves, regardless of gender, had a far higher level of empathy with the land and many believed that their magic came from the land itself.

Whatever the truth, Chard did not particularly care for he showed an uncommon ability with spell-casting, controlling magic that would have taken most humans many years of study to master. Chara poured her vast accumulated knowledge into the boy as quickly as she could for she sensed her time was rapidly coming to an end. He was insatiable and almost seemed to leech the learning from her, no matter how fast she tried to teach.

These thoughts, amongst others, crossed the child's mind as he went about his chores. He wasn't certain that his abilities made him happy and he knew that they did not mean he was liked by the other boys who lived in the village. Rather, they seemed to exaggerate the differences that already existed between them. Whereas they had to tend crops, milk cows and watch sheep, Chard spent his days wandering the paths of the woods and fields picking flowers or occasionally digging up roots. The brutal world that the rest of the village lived in did not appear to encroach upon this slim-built, aloof child.

Such was the mood amongst his peers and this was also reflected in the adults of the community. No one liked going to Chara's home and being given medicines mixed by a small child who merely sneered at you if you dared to question his knowledge or the ingredients. With Chara increasingly confined to her bed, the situation became such that her apprentice handled nearly all the day-to-day enquiries from the villagers and only occasionally asked for advice if he was unsure of a diagnosis. It had been this way ever since Shruna had married a local man and gone to live with him three years earlier. Over time, her visits had become more and more infrequent and they had drifted apart.

When they had first entered the village it had taken some time for them to be accepted by the people living there, but Chara's medicines and Shruna's gift of midwifery meant that they eventually became a part of life in the community. It was as Chard began to grow that the problems had started. Being able to read and write was practically unheard of and he had a worldly knowledge which exceeded all of his peer group and most of the adults. His attitude did little to help the situation for he regarded the other residents of the village as fools who existed merely as vessels on which to test the medicines he concocted. With Chara bedridden for much of the day, Chard had tinkered with the potions to improve them and made up some of his own. He enjoyed the mental stimulus that this engendered but it was the practical magic he was learning that really set his blood on fire.

When he found the patch of wild flowers he sought, he stopped. They grew in abundance in the country, sheltering in the lee of trees, their bright colours masking a deadly secret. Chard knew that when the petals were plucked, soaked overnight and ground into a fine paste, they became highly toxic, causing sickness in all and death if the dose was high. But if the dosage was low and strictly administered then it was highly effective in the treatment of diseases of the stomach. Chara was very agitated when the boy had told her of his findings and had forbidden him to continue with his experiments. Fearing that she would withdraw his training, he had soothed over the problem by simply keeping his knowledge to himself.

The boy knelt down, the dew soaking into his woollen trousers, making them damp, and picked a single flower. Almost lovingly, he held it between thumb and forefinger and watched intently as a small droplet of sap trickled from the broken stem onto his skin. Remembering his task, he quickly picked and stored half the flowers he could see – always wise to make certain that what you needed would still be there tomorrow. The thought made Chard smile just a little, a more genuine smile than most had seen him make as he recalled better times when Chara had been strong enough to accompany him on these excursions.

That had been a long time ago, almost another age, and now Chard realised that he was out here alone and prey to whatever resentment the other children chose to dream up and inflict upon him that day. This thought surged to the front of his mind as he sensed, rather than heard, people close by. Slowly he stood and turned to face the increasingly irritating sight of his fellow youths approaching him. His face remained calm. He had had a lot of practice at maintaining this façade which helped him when dealing with the bullying, but he knew that some day it would slip and who knew what would occur then?

There were four of them today, which was about usual. Chard recognised them all – the settlement was not large and strangers were infrequent outside of harvest time. The eldest two were both several years older than him, mindless gangly youths at the transition to manhood who felt the need to show their dominance at the expense of those weaker than themselves. The two others were roughly Chard's age and took great delight in seeing him brought down to size. They hated his intelligence, his freedom to do as he willed, but most of all they wanted to be accepted by the older boys.

'Picking flowers again, little witch?' asked the eldest with a smile.

Chard remained silent but slowly moved his head to watch as they circled around him. Somehow the mood seemed different today, there was more of a purpose about how they walked and Chard felt fear rise inside him. With an inward curse he suppressed it and did not allow it to show in anything he did or said.

'Something like that, Cracus, someone's got to.'

'Oh, and you reckon me and the boys here wouldn't have the knack, wouldn't have the knowledge to fetch and carry for your bitch witch?' Cracus brightened. 'Bitch witch! Not a bad rhyme, hey Chard?'

Chard smiled without humour. 'Must be all of an hour

since I heard that one. But I suppose when your short-term memory is centred around remembering to breathe in and out in the right order, things can get muddled.'

Cracus' face screwed up as he tried to work out what Chard had actually said. 'You trying to be funny, little witch?' Without waiting for a reply he nodded to his friend who had taken up position behind Chard. The second boy shoved Chard roughly in the back, causing him to stagger forward and collide with Cracus who gripped him by the tops of his arms.

'Hey, Hegieci, this witch is trying to get rough! Are we going to take that?'

Hegieci was a wiry youth, whose frame suggested that he was going to be a very powerful adult in a few years time, and he enjoyed nothing more than reminding the other children in the village of this fact. Roughened by his work in the fields, his open palm connected firmly with Chard's ear, the pain stinging and shaking the younger boy's head to one side. Cracus' grip meant that he couldn't move with the blow or raise his hand to rub his ear, but he refused to give them the pleasure of seeing him cry – not today, not ever!

A brief look of disappointment crossed Cracus' face when he saw that Chard remained as stern as ever but that was soon replaced by anger. Before he even knew what he was doing the fingers of his right hand curled into a fist and he crashed it into Chard's cheek. Anger and hatred burned in Cracus' chest and he didn't even really know why. Chard was flung to his left, his feet sidestepping to try and keep his balance but it was no good and he crashed to the ground.

The younger boys looked at their leaders with excitement, urging them on to greater excesses with cheers and shouts. It was as if a line had been crossed and now the two youths realised they could do anything they wanted. Glancing at each other they walked forward to tower above the fallen boy.

'No smart comeback, little witch?' asked Cracus, his face

flushed with excitement and adrenaline. 'Tell you what, you crawl ahead of us on your belly like the worm that you are and maybe we'll not beat on you any more today.'

'What about tomorrow?' asked Hegieci with a laugh.

Cracus crouched down and patted Chard on the head. 'Well I'm afraid that tomorrow's another day and we'll have to see.'

Chard rolled to one side and got slowly back to his feet, one hand clasped to his face. The pain was great and he could feel tears in his eyes. Searching his memory for the words of a spell that Chara had never taught him but that he had sought for himself, Chard built the power. Magic specifically designed to inflict harm was very rare in witchcraft, for witches believed that their purpose was to cure pain, not cause it, but there were spells if you knew where to look and Chard had made it his business to do so. Chara had only one spell book, which was old and tatty. It had no cover and nearly all of the pages were loose, but it contained a great wealth of knowledge for Chara had written it when she was young and still exploring her own magical boundaries. Many of the spells were quite simple and she rarely consulted it these days because she carried her best book around in her head, but Chard had found it most valuable. Inside its pages he had discovered a small section that Chara had never mentioned – the spells to curse, cause pain and even kill. She allowed him to read it simply because she knew that he would do so even if she tried to stop him, but she did not think that he as yet had the ability to understand, let alone use, those most destructive of spells. Had she known the time he had devoted to learning those words of power she would undoubtedly have destroyed the book, but Chard knew that she did not know. However, this fool before him soon would.

One hand still clutching the side of his face, he pointed at Cracus with the other and chanted the words in anger for the first time.

'Argus doth nurfdrar, argus mot nurfdrar!' shouted Chard, spit flying from his mouth such was the venom with which he spoke.

Cracus flinched slightly and glanced around him. Several seconds passed and then he started to laugh, his friends joining in. The colour drained from Chard's face and he slowly lowered his arm, staring at it as if he could not believe that it was a part of him.

Cracus swaggered up to Chard. 'I'm still here, little witch, not a frog at all!' He danced around Chard with the laughter of his friends driving him on. 'Or perhaps I am!' He bit on his fist with pretend amazement and started to hop about, croaking. Eventually he grew bored with this childish behaviour and stood in front of Chard who had not moved during the entire performance.

'Is that what you've learnt after all these years leeching from our village? A few words that sound like you're eating with your mouth full?' Without waiting for a reply his fist lashed out again, connecting with Chard's chin, snapping his head back and sending him sprawling for a second time. As he lay stunned in the dirt, the two younger boys ran forward and took the opportunity to kick him. The kicks lacked a lot of force but they hurt nonetheless, seeming to reinforce his failure. As he curled up into a ball to protect his head, his brain screamed one word over and over: *revenge.*

By the time Chard dragged himself back home, the sun had sunk level with the horizon and the shadows all around the village had grown long. He had taken the beating from the other children without complaint and without making a sound other than the occasional deep breath when one particular kick had hit home. This had infuriated the four boys all the more and they had continued the assault for several minutes until they decided that the time had come to return to whatever chores they had back at the village. When they left him, Chard had remained hunched in the dirt for a while, his mind still raging at him for his failure. The blood he had shed and the pain he now endured seemed almost just to his mind – what else did he deserve? Certainly he had failed the magic which he could feel coursing through his veins, boiling his blood and setting his soul on fire! But he didn't understand why.

Eventually he dragged himself to his feet and found a nearby stream to wash the blood from his face and soak his bruises. He splashed the cold and dirty water over his face, barely aware of the pain that his body was in, and contemplated what he had to do. Chara would ask questions and threaten to embarrass him by going to the boys' parents to complain and he would have to placate her. That was nothing new, these incidents had been a part of his life for two years now, although they had grown worse of late. It certainly hadn't helped when his mother had moved in with that bastard husband of hers who had point blank refused to allow Chard into his home and even appeared to resent the time that Shruna spent at his house, which wasn't much. Why had she left him? Chard still had no idea and Chara had merely patted his hand and told him that being an adult was sometimes complicated and that his mother still loved him.

Returning to the village he had barely collected a third of his usual amount of herbs and flowers and was two hours later than normal. These facts did not touch the boy and he paid them little regard. Instead, he continued to turn over the problem of what had gone wrong with the spell and what he could do to put it right. As his fingers touched the door to his home and he pushed it inward, he realised that there was only one person who could help him and it was unlikely that she would. Pushing his bitterness down he forced a smile onto his bruised face and walked into the house.

Chara was sat by the fire with her back to him as he

entered. The room was small and other than two chairs by the hearth there was a single dining table with three high-backed wooden chairs. Since Shruna's departure, Chard had discovered that he could have one of the comfortable seats by the fire – at least that was something, he mused to himself. He placed the small leather satchel he carried the herbs in onto the table and picked up an apple from a clay bowl. Tossing it casually from hand to hand he slipped into the spare seat by the fire and took a small bite, chewing slowly. He glanced at Chara who was sat quietly, gazing at the flickering flames without showing any signs that she had noticed his presence. Chard sighed inwardly. She was getting worse, that was obvious, and she still had so much locked away in that white-haired skull of hers that he needed! Damn her! Anger, rage, hatred, Chard felt them all as he stared at her, but not so much as a flicker revealed itself in his expression. He vaguely recalled a time when he had loved her and they had been happy, the three of them, but it all seemed so long ago, lost in the fog of memory.

'What do you see when you stare like that, young mage?' asked Chara suddenly, startling Chard. Slowly she moved her head round. Briefly he held her gaze but then turned away.

'How do you always know when I am looking at you?'

'Why do you always answer a question with a question?' replied Chara amiably.

Chard exhaled loudly and stared at his feet as they swung back and forth without touching the floor. These meaningless conversations happened frequently and they tended to end the same way, with him giving way.

'I see an old woman,' he said with characteristic bluntness.

Chara chuckled and poked the fire with a long-handled iron. 'If that is all then I haven't been teaching you very well!'

'No that is not all!' he hissed. 'I see the person who is holding me back, the person who could show me knowledge that I don't even know exists and who won't!' All attempts at pleasant coercion disappeared as all of Chard's rage spilled out.

'What gives you the idea that I won't help you?' asked Chara quietly. 'I thought that everything I have done since you came into this world was an attempt to teach you things. I wonder if your anger tonight is really aimed at me or if those bruises are clouding your judgement.'

Chard's face turned red behind the ugly yellow marks that covered it and then the tears started to roll. He made no noise as he cried, the tears simply slid down his face and quite suddenly he looked every inch the nine-year-old child that he was.

'Why do they hate me, grandma?' he shouted. 'What did I do to anger them all so much? Mother, her husband, the children, the villagers? They all despise me and I don't know why!' He got up from his chair and flung himself at Chara who held him tightly as he cried himself out on her shoulder.

Pushing himself out of her grasp, he stood in front of her, wiping his face with the back of his hand, ashamed at his display of weakness. Chara reached out and gripped his arms, her eyes boring into his so that he had no choice but to look back at her.

'Listen to me, Chard, you have a gift and there will always be those in the world who will hate you for it because petty men will always be jealous of that which they cannot have. You must rise above them, not be dragged down to their level, else you will end up like them!'

'I just want to be normal!'

Chara tousled his hair and gazed into the distance. 'Put such thoughts from your mind, little one, because that is something that you can never be. You have gifts beyond my ability to count and I will not allow you to waste them or to ignore them, and if that means a few bumps and bruises along the way, one day you will look back and know that it was a small price to pay.'

They stayed like that for some time, the only sound the occasional crackle from the fireplace. It had been a while since Chard could recall when he had last felt so secure and he hated himself all the more because he knew he had to shatter the peaceful moment with the question that was burning to escape. His tears had dried but as he stared at his teacher he realised that hers may well be falling soon.

'There is more, grandmother,' he said slowly, keeping his eyes on her, refusing to cower in the face on her forthcoming wrath. Without waiting for a response he ploughed on, the words measured and clear. 'I tried to use one of the spells from the last section in your book. I have been studying the words for months, in secret because I thought you would be angry if I asked you to teach me. I know what I did was wrong but at the time I was so angry they just kind of burst out of me and …' he stopped as Chara closed her eyes.

'What have you done?' she whispered.

'I just wanted to stop them hurting me any more, I was certain that you would have done the same in the same circumstances!'

Chara opened her eyes and shook her head. 'Oh Chard, is this the limit of your knowledge, your perception, your understanding?' She had not raised her voice and sounded sad rather than angry. 'I would never have done what you have done, not ever.'

'Would you rather they killed me? Because that is what will happen one day if I cannot learn to defend myself! One day soon they will go that bit too far, put that extra kick into me when otherwise they should have walked away and no one will care! No one! And now not even you!'

Chara shook her head more clearly this time, the speed increasing with every movement. 'Foolish child! What do I care for a few village boys or what their stupidity might lead them into? Let them trade blows with an apprentice witch, they will learn not to the hard way, as most do! Oh no, young mage, it is not for them that I fear but you! Why did you go behind my back for knowledge which you thought forbidden? Why did you not come straight to me when the desires to know what the words held became too strong? That is why I am angry, Chard, you have lost your trust and your faith in me when I swore a long time ago that I would never lose mine in you!'

'Then why did you hide these spells from me?' shouted Chard. 'I have memorised everything you have taught me. I can heal, make predictions, I could hear the minds of the animals and the trees at an age when you told me that you hadn't even started your training! Why forbid me knowledge?' The question was delivered at such volume that Chard coughed at the end, his throat raging in pain.

'Fool!' screeched Chara. 'Fool, fool, fool! I will teach you all that I know, including those spells you call "forbidden". There is no such thing as forbidden knowledge, Chard, knowledge has no morality, it just is. But the interpretation of that knowledge and the implementation of it! Now that is something else, for how can you make decisions as to the rightness of what you do if you do not have all the knowledge you need to make those decisions!'

'Then you will show me how to cast attacking spells?' asked Chard softly.

'Aye, Chard, that I will,' replied Chara equally quietly. 'And spells to kill. But be warned, such knowledge has a price, even if we don't see it straightaway. Are you prepared to pay, even though you do not know the cost?'

Chard stood as tall and straight as he could, his slender body silhouetted on the opposite wall by the firelight. 'Yes, mistress! I need to know everything!'

Denegtacus was sat behind his desk idly tapping his quill against his chin, completely unaware of the growing inkblot on his finger. The king had asked him to prepare a speech to give to the Council outlining what a wonderful period in history they were living in and how the elves leaving Bulair were ambassadors of their race rather than traitors.

'Or some such nonsense,' muttered Denegtacus to himself as he refocused his eyes to stare at the paper before him. It was no good, the words swam in and out of his mind like demented fish and he could not settle. Irritated with his own lack of concentration he finally stood and walked to the window which overlooked the garden at the back of his cottage.

It was a magnificent garden, the trees lovingly tended to grow in a wide semicircle at the end which gave perfect shade from the sun while simultaneously providing the ideal setting for outdoor talks and picnics. The flowerbeds were second to none, not even the king could boast such a variety of blooms in such a small space, a fact that he was forever teasing the old enchanter about whenever they met. It wasn't even as if Denegtacus had asked for these things, they had just kind of happened when royal gardeners had volunteered their services as a tribute to the much respected elf.

For many years there had been hardly any elves who lived on the ground, but since Denegtacus had moved down to what used to be called 'human level' it had become more fashionable and with the growing trend had come an increased desire for the aesthetic value of plants and flowers. This was something that the elves were truly gifted at due to the relationship that they enjoyed with their environment.

Denegtacus smiled to himself as he marvelled at just how adept his old mind had become at following a train of thought for no other purpose than to distract him from that which he really wanted to dwell on. The gardens were undeniably beautiful, that was true, but it seemed to him of late that everything he looked at was overshadowed by the constant thought of Chard.

Why was it that the centuries seemed to race past and he had shed tears at the funerals of his friends' great grandchildren, but these last nine years had dragged by with downright impertinence? Chard was ageing at a rate far in excess of what a normal elf child could expect and yet this was still not sufficient for the elf who had sworn to keep his distance until he had reached sixteen and the human age of maturity.

That did not stop him watching, or his mind going over the 'what ifs' a thousand times a day. He recalled the day he had watched the infant Chard scold his hand in a fire – no lasting harm had been done but it still made the old elf shudder to think of the things which could go wrong in any young life and bring it to an end prematurely. Yet there was something in his mind that assured him that Chard would survive and that he wouldn't fall prey to any accidents or mishaps, not with so many guardians looking over him.

Which brought him on to the next problem: what was that blackness which kept its silent watch over the boy? Denegtacus had long ago started to call it 'Chard's darker guardian' for no other reason than the fact that it had to be referred to as something. The elf had stood before the dark cloud many, many times over the years, just staring and listening, but nothing ever happened. Occasionally he tried to approach it but every time he did so it somehow managed to stay exactly the same distance from him no matter how quickly he tried to move. He had had vague notions of trying magic on it to see what might happen but discounted this; better not to know for the time being than risk an outcome he had no control over. The answer was there, even if it was not apparent to the elf, and he was in no doubt that one day he would understand and another piece of the puzzle would fit.

Denegtacus sighed loudly and turned his back on the window, once again regarding the clutter on his desk. So much work and so much of it unimportant, but if it filled the time between now and Chard's coming of age then all the better. When Chard was in his care and his training was underway he would inform the king that his days as an adviser were coming to an end. The enchanter smiled slightly as he once more pictured the king's face when he realised that not only had thousands of elves deserted their ancestral homes but that a human was living and learning on sacred elven territory! The colour he would turn at this news would be as nothing compared to that when he found out Chard was to be Denegtacus' successor and was here to stay!

If it were not borderline blasphemy to say it, Denegtacus almost wished that these years would speed by so that he could finally take his leave from his people and their troubles to prepare himself for the final great rest. It wasn't that he wanted to die or that he had grown bored of life, it was just that he had become so tired. How cold the winters now felt; aches he had never before noticed plagued him when the wind blew from the north.

Seven more years and then he supposed that he would know one way or the other. If Chard was the one, it shouldn't take more than a century or so to fully train him to a level whereby he could begin to teach himself what it meant to be L'tusian. If he wasn't the one … Denegtacus immediately ended that line of thought. The decision had been taken, doubt was a luxury he could no longer afford if he was to give Chard the best instruction possible.

Settling back in his chair he picked up his quill to continue and glanced irritably at the ink mark on his finger. Wiping it absently with the sleeve of his robe, he began to write.

5

On his eleventh birthday, Chara presented Chard with his own spell book. It was splendidly bound and embossed and the boy could feel the magic surging within its blank pages almost as if they yearned for him to commit his vast store of knowledge to them. He held it tightly for some time, savouring the moment, until he could bear it no more and slowly turned the pages, gazing at them as if they already had the words that he would write upon them. This was his, something that no man would, or could, take from him. He closed the book and held it to his chest, his thin arms encircling it so fiercely that they went white. Tears formed in his eyes but he blinked them away. No one who owned their own spell book should cry.

Luckily he had turned from Chara when she had presented it to him and she did not see his lapse. Stood at the open window where the light was best, he now turned to face into the room. Chara had made the effort to stand, and it was an effort, when she handed the book to him, but now she was once more slumped in her chair. He need not have worried because her eyes were closed and she gave no indication of any kind that she had sensed his weakness. Lines were gouged into a face that was screwed up in pain that no magic of hers, or her pupil's, could ease and her breath came in ragged gasps. The gift had brought the first smile to her face for what seemed like months and Chard was saddened to see how ephemeral the moment had been, how much of a shadow of her former self Chara had become.

Although he had always known her as an old woman with waning powers, he was not foolish enough to believe that this was how it had always been. Many times he had come to know her inner steel and strength and could well imagine what she must have been like in her youth. Chara rarely spoke of the past, either hers or his own, but when he pressed her she would occasionally retell tales that would have him enraptured. These days however, her memory played tricks on her and sometimes she could barely remember her name let alone things which had happened decades earlier.

Chard knew he had loved her, then love had watered down to respect and now it was akin to something like pity. But this gift had almost rekindled the old feelings, buried deep within the cold child he had grown into, and he suddenly felt the need to say something to comfort the old woman. Yet he did not, for he knew that any words of sympathy would be coldly rebuffed if acknowledged at all, and he had no desire to be the subject of her scorn. Instead he thanked her for the gift, ignoring the outward signs of her deterioration.

'Your words are unnecessary,' replied Chara. 'We both know you are ready to own your own spell book. You yearn to write the spells, to see them take form on the pages. Writing them for the first time is very much like casting them for the first time, the exhilaration, the knowledge of what you could make happen, that is why the magic user searches for more and more spells. It is intoxicating.' She came to a halt and winced as a particularly painful constriction wracked her chest.

Chard made no move to aid her but watched with an almost detached interest. He knew her malady was not one of the body, no cancer lingered in her, no disease infected her. It was simply that she had lived too long in a body never designed to last for the number of years she had accrued. Only her immense will kept her chained in the world of the mortals, her desire, *her need*, to see what became of Chard.

Chara drew another shuddering breath. They stared at one another until Chard asked the question that had suggested itself to him as soon as he had seen the book.

'Where did the book come from? I mean, the magic is strong and …' he paused, knowing that to complete the sentence would be like a dagger to the old woman.

Chara almost smiled but the effort of raising the corners of her mouth was too much and it appeared more like a grimace. 'Aye, the magic is strong and you think I am no longer capable of such things.'

Chard shrugged, there was no need to answer, it was obviously true.

'The book you hold is the same one I was given when I reached your level. All I have done is remove the spells I placed on the pages. It means that it has reverted to its original form and awaits its next master: you.' She sighed and shut her eyes. 'My spells live on in you, there is no more need for them to be written down.'

'But most of the spells I will write will be those you have taught me. What's the point in removing them so that I can write them back down?'

Chara's eyes opened just a fraction and she stared at him with some of her old shrewdness. 'Most?' she asked mockingly.

Chard berated himself silently for such a careless slip of the tongue. They both knew that he had made many discoveries for himself even though Chara had forbidden him to experiment until she deemed he was ready, but they played out the game all the same. His face flushed red, a mixture of shame and resentment.

The witch waved her hand, dismissing the point. 'You may write the same spells but they will change because the person casting them has changed. No two magic users are ever truly identical, least of all us.'

Chard picked up on the insult delivered so casually and felt himself growing angry.

'Then it is fortunate that you have no more to teach me!' he hissed through clenched teeth.

'If you really believe that, then I have taught you nothing,' replied Chara in a more amiable tone of voice. 'Before we go our own ways I have to show you how to let your soul soar. That is your last lesson and my final gift to you.'

Chard gasped in astonishment. He knew it was possible and had often tried it when he was alone but had never been able to do it, did not even know how to start.

'No come-back at all, my young mage?' said Chara without any attempt to keep the mockery from her tone. 'Strong in magic you may become, but at the moment you still need this old witch to keep her hand on your shoulder.'

Chard swallowed all of his ire. His anger he could vent later when he was alone, now he needed to know this last spell. He knew that a lot of Chara's hate was not truly directed at him, but the words still stung nevertheless.

'Now, mistress?' he whispered softly.

Chara reached out her wasted arm and Chard sprang forward to help her up, nearly losing his grasp of his new book as he did so. Carefully he placed the spell book under one arm and helped the old woman to her feet with the other. She swayed like heather in a breeze before making her way slowly to the door, her small weight borne mainly by the boy at her side.

Outside, the sun was just dipping behind the hills on the western horizon. It had turned the sky a glorious colour and the witch stopped in her slow progress to gaze at the red- and gold-streaked heavens. The shadows had lengthened and the animals of the night could just be heard stirring in the undergrowth. The old woman turned her head this way and that, taking in all that she could with her deteriorated vision. She was almost tempted to share what she could see with Chard but knew that he would never be able to appreciate these wonders, it was simply not in his nature. A caustic comment nearly slipped from her tongue but she managed to swallow it; better his final memories of her were of this great piece of magic than of the bickering that had so blighted their last years.

'Anywhere here will be fine, young one.'

Chard released his hold on the witch and she sank slowly to the earth to sit quite comfortably on the damp grass. Without a word, she patted the ground next to her and Chard hurriedly took his place beside her, making sure that his new book was safely on his lap.

'All this,' she began, gesturing briefly with her right hand, 'is a part of the wonders of magic, of the soul. Only by freeing yourself from the confines of the flesh can you truly appreciate its wonders and see with the eyes of your spirit rather than of your body. Hang onto this thought, grasp it and hold it close. Look for the wonder of the universe, Chard, and let go, for the flesh is weak but the soul is strong.'

Chard listened to her words with all his heart, for this was the one piece of magic that he knew he could not do alone. For the first time in months he truly attempted to accept her teaching and the meaning of her words. Closing his eyes tightly he opened his ears so wide he imagined insects flying straight through! Magic began to build up around him. He could feel it, making the air taste almost metallic and he yearned to immerse himself in it. But something was …

Abruptly he felt the hand of his teacher slip noiselessly from his and he risked a glance at her. The witch's eyes were closed, her face calm and serene and her soul clearly absent from the frail husk it inhabited. The peace Chard had been striving for left him as he realised that he had not joined her. He quickly closed his eyes once more but the moment was gone and in frustration he got to his feet, absently wiping the dirt from the seat of his trousers.

He paced slowly around Chara, his eyes never leaving her as his mind contemplated his failure. The word was like bitter medicine on his tongue and he felt a physical need to spit. Halting his walking he stared hard at everything and nothing, seeking a clue to aid him. She had gone beyond his normal sight and into a realm where he could not follow.

The thought came unbidden to his brain. Why was she beyond him? He had only her word that this was so and talking to her was only slightly helpful at the best of times, and the last few years were clearly not the best of times. As a witch she had the outlook of a witch but he was more than that, much more.

The bird he had been watching suddenly took to the wing and flew quickly out of sight. Had the boy wizard so desired he could have tracked it with the power of his mind alone, so could he not do the same with Chara? Why did adults always say, 'you'll understand when you're older'? Chard had the mental capacity of a man far greater in years and knew without a doubt that he was ready for the next step in his learning and that it had been waiting for him for some time.

He stared at the book he held in his hands and shook his head ruefully. So much wasted time. Without another thought he tossed it indifferently to the ground. What need had a *wizard* like him of such trinkets?

'I know what to do, Chara!' he called into the evening air. 'I do not need you to show me!'

Summoning his will he felt the magic surge into his body. His frail human form did not so much as waver as he drew the energy into himself, gaining strength from the magic all around him. Looking at his hands he saw the sparks start to earth themselves in the ground near his feet. All the colours of the spectrum flashed before his eyes and he smiled warmly and clenched his fists, the lights dripping between his fingers like coloured water.

Raising his face to look at the darkening sky above him, he saw the stars just peeking out at another night. This night, though, he looked not just with his eyes but with his soul and all at once the world seemed to burst into colour as he drank in the view of the spirits of the night. The souls of animals, insects and people who had died showed up as they made their way to their afterlife. Here and there he could make out the souls of new life hurrying to the Earth to replace those who had gone before them.

In that one moment Chard knew that he had the power to change the destination of all those souls he saw and even those he could not see. He could will them out of existence or control them in life; it was all up to him.

Other matters occupied him for the moment and he turned his head in a large arc in an attempt to locate Chara. They were linked, and in seconds he could see her, hundreds of feet in the air, standing quite calmly with her arms folded.

Chard outstretched his arms and called upon his magic. 'I do not need to flee my body, Chara, for my body is strong in magic, it is magic!' Slowly and deliberately Chard raised his physical form into the air. Soon his feet were above the blades of grass and Chard allowed himself a glance downwards and mocked the pathetic pull of the Earth that kept others chained to the ground.

He grinned hugely and with a roar of pure magic he surged into the night sky, his clothes billowing in the sudden gust of wind. Like a bird leaving its nest for the first time, he swooped and dived effortlessly, laughing in delight at the feeling of total freedom. Rolling onto his back he stared at the endless reaches of space above him. He kicked his feet and pretended to swim through the air, all the while making his casual way towards Chara.

Eventually he glided up to where the spirit of the witch

waited for him. She watched him closely but with an apparently neutral expression and remained still until he decided to come to a halt some feet from her.

'I am glad your powers amuse you, boy,' she said.

Chard shrugged, indifferent to the spirit of an old woman and what she liked or disliked.

Undaunted, Chara continued, 'But perhaps you have been given these gifts for other reasons and as such perhaps you should be …'

Chard held up his hand and Chara fell silent. 'There is nothing that I "should" witch, nothing. I do what I wish when I wish it.'

The witch bowed her head and had circumstances been different it would have been said that she was looking at the ground, but the ground was out of sight in the darkness some five hundred feet below. Her head came upwards sharply and the words were already tumbling out. 'No, Chard, you have these powers for reasons that as yet you do not understand, but I know that the universe would not have wrapped them up inside you if it did not have plans for you.'

'I have plans enough for myself. I do not …'

This time it was Chara who interrupted Chard. 'The mark of a man over a boy, Chard, is the ability to think of what others need above that which you personally desire,' she said sharply. 'You would do well to remember that.'

Chard inclined his head a fraction. It cost him little, he could feel the pull of death that surrounded the spirit before him.

Chara's soul would have sighed had she needed the air in her present form. In the moments that remained, she felt the need to make him understand. The difficult time he had had growing up she believed he would inflict upon the world as the adult he was sure to become. Knowing that time was running out she continued to try to bring him back from the brink he now stood upon, a brink she had helped push him to.

'I look back on my life, Chard, and do you know what I see? I see works of great good, great sacrifice tempered by some petty evils that I wish I had the power to change. I would like to believe that where I passed I left those behind with a better life than that they had before I came to them. I delivered a lot of lives into this world, Chard, yours included, and I never ended one on purpose.' She eyed him keenly. 'When you stand in my position, talking to whomever you have decided is almost good enough to follow after you, will you be able to say the same?'

'Petty insults to the last, mistress? That is beneath you.' He glanced over her shoulder as a brilliant blue light shot through the air towards the Earth, the soul of a new life eager to find its home. Chara turned to look at what he had seen and raised an eyebrow when she realised what had caught his attention.

'Rather than quibble over the deaths of the lives I choose to end, I would say to the person who follows me, "Think of all those I allowed to be born".' He gestured at the soul lights. 'Look at them, countless thousands of pointless irrelevancies who owe me their very existences. Not only do I expect their thanks, I shall demand it. Will not serving me give them a sense of purpose? A feeling of order in a world of chaos? An awareness of their place? Therefore, should I decide to end some lives, it is my place to do so.'

The witch's soul shook its head slightly. 'You are older than your years, child, but your thinking is warped and I must carry some of the burden for that fault. Do not walk down this path I beg you, for it will lead you to your death and the deaths of others.'

Chard stared hard at his former tutor and tried to recall the good times, the memories which would allow him to ease her pain, but none came. It was as if he was looking at a stranger and he felt a certain detachment from the conversation. He opened his mouth to reply but instead of speaking he simply closed it again. Chara watched and then this time did sigh.

'I do not wish to leave you like this, Chard, and yet I know that I shall not see the dawn.' She turned from the boy, looked at the night and smiled thinly. 'I shall miss it, Chard, all of it.'

By the time she had finished the sentence the transformation was already underway. The years began to melt from her face, the lines disappeared, her hair turned from white to auburn. In a matter of moments she had become a young woman of some beauty but it was her manner which showed the greatest change. Gone was the weariness that had so plagued her in recent years, to be replaced by the steel of youth that had supported her throughout her long life.

Chard glanced downwards and thought he could see where the witch's body lay, awaiting burial. From inside his tunic he brought out a dirty copper coin with a faded image of some faded king. 'Do you need this for the ferryman?'

Chara shook her head and produced the ethereal shape of her own coin from somewhere inside her clothing. 'I came prepared, young one.' Already she was beginning to waver as the pull of death took her. 'Bury me where I lie, Chard, and plant some flowers, buttercups would be nice ...'

And then Chard stood alone in the sky, holding the coin which he returned to his pocket. He felt nothing at her passing, not despair or sadness, not even relief, just nothing. Any emotion within the boy wizard had simply withered away to leave the husk of humanity that now was truly alone in the world. His thoughts turned to his mother who barely spoke to him these days because her new husband had forbidden it. What sort of person cast their child aside like that? What had a child done to deserve such treatment? Chard no longer knew and no longer cared. He was alone and the world would not be able to touch him if he remained so.

The fun he had enjoyed as he soared in the air seemed to

have evaporated and he cast about to get his bearings for the return journey to his home. But something prevented this. Whatever it was it simply could not have just appeared so close to him, he would have seen its approach or at least felt it on some level. And yet the wall of blackness was there, right before him and all around him, shrouding him in velvet. Close enough to touch, it oozed an evil that was palpable and Chard began to recoil from it until he realised it was right behind him as well and he came up short. Looking over his shoulder he saw that he had nowhere to run. Cautiously he extended his hand and watched as it vanished into the dark. There was no feeling to suggest that he was even touching anything but he believed what he saw since he had been brought up by Chara to do just that. If you couldn't believe your own eyes, then whose could you? As he tried to withdraw his arm he felt something unseen grip it with force. The first surge of panic gripped him, threatening to destroy his thinking and he struggled to overcome it. His will commanded him to remain calm but there was something else, operating on a far more primal level, that was making his mind a blank. Drawing in a lungful of air he tried to scream but before the sound could escape his lips, the inky blackness swallowed him.

Denegtacus was kneeling on the sodden earth, a trowel in one hand and a collection of weeds in the other. In truth he was no gardener but he was a patient elf if he put his mind to it and tending flowerbeds needed patience. The efforts often took years before they were rewarded; he had heard the king's gardener say only recently that at the age of two hundred and forty he still wasn't happy with the palace lawns and that his only regret at getting old was that he wouldn't live to see if the new fertiliser would be as good as he hoped.

Results in other areas of life often took even longer,

Denegtacus thought to himself. Take all this nonsense with the arguments over elves leaving Bulair and going out into the world. Sure, bad things were bound to happen, and Denegtacus was pretty certain that there were elves in Bulair who actively wanted them to, but think of all the benefits that were to be had. Change is hard, change can cause problems, *change is not always for the best.* The elf smiled at the thought. Change had so far affected others, but with the coming of the human boy it had finally caught him up too.

The sun was sinking and another day was ending. Night came quicker to the forest, the thick canopy of Bulair screening out so much of the light. Denegtacus turned his head and looked up at the sky. The trees surrounding his home had been deliberately thinned in order to allow the elf to keep a garden which boasted a greater variety of life than it might otherwise have had. It looked like being a clear night and the temperature was bound to fall. More firewood to stack, more blankets to keep out the chill. Chuckling to himself, he wondered what all those elves who told such fanciful stories of the magnificent enchanter would make of the reality. He looked down at his muddy hands and clothes and wiped the worst from them. Magic was far too precious to waste on such trivialities as cleaning an old elf or warming his cottage when a bath and a decent fire could do much the same. It wasn't as if he had to gather the wood for himself, there were plenty of people who did it for him, who even considered it an honour.

'Ah what it is to be famous!' he said quietly and started towards his cottage. Abruptly he came up short, his previous happiness draining away. Something was wrong, very wrong; it was almost as if he had forgotten something important. The old elf walked back to his cottage still wiping the dirt from his hands. He paused to place the weeds he had picked onto the compost heap before he finally went inside.

Enchantment brings great power but he was no god.

Denegtacus hurried across the room to his desk. The sense of foreboding was growing with every second and he knew it had something to do with Chard, but as yet he did not know what. Casting papers aside with careless disregard, he quickly found what he was looking for: a human calendar with Chard's sixteenth birthday marked some years in the future. Humans never got magic before adulthood, he was certain of that, and yet even across the hundreds of miles that separated him from Chard he could feel the waves of magic being disturbed, shifting in pattern and strength.

The answer hit Denegtacus almost as he thought of the question and he raged silently at his own stupidity. No elf magic user ever got magic during childhood, not even himself, but Chard was human and humans went through puberty decades before elves. Adolescence was the moment that most felt the first stirrings of magic, it was yet another problem to add to all the others that youths went through. Chard was not as yet an adult in terms of years but he was becoming one biologically and as such was gaining an awareness of the magic that surrounded and engulfed the world.

Denegtacus physically staggered as his thoughts were interrupted by what could only be described as a punch of pure emotion emanating from the east. He clasped hold of his desk and waited until an unfamiliar sense of nausea passed. Powerful magic was being worked; magic that only Denegtacus or someone like him had the ability to use.

Forcing himself upright he called upon his will and summoned the magic. Sending it out to locate Chard he wanted it to show him what Chard could see, to tell him what Chard was saying. Nothing happened, the spell simply fizzled out. Denegtacus felt sick, it was all he could do to stop himself throwing up his supper. He could not actually recall the last time his magic had failed in any way; it must have been centuries ago when he was still learning how to use his power.

His mind raced as he struggled to understand. Nothing had been wrong with his use of enchantment, so that meant something had to be wrong with Chard. A fleeting image of the boy lying dead went through the elf's mind and he forced it away. Even if he was dead the magic should still have taken him to the body. He breathed out hard and decided to try once more. Repeating exactly what he had done before, not expecting anything different to happen, he prepared himself for the journey to Chard he would have to make immediately after the spell failed.

Only the spell did not fail, it worked perfectly. Denegtacus stood open mouthed before an oval-shaped hole in space and time that allowed him to view events happening hundreds, thousands, of miles away. The magic shimmered over the molecule-thick image of a young boy planting what appeared to be buttercups onto a freshly dug grave. Denegtacus watched as Chard patted the soil into place and sat, without making a sound, next to the grave he had excavated with his bare hands, to judge by the thick layer of dirt that was upon them. The night had closed in and only the light from the moon lit the scene the elf was spying upon. Sounds from another part of the land drifted to Denegtacus, animals and birds of the night, nothing sinister, and the old elf suddenly felt a great desire to begin the boy's training immediately, this very night. Far better that the world had a new L'tusian sooner rather than later if he could no longer rely on his magic. He waved his hand at the image which abruptly disappeared to leave the familiar sight of his home, but somehow it did not raise his spirits. Five more years until Chard reached adulthood: he had a feeling that they would be long.

Chard patted the last of the flowers into place on the grave. It wasn't really the right time to be moving plants around, but he had wanted to obey Chara's last wish straightaway. He scratched absently at his nose, ignoring the soil on his fingers and the line of dirt he left behind. Something had happened, something was bothering him, but for the life of him he couldn't think what. He could remember the feeling of exhilaration as he had learned to fly and the lack of feeling at his teacher's death and then … and then … he was burying her as she had asked him to do.

He shook his head just once. Whatever it was, the memory was gone, but unease gnawed at Chard. His thoughts were interrupted as he became aware of being watched. Turning his head he thought he caught a glimpse of an old man watching him from the end of a very long tunnel, but the image vanished even as he tried to focus on it. The man seemed to have pointed ears and eyes like creatures in books. Chard smiled. Clearly he was tired and not thinking straight. Tomorrow he would mull over what had happened when he was rested. Pushing himself to his feet he made his way back to the house that was now his.

6

Chard had waited until the end of the working day to visit the home of his mother. There was a part of him that relished the idea of confrontation, and besides at any other time it would have been utterly futile since there would have been no guarantee that there would be anyone home. Ignoring everything else he strode through the village, eyes fixed on the house fifth on the right past the main hall that served as the focal point of the community. A few of the villagers who were only just returning from their labours glanced at the boy but none offered a greeting or even a second glance and Chard did nothing to encourage either.

He stopped in front of the house just long enough to cast an enquiring look over it. Nothing had changed; the home was well made from local materials although the roof was still a patchwork of repairs after a particularly vicious storm during the winter had caused damage to the north side. The windows were empty and small, allowing light in but trying to keep the cold out, and were now blocked by heavy woollen curtains as the evening drew in. All of this Chard knew as he knew what to expect when his knock was answered. Without further delay, he rapped his knuckles firmly on the wood of the door three times and took a half step backwards.

From inside he could hear the muted sound of conversation and the approach of footsteps. The door opened and the face of his mother appeared. Shruna was wiping her flour-covered hands on a towel hanging from the cord around her waist and her eyes widened in shock at seeing the boy, the towel dropping from her grasp.

'Whatever are you ...' she began and then cast a quick, nervous glance behind her before stepping out onto the street and pulling the door closed. Surprise was evident in her voice as was the merest touch of fear. 'I mean ...' she paused again. 'I am being rude, Chard, and a little silly, I do not want the words to sound unwelcoming.'

'Yet they do,' sneered Chard in a tone way beyond his years, the hurt of rejection surfacing briefly, only to be quickly stifled by the needs of what he had come to say. 'Do not worry, mother,' he said in a more level voice, 'I will not trouble you long.'

Shruna watched Chard and something surfaced in her mind. 'Chara!' she asked, her voice rising.

'Now you think of her,' replied Chard evenly. 'She died last night. I buried her as she requested not far from her back door with some buttercups to mark the grave.'

'Oh, Chara,' she whispered, and stared at some point over Chard's shoulder, her gaze lost in the past. 'Sleep well.'

Chard shook his head. Not one remark directed at him from his own mother, a woman who lived in the same village as he did and yet he had not seen her in two days or lived with her in years. They had nothing in common; he sometimes found it hard to believe that they shared blood, for he knew they did not share the bond of family.

'If anyone should ask, nothing will change as far as the treatment of ailments is concerned, except that perhaps without her interfering they may be a little better. Babies on the other hand ...' The boy paused and gave a rueful smile. 'I suppose that will be more work for you because I don't suppose there will be many people who want an eleven-year-old boy tending their women.'

Shruna shook her head as something Chard said penetrated her thoughts of the old witch who had been her friend for so long. 'Eleven?' Her brow creased in thought until she remembered her son's birthday, which had come and gone yesterday. 'I'm sorry, Chard, but with one thing ...'

Chard held up his hand, the sneer turning into a snarl. 'Forget it, Shruna, I already have. I don't suppose remembering my birth is very important to you.'

Behind her the door suddenly opened causing Shruna to stumble slightly as she still had hold of the handle. Quickly she recovered and stepped between Chard and the man now silhouetted in the doorway. Her eyes cast from one male to the other yet never held either's gaze.

Chard stared balefully at his stepfather, Greevish: the man who had stolen his mother, made her move out and destroyed his home and happiness. He was only average in height but the years in the fields had given him a powerful frame. His chest was barrel-like and his arms enormous. His stomach overhung, displaying his liking for wine and food, but as he would remark if asked, he had grown it so why shouldn't he enjoy it? His face had at first shown only an interest in who was at the door and why that person was delaying his well-earned meal, but when he saw the boy his expression darkened noticeably.

'What did the runt want?' he asked his wife, his hand already guiding her back indoors, his speech already dismissing Chard into the past tense.

'To speak to his mother,' replied Chard loudly. 'Without interruption from boorish fools!'

Shruna's eyes closed slowly as the words hit. She knew the temper of her husband could unleash itself suddenly, especially if his food was late. Greevish stepped outside, one large pace bringing him directly before Chard. Although there were only a few people in the street they had all stopped at the sound of an argument and were settling themselves to enjoy a free piece of theatre.

'What did you say, child?' Greevish asked, in an ominously quiet voice.

'You heard,' replied Chard, refusing to lower his eyes from the big man before him.

Greevish turned his head and looked at the dozen or so people who were close enough to hear their conversation. 'Yes I did, and now so will all these good people of my village hear what I have got to say to you.'

Chard shrugged, insolence and hatred evident in all his mannerisms. 'There is nothing you can say or do that can touch me, Greevish, you have already done the worst that you could do by taking my mother from me. The whole village knows of your coldness towards me and yet they say nothing because it suits them not too. We all know of the death of your first wife and I am more aware than most of your inability to father children. Did you really think when you asked the old woman for her help that the news would not get back to me?' Chard chuckled without any sign of humour. 'Stupid as well as barren!'

The boy stood quite still, waiting for the blow that would knock him from his feet, the pain that would sting him, the blood that would be spilt, but none of it came. Colour rushed to the older man's cheeks and the temptation to lash out was written across his face, but he did not. Instead he gave a tiny nod, almost as if recognising a cogent point made by an enemy. 'Possibly, Chard, although when it comes to stupidity I must say that your own far outweighs mine.'

The dangerous leer on his face, the expression in his voice, the way he was holding himself; Chard knew that whatever came next was the truth and that Greevish had waited until exactly the right moment to unleash it. He could walk away now and never listen to it. Go back to his cottage and mix his potions, practise his spells and try to live with the humiliation of backing away from this pathetic man, and yet he knew that he could not, he had to hear the words, whatever they were.

'Please, husband,' cut in Shruna softly. 'There is no need.' She reached out a hand and laid it gently on his arm. For just a second his eyes flicked to his wife's hand and then to her eyes, and perhaps a piece of his anger faded.

'You have something to tell me?' said Chard, breaking the moment and serving to light the fire beneath his stepfather once more.

Greevish smiled cruelly. 'Indeed I have. You really believe that a mother could be forcibly dragged from her child and that she could learn to love the man who had made her make such a decision?'

Chard shrugged again. 'What I believe is unimportant, it has happened.'

The smile twisted into malice and Greevish gazed again at the slowly gathering crowd which now numbered nearly twenty. 'Such thinking is what I would have expected from someone like you Chard, a bastard with no ties to this world of blood or love. Shruna is not your mother and the old witch hated you, can you not see that you are just a burden to all whose path you have crossed? Be gone from my doorstep, bastard, I have no coin or food to spare you!'

The laughter was real, the hatred was real. Chard stared into the face of the man he had thought had stolen his mother and who had now shattered the illusions that had held his life together. He did not have to look at Shruna to know that Greevish spoke the truth, in his heart he knew. Greevish pushed his wife back into his house and disappeared after her, not even giving the discarded child another glance.

The shadows had lengthened even in the few minutes since he had knocked on the door but it did not hide Chard's burning face. He had not seen them when he had walked to the house but he did now, as he practically staggered away:

the expressions of distaste across the watching crowd as he went past them. He had always known he was disliked, how could he not? Now he was a pariah, totally excluded from community life with no rights under the law and no family to defend him. The one constant he had had, even if she lived in another part of the village, had been denied him. His eyes went from one face to another. People he knew, had treated, cured, turned from him and went about their own business. It seemed like only seconds and he had the main street practically to himself.

Picking up the pace he ran back to his cottage, his eyes fixed only on his front door. He thumped against the wood that felt cool against his skin and stood there for a time, just resting his forehead on the door. The cold began to eat into him which reminded him of the need for warmth. He put his hand to the latch and kicked angrily at the bottom corner he knew always stuck and went inside, slamming the door behind him with enough force to startle a few roosting birds from the branches overhanging the roof.

Crossing the room he sat in the more comfortable chair that Chara had always occupied. It was an unconscious act and yet it symbolised the change that had occurred. The fire had been lit during the day but had died down and now only a few embers glowed dimly in the grate. Chard glanced irritably at it, almost willing the flames to spring, but nothing happened. At least some small part of the tension slid from his shoulders; here was something menial that had to be done and he could use it to occupy his mind. Standing once more he sought his kindling and set about relighting the fire.

The knock was insistent, as if it was wary of being ignored. Chard roused himself from wherever his mind had been dwelling and glanced at the door. The night was dark but the flames in the fireplace still burned strongly; it could not have been more than an hour since he had lit it and slumped into his chair to think. He hadn't been aware of falling asleep, and he found it difficult to believe that he would ever sleep soundly again, but another firm rapping on the door dissuaded him of this and he finally propelled himself to his feet.

Crossing to the entrance he pulled it open savagely, long years of remembering to only open it as much as needed so as to keep as much heat in the room as possible were forgotten. Expecting some villager wanting a medicine for suspected stomach cancer but which would undoubtedly turn out to be wind, his face was already angry. Mouth open to deliver an outburst at being disturbed at such a time of night he closed it again as he looked at Shruna.

His foster-mother gave a somewhat wan smile as she stared at the child she had helped bring into the world and whose face bore such bitter scars. In her hands she clasped a small posy of flowers which she held out to Chard. The boy's eyes glanced down but he made no move to take them. After a moment she lowered the gift and the silence began to stretch out.

Eventually Shruna spoke. 'I would like to put these flowers on the mistress' grave, if that is all right with you?'

'She is dead, what do I care if you want to put flowers on her grave? I have fulfilled my promise to her and from this day forth I am free of any obligation.'

Shruna flinched at the sheer force of hostility that spewed from such a young being.

'Where did I go wrong with you, Chard? Even as a babe you were cold, but now …'

'Does your husband know that you are here?' he asked, cutting through talk of the past.

She shook her head. 'No, Chard, there are things we must discuss and they simply will not wait until sun up.' She looked over his shoulder into the empty room. 'Are we going to talk out here or are you going to invite me in?' She tried a smile but it soon fell from her face as Chard's expression remained fixed.

'I think not.'

'You'll lose all the heat from your fire with the door open.'

Chard finally broke eye contact with his visitor and glanced back into the room. Coming to a decision he turned and walked back inside and sat in his chair, leaving the door open for Shruna to follow.

The woman stepped across the threshold, quietly closed the door behind her and moved to stand before the fire, directly in Chard's vision. The boy gave no indication that he was even aware of her presence and so she crouched down, her eyes boring straight into his. She reached out and took one of his hands in both of hers. Feeling him tense and start to pull away she held on more tightly.

'Listen to me, Chard; it is time to tell you of the past.'

'The past is dead, it ...'

She gripped his hand so fiercely that a sharp hiss of pain escaped through his clenched teeth. His expression blazed in anger but Shruna pressed on.

'Let go of your hate for just a moment, Chard, and listen to what I have to say!' Easing the pressure she was exerting but still maintaining a firm hold, she began to relate his background and her own part in it.

For some time she talked and Chard listened without questioning as she spoke of Chara's belief in his powers and her desire to train him in order to use them wisely. She told him how they both knew how he had suffered at the hands of the other children who so resented his way of life and the witch's presence in their village no matter how many times they sought her aid. Then she told him of her genuine love for her husband and how she desperately wanted Chard to be the son for Greevish that he was unable to sire for himself, but that his heart had been soured against Chara and the boy for failing to stop his first wife from dying.

She talked and talked until she had literally poured herself out. The fire was still alight, but only just, when she finally stopped and throughout it all Chard had remained resolutely silent. Noticing the dying embers, Shruna quietly busied herself rebuilding the fire from the stock of wood in the rusted iron bucket on the hearth.

'What did Chara know of wizardry?' asked Chard quietly.

Shruna was slightly turned from Chard when he spoke and remained so when she answered. 'Not much in truth. She always said that male and female magic had no business getting mixed up with one another.'

'Yet she chose to mix them up in me,' mused Chard aloud. 'I doubt there is a witch alive that knows more about herb lore than me or has successfully come up with more new potions than I have. Yet I have begun to feel in me a certain unhappiness with my magic, like it was not giving me enough …' He paused, trying to think of the word that would fully explain how he felt.

'Power?' asked Shruna gently.

Chard looked at her in surprise. 'Yes, power. It is one thing to extend life; it is something else to take life away. I know that there are spells within witchcraft that can do just that, but mostly they are just common fakery. I have read and learned all that Chara knew and I can tell you now that for a witch to kill it would be easier to stick a knife in someone. They suggest to the victim that they are dying, put ideas into their minds, play tricks and deceive, but any with a strong will can resist. But a wizard, now that is something else!'

'Real power comes from within the soul and is harnessed for good. What you are suggesting is evil.'

'My power comes from within!' shouted Chard, standing up. 'My gift for witchcraft is linked to my power as a wizard, none have had such strength as I! I have learned to draw more energy to myself from the world around.' Chard was in full swing as his mind raced with new ideas. He gripped

Shruna by the shoulders. 'Don't you see?' he shouted in elation. 'I am the only man in the world who has control of all magic! Of witchcraft, of wizardry, and yes, even sorcery! There is nothing that I cannot do once I have learned how to harness it, nothing!'

Shruna shook herself free of his hold, dread rising in her. *This is a child, your child! There is nothing to fear* and yet she did. Chard's eyes were alight with a desire that Shruna had never seen before and she shrank back from him.

'But there are always things that you shouldn't do regardless of whether or not you are actually capable of them,' she said in a pleading voice. 'What use is strength if it comes at the cost of making others weak? What good comes of power that is not held in check by notions of morality?'

Chard seemed to tower over the kneeling woman, his face suddenly twisted into almost bestial rage. 'Morality!' he roared. 'Where was your precious morality when the others used to beat me? Where was your morality when you stole me from my true family in the night? Morality is a concept for the weak; I will have no use for it!'

Shruna shook her head in despair. There was no hope for this boy, both she and Chara had failed utterly in their attempt to bring him up. She wept gently into her hands, still kneeling on the hard wooden floor.

The pitiful sight before him merely sent Chard's anger to new heights. All rationality and control fled him. Here, right in front of his eyes, was one of the adults who had failed him throughout his short life. He had wanted to run with the pack and be normal but she and the witch had kept him apart and made him a figure of fun and hatred. In that moment he despised her with every fibre of his being, he forgot the times she had tended his scraped knees and put food on the table, and gave way to the darkness within.

With a shout that was more animal than human, his hands swept up, the palms facing away from him and his fingers pointed at the ceiling. Red flame erupted from the flesh and flowed around Shruna, whose screams bounced from the walls of the room. The cry for help served only to infuriate the boy wizard. The flame leapt forth with renewed vigour, turning blue and then white as the temperature rose. The screams soon stopped and the charred corpse slumped back, but still Chard poured the magic of hate at the body. Stray gouts of fire soon set the whole house ablaze. The chair where the witch had so liked to sit was incinerated, the old cloth and stuffing burning in seconds. The heat appeared to have little effect on Chard who finally ended his attack and stood quite calmly in the centre of devastation he had caused.

His arms slipped to his sides, the left catching on the ruined chair. The pain hit him and he looked down at his palms where the skin was blackened and peeling. He staggered back, stepping through flame that reached up to consume him. Screaming in agony, he ran through the burning building and flung himself against the door, his ruined hands struggling to open the latch. Sobbing with relief as finally the door came open, he fell into the night and pushed himself backwards on the ground to a safe distance from the inferno that had been his home for so long. His back connected with a tree and he forced himself into a sitting position and watched the house burn, the pain in his hands almost forgotten as his brain failed to cope with all that was happening.

The first footsteps came along quickly as the villagers arrived to see what was causing the fire. The old witch's house was far enough away from the main part of the village to mean that there was no danger of the fire spreading and all could tell that there was little point in trying to halt the spread of the flames which had already all but gutted the building.

It was one of the farmhands who first spotted the boy,

propped up against the tree like a broken puppet, and he made his way over to him. He crouched down before him and felt for a pulse in Chard's neck. Satisfied that the child was alive and likely to remain so he called to the others for help. By now there was quite a crowd gathered and a few drifted over to look at the boy, but most remained where they were, happy to watch the fire and let others deal with the injured, especially since it was only the bastard witch boy.

The farmhand placed his thumb on Chard's eyelid and gently lifted it. The boy's stare was focused and the pupils large, reflecting the firelight.

'You OK?' he asked, not unkindly. 'What happened?'

Chard smiled, his soot-blackened face creasing as he did so. Without reply he raised his hands and showed the man the palms.

The man recoiled at the sight of the ruined flesh and made the ancient warding sign to protect from evil. He made no further attempt to touch the boy and instead just stared at him, his expression locked into one of disgust.

Chard's hands slumped back down, the effort of holding them up too much. Then he started to laugh, and did not stop until consciousness left him.

He awoke to find himself lying on a hard wooden bed with the thinnest of blankets tossed casually over him. The pain still gnawed away at his hands and he gradually eased himself upright, taking his weight on his elbows. The village he lived in didn't have a jail, it had never really needed one before, but Chard was silently impressed by how quickly they had managed to improvise. In a bare wooden room he was lying on the only furniture. The window was letting in only a minimum of light due to the fact that pieces of wood had been nailed across it from the outside. The door had a lock on it and Chard did not need to test it to know that it would be in use. Judging by the structure, Chard believed himself to be in the main town meeting hall, most likely some storeroom that had hastily been converted to his temporary home.

Swinging his legs round he sat up and studied the damage to his flesh. The hours of darkness had helped to numb some of the pain but in the semi-light of the room it was clear that they were permanently ruined beyond even his ability to heal. He drew in his breath and tried to flex his fingers. Tears sprang involuntarily to his eyes as the sores split and fresh blood mixed with pus oozed from the gaps. He gasped out loud and then angrily bit his lip, determined to suffer in silence.

The sound of a key entering the lock made him look up. The village headman stood looking down at him, a thoughtful expression on his face. One hand idly scratched at the grey hairs on his chin while the other turned the key between his fingers. Welcrar had aged well, his hair had not fallen out, just turned grey and his figure remained lean and strong. His faculties were intact and as headman his position was well respected.

'When I first met Chara, I told her that trust was something few could afford. Seems you weren't worthy of it.'

Chard said nothing, it hardly seemed necessary.

Welcrar leaned casually on the doorframe, still keeping his distance but apparently perfectly relaxed. 'There's a lot of folk who want to burn you. Reckon we should finish what the fire started last night.'

'Where am I?' asked Chard, his eyes locked with the older man's.

'Village hall. I use this room as storage for anything valuable, only place with a lock on it.' He gave a small chuckle. 'Not that we have anything of value, mind.'

'What's going to happen to me?'

Welcrar didn't like the boy sat on the pauper's bed. He

couldn't think of a single redeeming feature in his character and yet there was something wrong in killing an eleven-year-old child, regardless of what they had done or were.

'Did you start that fire?' he countered.

Chard nodded and lowered his head but found that he didn't want to look at his hands and so he gazed out of the window at the limited view afforded him.

Welcrar sighed loudly. 'Then I guess we'll have to have a trial and I think we both know what the outcome will be.'

'What if I just left? What if I went away and promised never to come back?'

'That would suit most people down to the ground, me included. But most ain't all.'

'Greevish,' said Chard; it wasn't a question.

'Aye, Greevish. That's the second wife that's upped and died on him and you've been involved with both.'

'His first wife died of cancer, I did everything I could do and so did Chara!'

Welcrar held up his hand in a placating gesture. 'I believe you, son; you're not being accused of anything concerning her as far as I know. But you can see his point can't you? He wants justice and that means bad things for you.'

'You could say I escaped. You could say that I used my evil magic on you and when you came round I was gone.'

Welcrar finally crossed the room and stood by the window. He leaned forward to gaze out between the slats of wood and gave the thinnest of smiles as he saw groups of people milling around, all looking at the boarded-up window while trying to avoid each other's stares. Murder wasn't common and no matter how important work was, Welcrar had a feeling that not much would get done today.

'Don't think you'd get too far, kid. Lot of folk out there who should be working are just looking for an opportunity to let loose some justice of their own.'

'When will the trial be?'

Welcrar glanced back at the boy. Chard was sat hunched up, his whole posture one of misery.

'Next hour or so. Best that this is all over with today and then we can get on with life.'

'Except me of course.'

Welcrar laid his hand on Chard's shoulder. 'If it was down to me, son, I'd turn around and hope that when I looked back you were long gone. But it's not just down to me; the village wants someone to pay for what happened to Shruna.' At the doorway he paused and turned back. 'There wasn't much left of her by the time the fire burnt out. I find that a little odd. I mean, the fire sure took hold and there's not much left of anything but the body was nothing more than ash, even the bones had melted. I spoke to Thrisam over at the blacksmiths and asked him how hot a fire would have to be to do that to a person and he said a lot hotter than any wood fire he'd come across.'

Chard remained silent and didn't even look up at Welcrar's questioning expression.

The headman clicked his tongue. 'A mystery,' he said slowly, his gaze flicking down to Chard's blackened flesh. 'Someone will come for you; it'll all be over soon.'

The door shut, the key turned in the lock and Chard was alone.

7

The hall was packed to bursting. Chard estimated that there was upwards of three hundred people present, with many more milling about in the entrance and outside. Obviously this was a high point of interest for the village and Chard reflected that only now, after doing what he had done, did anyone take any notice of him. The audience was lined up in chairs on three sides with one side clear for Welcrar's desk and a space where Chard was to stand, directly before him. The headman was acting as judge and jury and was willing to listen to any testimony he believed had relevance to the issue.

Welcrar surveyed the villagers and sensed the palpable excitement in the crowd. No doubt there was someone outside already stacking the timber, ready for the execution. He raised his hand to try and start the proceedings but in the general noise, no one noticed and he was forced to raise his voice above them and call for quiet.

'Is there anyone prepared to speak for the defendant?' he asked the gathering.

Not a sound could be heard as hundreds of people glanced at each other, wondering whether or not the headman had made a joke.

He smiled humourlessly. 'I take it then that the boy will have to speak for himself.'

'Who wants to hear the lies of a bastard?' shouted a voice

which Welcrar failed to locate as the others rumbled their agreement.

'The boy has the right to speak, he has been found guilty of no crime,' responded Welcrar.

'Yet!' called another man to laughter from the villagers.

Welcrar glanced at Chard who stood quite still, his head hanging down.

'Is there any to speak for Shruna?' This time his question was answered by a roar from the crowd and a sea of hands went up.

From the front row to Welcrar's left, Greevish stood up. He stared at the headman, his eyes calm and empty.

'I will do it.'

Welcrar nodded. Sitting back, he gestured for Greevish to make a start. Greevish inclined his head and turned to look at Chard who stared back at his accuser.

'Did you start the fire at the house belonging to the witch Chara last night?'

'Yes,' answered Chard simply.

Greevish continued. 'Did you do it on purpose?'

Again Chard responded with a solitary word. 'Yes.'

The widower closed his eyes and paused before asking. 'Did you murder my wife, Shruna, a woman who had looked after you as her own for many years despite knowing all too well that you were not hers?'

'I did,' said Chard in an unwavering voice.

Such a public confession was greeted by a barrage of noise from the assembled villagers. Insults were hurled but thankfully no one attempted to physically attack the boy. Wary that this state of affairs might not last, Welcrar made certain that the men he had instructed to ensure nothing untoward happened to Chard were in place and aware of the danger. The men, all workers on his farm, nodded back at the headman and, reassured, Welcrar cut in.

'All right, keep it down!' he shouted, and gradually the

noise subsided. 'Do you understand what you have said, boy? The punishment for what you have done is hanging, no matter what your age.'

'I understand perfectly,' said Chard. 'But surely the punishment is burning, not hanging, for I killed her with magic, not ordinary fire.'

'Bastard!' screamed Greevish, and rushed at the boy. One huge sweep of his arm knocked the child from his feet and sent him sprawling to the floor. Two of Welcrar's men leapt forward, held Greevish's arms tightly and looked to Welcrar for instructions.

Welcrar said nothing and made no move to help the fallen boy. After a delay of over a minute, Chard finally picked himself up and stood once more before his judge. Greevish allowed himself to be taken back to his chair, although he shrugged off any who tried to comfort him.

'You're quite right, Chard, if you commit a crime using magic you are indeed burned, but as I understand it, you simply set fire to the house and trapped Shruna inside.'

Chard shook his head fractionally. 'You asked me how a body could be so badly damaged and I shall tell you.' Raising his hands he showed the headman the blackened flesh and then turned in a circle so that all could see. 'The fire came from within me, magical not wooden. It was the first time I have ever used such a spell and clearly I cast it wrongly for I should not have been injured like this.'

Welcrar sighed. 'I have but one last question for you, young wizard: if this is indeed what happened, will you tell us all why you did it?'

Chard's shoulders slumped. 'Because I despised her. When she told me the truth about my past, I felt all the rage I have kept in burst out. She did not deserve to die like she did, my hatred killed her, my lack of control killed her.' Suddenly he brought his head up and stared hard at Welcrar who could not help but flinch as the boy's eyes blazed. 'It is not a mistake I shall make the next time!' he bellowed.

Welcrar was afraid and he didn't know why. There was nothing this child could do, there were dozens of men, all armed with a variety of weapons, who could bring him down in seconds, and yet Welcrar could feel his insides tying themselves into knots. The headman barely heard the jeers from the crowd, the scrape of chairs as people got to their feet and surged forward, his focus was completely centred on the child.

The first hands grabbed at Chard, his protectors totally swamped by the mass of humanity that confronted them. He was dragged from the hall and through the open doors to the road outside where a pole had been hastily secured into the ground and surrounded by kindling. Chard's clothes were ripped and blood-stained by the time he was finally bound to the pole and the mob backed far enough away to enjoy the show.

It was Deris who stepped forward and handed the torch to Greevish, motioning him to do the deed. Greevish did not so much as glance at Deris as he took the torch and walked as close to Chard as he could get without risking injury to himself once the flames took hold. He held the glowing wood at arms length and showed it to Chard, who merely sneered his contempt.

'You'll soon know what burning alive feels like, just like my Shruna did. Better get used to it since your soul will spend the rest of eternity in the flames of Hell.' He lifted the torch high and bellowed his dead wife's name before plunging it deep into the oil-treated tinder. The fire took hold at once, forcing Greevish to retreat and shield his eyes from the acrid smoke. Behind him the crowd cheered their support and listened for the first cries of panic and pain from Chard.

The boy wizard stood peacefully in the centre of the flames, his eyes clear and untroubled, taking in all that he saw, apparently unaffected by the smoke. Then his hands were clasped silently before him, the shards of rope that had bound him still visible about his wrists. Slowly, very slowly, he walked through the flames that seemed to part like a crowd and stepped back onto firm ground, his clothes and hair not so much as singed.

There were audible cries of astonishment and fear from the assembled villagers. Some of the brighter ones were already making for their homes and perceived safety while others remained immobile with shock. Chard stopped as he stood before Greevish, his face the picture of serenity.

Greevish spluttered something unintelligible but Chard touched a finger to his lips and the man fell silent. The boy leaned forward and whispered into the man's ear. The crowd watched as a look of horror spread across Greevish's face. Chard smiled. It was the like the grimace on the face of a corpse and Greevish would have recoiled from it if he had been able to will his legs to move.

Pain the like of nothing he had ever experienced before lanced through Greevish's body, bending his frame and sending him onto one knee. Moaning he reached for the knife he kept in a sheath on his hip. In one move he pulled it clear and thrust it into his throat, giving no more than a small gurgling sound as he choked on his own blood.

Chard chuckled to himself and glanced at the assembled mob, all of whom were trying to hide behind one another. 'You came looking for death and now you have it, but I sense that you are not satisfied.' He touched the body with his toe. 'Is this not what you wanted!' he roared.

Chard noticed a few of the villagers glance at something behind his back and turning he saw Welcrar appear in the doorway of the meeting hall. The headman had remained at his desk when the villagers had borne Chard away, not wishing to see his end, but as the minutes had ticked by, he become aware of a growing sense of foreboding and made his way outside to see for himself what was transpiring.

The smoke from the still burning fire cast a dark pall across the whole spectacle, the sound of crackling timber adding a background noise to a view which would otherwise have been devoid of sound. Welcrar seemed to age visibly as he looked out onto the horrors taking place in his own village. His shoulders were stooped, his face ashen.

'Go, Chard,' he whispered. 'Take your wizard powers away from here and leave these people be.'

'Why?' asked Chard. 'I might wish to stay.'

'Someone will come once word gets round and they will kill you. You may be powerful to us, Chard, but you are still a child and another wizard could destroy you.'

'You know nothing about which you speak,' retorted Chard. 'Besides, I killed that fool Greevish using nothing but suggestion and his own paranoia, not wizardry.'

The headman shrugged. 'He is still dead, another murder to be laid at your feet. Is that how you want to live your life, Chard? You had better go and make sure you have a good head start, for the king's men will soon be on your trail.'

'Then you want to hope they make a better job of killing me than you managed to do!' Chard swung angrily round, his ruined hands sweeping up. The villagers recognised the warning and most turned and fled. Two lightening bolts leapt from his outstretched fingers, one connecting with the ground a few feet from a man who was sent sideways by the impact, the second hitting a fleeing woman squarely in the back, killing her instantly.

'*That* is wizardry!' shouted Chard gleefully to the horrified headman.

Welcrar shook his head. 'No, Chard, that was murder,' he replied sadly.

Chard slowly brought his hands down, the smile slipping from his mouth.

'Send word to any who will listen to you, Welcrar, I care

not. Make sure you tell them that anyone who stands against me I shall kill. Tell them I said that.'

'I will tell them, Chard.' Welcrar pointed at the road that led from the village before turning his back and disappearing inside the hall.

Chard watched him go and then gave one last cursory glance around the village. There was not a soul in sight, although he could feel the stares from unseen watchers. This was not his home, he had no home and no need of one. Walking from the village he did not look back.

Elf politics was a very involved subject to which a great many elves dedicated their lives. Humans said that politics was the reason elves lived so long; it took centuries to fully understand just how things worked. Be that at is may, if anything was to be done then it would only be achieved by someone who knew the ins and outs of the system and that meant professional politicians and all that they brought with them.

Denegtacus sighed deeply as he re-read the letter on his desk for the hundredth time. A human delegate from Curinlas had sent it to him via the monthly diplomatic postal service that had been instigated by the king when elves had started freely roaming the continent. If his children were 'gadding about the world', as the king put it, then the least they could do was make sure they kept in touch. The post had soon become an enormous operation both in terms of money and volume but all could see the benefits that it had brought and the potential that was as yet not fully realised. The human nations that surrounded Bulair had become involved in it and now, less than a year after it had all begun, it was the accepted means of communication between states.

All over the continent, state postal services were springing up as demand grew. The best horses in the world were used at the hundreds of staging posts across Eurasia, all kept ready for when messengers carrying saddlebags stuffed with correspondence rode in, needing fresh mounts for the next leg of the journey.

The old elf mulled over all that had happened in his mind. Change was the nature of things, no matter what a lot of the old elves said as they grumbled to any who would listen. But this request was something that Denegtacus was certain would not be welcome: a change too far, too quickly. That was the problem with humans, their short lives meant that they were always in a hurry; they never took the time to simply stand back and watch things evolve on their own rather than trying to force the issue. Even as these thoughts crossed the old elf's mind he realised that this was also the humans' greatest talent and the reason why they had swarmed across the continent like an unstoppable wave, forcing the other races into smaller and smaller pockets of land. Denegtacus knew that at some point in the future the humans would turn envious eyes to these places as well and the war that would follow would be disastrous.

He shuddered and put such thoughts from his head. At present, there was an unrivalled sense of alliance between elf and human and it achieved nothing to ponder future 'what ifs'. The future would take care of itself, the present was what needed the enchanter's concentration.

The letter itself was couched in all the usual diplomatic language and ran to four pages when a paragraph would have done. It begged its reader's indulgence for encroaching on his time and went on to recall past meetings and the beginnings of friendships between individuals as well as between nations. All this Denegtacus skipped as he sought to find the real message. When he had first realised what Curinlas was asking he had frowned, when he realised what his king's reaction would be he had almost laughed aloud.

In essence the request was simple: Curinlas had built a new

post station only a mile from the border with the western edge of Bulair, its function to deal solely with Bulair and so speed up rates of communication by days if not weeks. Messages from Armishmer could be sent to Elvern in three days and if the elves responded in kind it would be possible for the kings to correspond directly with each other in less than a week!

Of course there was a catch. Curinlas was well aware of how slowly things moved in Bulair and that any letter sent from the humans to the elves would never be regarded as urgent no matter if it foretold of the end of the world. The Royal Government of Curinlas was therefore suggesting that a post station should be built inside Bulair to receive these letters and that it should be staffed by Curinlasian officials who would be able to sort out quickly what was urgent and requiring a prompt reply. The station itself could be built in less than two weeks and it was estimated that a staff of twenty should be more than enough to see that things ran smoothly.

Denegtacus could already see the king's face when he told him of the request, he could already hear the bellowed answer and was pretty sure that the humans back in their own capital would hear it too. However, politics was all about controlling change, and although Denegtacus knew that the king would never agree to humans working inside Bulair, he would see it as a victory when Curinlas backed down and accepted elf officials running the station, whereas of course all Curinlas really wanted was the station built in the first place. Everyone would get what they wanted and then they could focus on the next problem when it cropped up.

Denegtacus would go to the king and explain the situation. He smiled with genuine warmth at the thought of his comrade and wondered what he would have said in years gone by if Denegtacus had told him that his reign would see more change than any other king's to date. He knew his friend well enough to know the answer. At least his wife would always be ready to calm him down and make him see sense.

It had been the question of humans on elf soil that had jolted Denegtacus' thoughts back to Chard. The enchanter had no doubt that he would get his own way and that permission would be given for Chard to train alongside him, but the issue of time bothered him. A common joke among the tradesmen of Eurasia was that if a human merchant wanted to visit an elf inside Bulair then he should make certain that he put his grandson's name on the form requesting permission to enter the forest. It wasn't overly far from the truth.

Chard. Chard. Chard. Everything always came back to the boy in one way or another. He was eleven now, a few more years and he could begin the training, but there and then Denegtacus resolved to bring the matter to the attention of the king in order to give him time to get used to it. Five years! Denegtacus had known the king take longer than that to get used to a new bowstring!

Gathering his will, he cast the magic that opened the passages that allowed him to travel anywhere he chose almost instantaneously. An oval hole opened in the air before him, showing the palace. He adjusted the image slightly until he had located the king, who was sat on one of the balconies with his wife and a few other elves that Denegtacus vaguely knew. As soon as he stepped through the gateway, it instantly closed behind him.

The King was used to his old friend simply appearing and hardly raised an eyebrow, but some of the other elves were more nervous. One drew a sharp intake of breath and almost raised his hand in the ritual gesture of protection but remembered himself just in time and instead changed it to a nervous wave of greeting.

'Ah L'tusian!' said the king happily. 'Always a pleasure. The councillors were just leaving in any case.'

With deep bows to the monarch and his wife, the three other elves slipped away, all looking relieved.

Denegtacus turned and watched them go, a scowl on his face all the while. When they had gone he gave a smile. 'Does the people good to be frightened every now and again. They'll run off and tell their friends of my dark powers and fierce countenance.'

The king chuckled and gestured to a chair which Denegtacus took. Barely had he sat than he was up again and pouring the king and queen a fresh glass of watered wine. Then he poured one for himself and resumed his seat.

'What brings you here then, old friend, or did you just want to scare a couple of politicians for me?'

'Not that it isn't always a pleasure to see you, Ancient One,' intervened Queen Amaril gently, her hand straying to her husband's arm and giving it a small squeeze.

Denegtacus smiled at the words and savoured them, for they were likely to be the last complimentary ones he heard for some time. 'Do you not find that when you see less years in front of you than you have accumulated behind you, you want the world to stop and just stay the same?'

'I believe you are teasing my husband,' replied the queen, her expression showing her jest.

'Yet it never does,' continued Denegtacus, as if he hadn't heard. He looked at his sovereign with piercing eyes that Theaspida found hard to hold.

'Come, come, my dear Denegtacus. Whatever is the cause of such melancholy sentiments? Have you forgotten that I have lost a son to the world only recently and yet I took it like an elf.' He paused and his smile slipped. 'But I wish I had not lost him so.'

'Other changes are coming, my king,' said Denegtacus softly. 'Perhaps some with an even more bitter taste than those we have already endured.'

The queen took a sip of her drink, the glass hiding the lower part of her face as she spoke. 'My husband has spoken of your hope of finding another with powers such as yours. Is this something to do with that search?'

The enchanter walked to the edge of the balcony. He leaned on the stonework and took in the magnificent view of the city, built as one with the forest that shaped it.

'I don't even know how old I am any more,' he said quietly. 'The years have all blended into one long continuation that I cannot see the end of. My power is as strong as ever it was but I feel … old. There is no other way of saying it.' He glanced back over his shoulder at the royal couple before enjoying the view again.

'You have always been there, my friend,' said the king kindly. 'We elves would not be the noble race that we are if it were not for your steadying influence over the centuries.'

'It is kind of you to say so, my lord, but I have found the person I believe has been sent to replace me and my time here is, perhaps, coming to an end.'

The king and queen got up and made their way over to Denegtacus, each taking up a station on either side of him. Amaril placed her arm around the L'tusian and waited, sensing the need for the elf to talk.

'You are wise, Amaril, you have seen that I am becoming less settled at a time in my life when I should be content.'

'I had a good teacher,' she said kindly.

A sigh came from Denegtacus that seemed to shake his entire being. 'I may as well tell you some of the inconsequential news before we argue about matters of importance. The humans of Curinlas have asked me to speak on their behalf regarding the building of a post station inside Bulair. They want twenty men to man it and believe this will help relations between our two nations.' He raised a hand when he saw Theaspida's face literally sag. Strange how the sight did not strike him as funny in any way. 'Of course it is unacceptable, they will be more than happy to simply see the station built since it will aid them and us.'

The king rubbed his chin. 'I suppose it could be done. Don't really see the need myself but then I can't recall the last time I did see the need for change and that never stopped it happening anyhow.'

Amaril smiled but silently urged the enchanter to continue.

'But although trade is important it is as nothing when weighed against the importance of magic to this land, to this world. While we can laugh at their suggestion of allowing a permanent garrison of humans on sacred soil simply to sort a few letters it does not mean that we can laugh off all suggestions of foreigners coming to our land.'

The king turned his glass around absently, the noise of it scraping on the stone sounding louder than it actually was. 'We are not totally closed to outsiders, Denegtacus, never have been. Anyone can ask for permission to come into Bulair regardless of their species.'

'True, my lord, but did you know that the longest visitor to our land stayed just nine days? That's hardly long enough to shake the mud from your boots. Whereas on the outside our elves are allowed to roam practically at will.'

'More fool the humans for letting them,' muttered the king.

'No, my lord, we are the fools for thinking that we can lock ourselves away in here. The more we try to shut the world out, it is my belief that it is us who will suffer.'

The king did not look at the older elf but his expression was flat and devoid of emotion. He did not wish for an argument with Denegtacus but if it came to it he would remind him just who was king and who was subject! No matter what his powers!

'I have found the man to replace me,' repeated Denegtacus. 'His name is Chard and he will be joining us in five years.'

'Joining us from where exactly?' asked the queen, her nervousness showing through as her gaze flickered from elf to elf.

'The east, beyond the trees. He is human.'

Theaspida's fist crashed down on the balcony wall and he rounded on his closest adviser. 'Never!' he bellowed. 'I have done all that I can to bend like a tree to the winds of change but I will draw a line here! No human will pollute the air of Bulair for a minute longer than is necessary and none will ever call this land home. Denegtacus, what has happened to you? Do not give me any of your nonsense about getting old, it happens to us all. There must be more!'

'I have sensed this boy's power, his strength, and it rivals my own. He must have training or he will never understand that with his gift comes a burden of responsibility and there is none other than I who can give him that guidance. In all probability he could be our greatest ally or our worst enemy. What would you prefer?'

'The answer is obvious if that was the question but it is not. The real question is how do you expect our people to allow this blasphemy? Is it not enough that I am criticised openly by those elves who are supposed to implement the king's will? This will drive a wedge through all elf society. It could mean civil unrest, war! I will not go down in history as the king who spilt the blood of his own! Not even for you, Denegtacus, will I allow this, the matter is closed!'

Denegtacus' eyes flared angrily and he rounded on his king. 'No, Theaspida, it is not. I will train this boy here inside Bulair or I will go to him and train him on the outside and never return to this land! You will be the king who drove the most powerful magic-user the world has ever seen from the land I vowed to protect centuries before you were even born!'

'You must do as you see fit, L'tusian, after all, it is what you usually do!'

The old elf could feel the rage within and struggled to control it. Taking several deep breaths he said in a measured tone, 'I am the protector of this land and of our people and that will never change, even if I must protect it from itself. But I have a duty to the world and to history. If I miss this opportunity to secure my successor he could easily turn to evil and destroy all that we hold dear. For the sake of the generations yet to be born we must take off our blinkers and let this child into our society so that he can see its wonders for himself. It could be the beginning of a new and greater understanding between our two peoples.'

'And it could very well destroy all that our ancestors worked for,' retorted the king in an even voice. 'I cannot make such a decision and I cannot allow you to make it for yourself. If you attempt this, Denegtacus, I will declare you a traitor and I will cast you out.'

'Do you really think you or anyone else could make me leave if I chose otherwise?' asked Denegtacus ominously.

The king stared hard at the elf before him. 'A moment ago you proclaimed that you were the guardian of our people and now you are threatening to kill them should they make a decision you do not agree with. You cannot have it both ways.'

Denegtacus could not have been more stunned if Theaspida had struck him. He took a step backwards, his back colliding with the stone. 'All my life I have spent serving this land and you accuse me of …' he spluttered to a halt. Drawing himself upright, his face was like iron. 'I leave today for the outside, I shall return when the land cries out to me for help regardless of what you say. None shall enter my home, for the day will come when another will seek me out.' He gave a curt nod to the queen. 'My lady,' he said, then turned his back on the couple and stalked away.

'My dear Pida,' whispered Amaril. 'What has happened here today?'

'I am king and he will obey me, as will you.' Rounding on

his wife the king continued, 'From this moment forward there will be no more talk of Denegtacus. He made his choice and must live with it.'

'As must we,' whispered Amaril.

Denegtacus travelled to Chard's village as soon as he left the king's presence, certain that he was right and that he would see this through to the end no matter what. Once there, he found the village in a state of confusion and anger, all of it directed at the now absent Chard. By probing the minds of the villagers he was quickly able to ascertain what had occurred and he made off in pursuit. It did not take him long to find the boy, who was some miles to the south-east, sheltering in a glade of trees from a sudden rainstorm.

The trees had been shaped by magic to form a perfect, waterproof tent for him and the remains of a rabbit ensnared by magic lay discarded outside. Chard himself was dozing off his meal, curled up and warm beside a fire – lit by magic.

Denegtacus sighed heavily. If magic was money then Chard had been spending recklessly. Everything he did he used magic to do and that was the surest way of emptying yourself of strength and power. Magic had to be used wisely and never frivolously since it was a gift from God. All this and more he would teach him, but in the meantime he would be satisfied to watch and observe.

This train of thought reminded the elf of the darkness above and he soared the winds to see it again. He cast about the sky above Chard but could find nothing of the dark guardian, no trace at all. The answer hit him hard. The deaths back at the village, the all-pervading aura of hate that lingered there ... the darkness was no longer without but within the young boy sleeping peacefully below him.

Denegtacus slipped away to a safe distance to watch and think. He would stay there for the next five years.

8

Chard glanced around at those who shared the fire with him. Six men, including himself, all seated close to the flames with the smoke playing around and between them. The stew bubbled gently on the flames, the long wooden spoon poking from it and propping up a lid that did not match the pot. Every now and again one of them would lean forward, give the food a cursory stir and sniff the air above it like a hungry dog. Chard watched as a man did just that, smiling inwardly to himself at their petty needs. The man's desire not to share this meal was the only thought Chard could hear bouncing around inside his thick skull. It was probably the only thought he'd had that day.

Three of them were known to Chard – he had spent the last year or so journeying with them as a sort of self-employed problem-solving service. They rode into town and did jobs in exchange for monies or rewards of other natures. Their last enterprise had seen them kill the leader of a small band of rebels who had been stealing food from a village and persuade the rest of the group that they should seek easier pickings elsewhere. They had been rewarded well for that: good food and a particularly pleasant evening with two whores had been Chard's share. There was no real need for Chard to use the men he travelled with but he had found them good cover for his powers. Few people would employ a sixteen-year-old and so he had joined up with his present companions to hide his abilities. All in all, he rather enjoyed what he did since it gave him ample opportunity to practise his magic, but he could feel that he would soon strike out on his own since he had long grown tired of his acquaintances.

From one to the next he watched; playing with the gloves he always wore, recalling all he knew of them. Asnaxly, the easterner who maintained his strange name was due to the fact he had arrogol blood in him. The others said it was because his parents couldn't spell and spent many hours telling the same joke simply to pass the time on the road. Out of the three, Chard liked Asnaxly the most but that didn't really say much since he practically loathed the other two. Juster: tall, thin and with a pockmarked face from childhood smallpox. Easily the most dangerous, the one who made certain they got paid and took the greatest delight in meting out the group's very special brand of justice. Chard had no reason to fear any man and yet there was something unnerving about Juster's cold face that made even the young wizard set a guard spell around him before he closed his eyes for the night. Lastly there was Pridmore, a man from Curinlas, strong, well-built and with a desire for revenge. Years back he had been a fisherman, until bandits had raided his village when he had been away at sea, killing his three children and raping his wife before hanging her from the apple tree Pridmore had asked her to marry him under. Overnight he had changed and become the desolate killer that now sat opposite Chard. Speaking only when spoken to, he hated all he came into contact with. He hated the men who preyed on the weak, he hated the weak for being weak but most of all he hated himself for not being there that day when the raiders had come.

Idly Chard scratched his chin while he waited for his share of the food. He always got the most by a simple illusion spell which made his plate look emptier than it really was, causing it to be heaped high. It wasn't even as if he wanted the extra food – Chard had grown into a slender-built young man – but he liked being able to prove his cleverness over the others, if only to himself.

The last two who made up the group were fellow travellers who had been close by when they had made camp. An unspoken rule of country travel was the sharing of campsites and food, the need for safety in numbers. The two men had turned out to be brothers on their way to the capital to seek their fortunes. They had next to nothing and Chard was certain that if any of his comrades had believed otherwise they would have slit their throats and dumped the bodies in the undergrowth. Perhaps these two had been fortunate to catch Chard's group in a good mood, for as Chard watched the older brother finish stirring the stew Juster actually started a conversation.

'Been on the road long?'

The older brother, a dark-haired man by the name of Gerlharvil, shook his head slowly. 'Me and my kid brother here set out last week for the city. Armishmer!' His eyes stared dreamily at nothing. 'One of the old men from the village said he'd been there once, said it was magnificent, all marble and three-storey buildings. So me and him reckoned we'd see it for ourselves.'

Juster nodded. It was the sort of crap he heard all the time from boys like these two. Probably be begging for a living within a day of getting there. He picked up the bowls and began sharing out the food, making certain he picked the most pieces of meat for his own plate.

They ate in silence and soon retreated to their own blankets. Chard settled himself down, he was actually happy. Food had been relatively good since they'd still had some of the beef the villagers had given them and his stomach was comfortably full. A simple spell kept the insects at bay and the autumn evening was warm enough to enjoy without the need for a second piece of magic. As he drifted off to sleep, the sounds of Pridmore's snoring soon faded away.

The darkness had been replaced by light. Light of such intensity it hurt his eyes! He raised his hands to protect his face but it seemed to make little difference, still the light seared into his brain, burning, burning! He screamed at the pain, unable to focus his magic or bring his will to bear.

'Where is the darkness, Chard?' boomed a voice.

Chard's only response was an agonised sob as he sank to his knees.

'Where is the darkness, Chard?' repeated the voice at such a level Chard thought his eardrums would burst.

'I don't … know what … you …'

'Liar!' screamed the voice. 'Liar! Where is the darkness?'

'What do you want from me?' begged Chard. 'Tell me what to say and I'll say it!'

'Truth! You must answer with the truth, only the truth will end the pain!'

'Gone!' shouted Chard, although to him it sounded like a whisper when compared to the commands of the unseen speaker. 'Gone the night Chara died. Came at me, swallowed me … can't remember what happened next!'

'You must!' urged the voice.

Chard slumped to the ground he couldn't see and tried to find an answer he didn't know.

'I was burying her …'

The light and the noise were gone. Chard remained where he was for a moment longer before dragging himself to his feet. Before him stood an elf dressed in white robes, a neutral expression on his old face. The boy wizard glanced nervously around but there was nothing to see, nothing. The two of them were the only objects of any description as far as he could tell. A feeling of queasiness welled up inside and he attempted to focus on the being before him.

'The darkness found your soul willing to embrace it, Chard. It has taken root inside you. All of your hate and malevolence is feeding it, can you not feel it? Cast it out and look to the light, for the light shall banish the darkness and shall set the soul free.'

Chard screamed in agony as something retched in his soul.

Chard woke with a cry and was on his feet before the covers had even hit the ground. In an instant the camp was roused, men reaching for weapons and scanning the trees for danger. Within moments it was clear that there was no threat and soon they rounded on the young man who stood, chest heaving, near to the fire.

Juster stood before Chard, arms folded angrily across his chest, the only light from the stars and moon casting ghostly shadows on the spectacle below. 'Well?' he said gruffly, jabbing a hard finger into Chard's ribs.

The mage didn't appear to notice, his eyes were glazed, focused elsewhere.

This did not sit well with Juster who had never really taken to the young man and at this moment couldn't remember why he'd even agreed to let the little bastard tag along. 'I'm talking to you, boy!' he hissed, pushing Chard in the shoulder with some venom, spinning him round and nearly sending him to the ground.

Memories of childhood rose in Chard's mind. All his life he had suffered at the hands of people like this. Jumbled thoughts that were raging in his mind were put aside and instead he brought his will to bear on the creature before him.

Chard lost control. His hands flew up, his fingers spitting bolts of white-hot lightning in all directions. Three hit Juster in the chest, one in his face, destroying most of the features and sending pieces of brain across the camp. What was left of his corpse collapsed to the ground, blood seeping into the earth.

None of the others had been hit by Chard's magic but all had seen it and they retreated to the hoped-for safety of the trees that surrounded the small camp. Soon the only sound that could be heard was Chard's harsh breathing as he fought to get his heartbeat back under control. Eventually he looked up and although he couldn't see them, he could feel the emotions of the other men watching him, a mixture of fear and astonishment. Asnaxly was confused more than frightened, while Pridmore just wanted to get his things and make good his escape. Chard gave a small sigh. Let them do what they liked, he knew his time in this group was over.

The dream, Chard knew, was more than that. It was a vision, it had been real, and that worried him more than he cared to admit. The old elf had immense power, that was obvious, and knew of the darkness that had haunted Chard as a boy. He remained where he stood, oblivious to the murder he had just committed and the fear his actions commanded. Escape wasn't an issue, it was unlikely there were any militia units within a hundred miles, but he did need time to think. Stepping over what was left of Juster he gathered up his few belongings into his bundle and walked slowly away.

At a small stream he decided to fill his water canteen. Placing his pack on the soft ground, he flicked the lid from the bottle, emptied the small amount that was inside and then filled it with fresh water. Taking a swig he sat back, staring at nothing. Chard knew he was somewhere in southern Curinlas, probably fifty miles from the far south-western border of the elf lands and not very far from the newly-formed nation of the dwarves. He'd heard the new name somewhere but had forgotten it, the dwarf language being harsh and unwieldy to those unfamiliar with it. None of this was of any real consequence, he was safe from any who would do him harm with the possible exception of one old elf.

He had another small sip of water and rinsed out the taste in his mouth, spitting the fluid onto the grass. It was a beautiful country he found himself in, that was for sure. The trees looked splendid with their autumn colours and the mountains that bordered the dwarf lands towered away to the south-east, the snow-topped peaks just visible through gaps in the canopy. Sighing, Chard realised that he had never really appreciated things like this, it had always just been scenery, there but ignored. As he glanced all around him, no direction particularly appealed, all looked pleasant and devoid of people. Replacing the cap on his water bottle he thrust it savagely into his pack. Enough nonsense! The elf would come for him or he wouldn't, there was nothing he could do about it, so why worry?

He stood up and stared into the expressionless face of the elf from his dream, who was standing less than six feet from him. Chard was motionless, his hand halfway towards his bag, clutching at nothing. A moment or two passed and Chard flexed the fingers of his outstretched hand, the movement drawing the elf's eyes briefly before they flicked back to Chard's own.

'Going somewhere?' asked Denegtacus pleasantly.

Chard nodded slowly. 'Somewhere, yeah,' he replied cautiously.

'Somewhere?' The elf gestured vaguely back in the direction Chard had come from. 'I'd have thought anywhere was better than hanging around the scene of a murder, but then I don't believe I've ever committed one so I don't really know.'

'It was an accident,' said Chard, rather too quickly. 'I didn't mean to do it.'

Denegtacus walked up to Chard and then around him. Chard stayed where he was until the elf was back before him. 'You decapitated a man with a blast of magic that could have brought down an oak tree and you didn't mean to do it?' The elf gave a soft chuckle which lacked any humour. 'What would you have done if you had truly meant to kill him?'

'It's not as if he was an innocent,' retorted Chard, some of his old cockiness returning. 'The world is doubtless a better place without men such as Juster.'

Denegtacus nodded sagely. 'Perhaps. But who are you to judge him?'

Chard shrugged and hefted his pack onto his back. 'His actions judged him, not me. If I hadn't killed him he would have found his way to the hangman's noose before long.'

The elf agreed with the boy if the truth be known, and yet something bothered the enchanter. The child had absolutely no remorse over the taking of a life, no doubts as to the rightness of his deed. Killing was not something that should ever become easy or be done lightly and yet this boy had already dismissed it.

'Your magic is strong, Chard, but I feel that it could yet be stronger.'

Chard was still stood in front of the elf and looked down at him. He was by no means tall, average for a human, and yet he was nearly a foot taller than the elf. 'I know you have magic, elf, which is why you came to me in the night. But if you were a threat I would be dead by now. So I believe I shall be on my way.' He pushed past Denegtacus and walked through the trees.

The elf sighed and rolled his eyes, suppressing his desire to curse.

'You want me to make you listen to me, boy?' he asked quietly, the unspoken threat hanging in the air.

Chard was now behind the elf, although he had his back to him.

'You are old and I am young. I believe in my magic, it has always protected me and always will.'

Denegtacus rounded on the human and placed himself before him once again. 'Always is a very long time, boy, remember that.'

Chard snorted with derision and his hand flew up. Suddenly he was catapulted backwards by an unseen force, arms and legs flailing at the sky. He landed heavily, his back arching over his pack at an unnatural angle causing him to cry out in pain. The elf hadn't moved a muscle and yet Chard found himself defeated and in agony.

He gave a soft groan and forced himself back to his feet, ignoring the protest from his body. This time he raised both hands and smiled in triumph as they spewed forth fire that engulfed the elf. More and more energy he hurled at the elf, not caring what state he would find the body in.

After several seconds he ended the spell and the smile dropped from his face. The elf stood quite unharmed in the centre of a blackened patch of grass, his arms folded casually across his chest.

'Why do you persist in this nonsense?' asked Denegtacus, his lip curling into a sneer. 'Can you not see that your magic is feeble when compared to mine? Can you not sense the power I am holding? Do you not realise that I could destroy your very soul with less effort than others would use to tread on an insect?'

'How ...?' began Chard.

'You are good boy, I will give you that. But untrained and reckless. I have met dozens of wizards who could defeat you quite easily. If you are to become as good as your potential suggests, you are going to need some help.'

'You are offering to teach me?' The old Chard began to reassert itself. 'Why would you do that? What's in it for you?'

The elf walked up to Chard, who took an involuntary step backwards. Without giving an answer he lashed out and struck the boy a ringing blow across his cheek.

'From this moment forward you will refer to me in a polite manner or you will be punished! Do you understand?'

Chard's eyes blazed with hidden fury but he managed a curt nod.

Denegtacus backhanded the boy, opening a small cut at the corner of his mouth.

'I spoke to you!' he roared. 'Do you understand?'

'I understand ... master,' replied Chard.

The elf shook his head. 'No, you do not, but that is immaterial at the moment. Soon you will see what the universe has in store for you and only then will you even begin to understand the duty that has been hung around your neck.'

Denegtacus reached out and took Chard's hands in his own, studying the well-made, soft leather gloves that he wore. 'Explain this nonsense to me.'

Chard forgot all about his hatred for the elf and looked inwards to memory. He drew his hands back and turned them slowly, studying their shape through the gloves that he had tailor-made for him at one of the larger towns his journeys had brought him to. Pictures of his adopted mother flitted across his mind and he almost smiled, but the thoughts, as always, were interrupted as he saw again the moment of her death at his hands.

These hands, which still bore the marks of his punishment.

'I was angry when I cast the spell, angrier than I think I have ever been before or since. She didn't deserve to die, I know that now, she had always tried to live a good life.' Chard sighed desolately. 'She had forgotten my birthday, that's all. And I killed her for it. But then I suppose I had been building up to it for some time.'

'You have much blood staining your soul, Chard. Perhaps I am wrong, perhaps it will never wash off.' The elf stroked his chin thoughtfully. 'Perhaps I am wasting my time.'

The young man's eyes flashed with murderous intent but he refrained from lashing out. 'I regret her death like I regret nothing else!' he hissed from between clenched teeth. 'I was a child when it happened, I wouldn't have done it now!'

'Really?' mocked Denegtacus. 'Back there is a corpse being picked over by foxes that would argue otherwise.'

Chard breathed deeply and fought for calm. The elf was deliberately trying to insult him, to make him lose his temper and he wouldn't give him the satisfaction of doing so. 'Juster was nothing compared to Shruna, it is like putting dung next to a rose.'

'From good dung roses will grow,' said Denegtacus with a smile.

'Your word games serve no purpose!' said Chard evenly. 'We are fencing verbally when I should be telling you this story.'

The elf inclined his head, acknowledging the point and gestured Chard to continue.

'The magic roared from me,' continued Chard. 'It felt like a release that I had been building up to for years. I paid the price for my actions. The skin across my palms was burnt away by the magic. I wear these gloves that I imbue with a herbal lotion I concocted myself from fennel and poppy. The ointment soothes the pain and allows me to use my hands normally. If I don't change it every two or three days my hands become dry and cracked, then the flesh splits again and it oozes pus and black blood.'

The elf nodded. 'I have heard of such things occurring when the mage is inexperienced and clumsy with the spell, although I never heard of the effects lasting for the number of years you are suggesting. It must have been an extremely powerful piece of magic.'

Chard smiled. 'It was, master, the air itself crackled with the heat.'

The elf took the boy's hands in his own and gently eased the gloves off to study the damage for himself. The flesh was pink and angry and Denegtacus felt Chard flinch at his touch. Even as he turned them he saw a blister on Chard's left hand pop and send pus leaking out.

'You have not tried to put it right with your magic?'

Chard bit back an angry response and replied steadily. 'Yes, master, but to no avail. I am good with potions and witchcraft, the mistress taught me that much, but it appears that my magic cannot be used thus.'

The enchanter was worried. This was not right! The power to heal was the strongest power that the elfin mages had at their disposal, it was one of the myriad of reasons that they lived so long as a species. Minor and major ailments could be treated by any apprentice wizard, even those ills that would be considered terminal by humans, and yet Chard could not mend the after-effects of a magical burn!

Weighing up a decision in his mind he acted instantly. The scars across both the young wizard's hands were cured by a single thought from the enchanter, the flesh now fresh, pink and healthy.

Chard was stunned; he had gazed at the ruin of his hands for many years now and had become resigned to them always looking this way. He had even swallowed his ample pride and consulted with a few doctors who specialised in such injuries.

He dropped to his knees and pressed his lips to the enchanter's fingers.

'Thank you, master!' he said joyfully. 'I shall follow where you lead!' He averted his gaze and grinned boyishly when he saw his fine gloves lying in the dirt. Let them stay there! What need did he have of them?

'You realise what you are saying, young one? From now and for always we two will be linked, will be one. Nothing we do shall be as an individual, only as teacher and student.'

'It is all that I have ever wanted!'

'Know then that I am L'tusian, the greatest mage of this and any other time! I am the Godsman! I am the Chosen! I am the One of the Day! I am the Enchanter!'

'And I am yours, master,' whispered Chard.

Those elves that had left Bulair found the human world a strange place. Elves were at one with their own environment but many were finding it hard to make the transition to the human way of life, and others did not even bother trying and returned home. Everything the humans did seemed ludicrous and illogical to the elves, from living on the ground like animals to building their homes from stone and so holding back the power of the land. It was no wonder humans lived such short lives since they tried to tame nature, to imprison her rather than prostrating themselves before her power as was proper. Perhaps their short span was a punishment for this.

Private ownership was not a new concept to the elves, they had traded as groups long before the humans had even discovered fire, but the idea of owning land was alien to them. The hills were there before all now living and would still be there when all were gone, so who could claim to own them? Yet that is exactly what humanity did. Countries were one thing, the elves saw the necessity of that, but surely the land of that nation should belong to the spirits of the ancestors and those yet to be born there rather than friends of the king?

Still, there were many elves that had made the transition to living and trading amongst humans. Business with humans had to be conducted with your eyes wide open, as the old saying went, since it was well known that humans could not be trusted. What more proof was needed than the story of the elf who had been talking inside a human tavern and had overheard a human merchant saying that he had been cheated by an elf and warning his colleagues to beware trading with them! As if any elf would betray his honour – his ancestors would turn in their graves!

However, trading with humans was one thing; living alongside them was something else. Whole elf communities were growing inside Curinlas and the Isle of Rittan in particular, and although they considered themselves a part of Bulair, the human governments still wanted their taxes. These conflicts were minor at the moment but everyone knew that old tensions and hatreds could only be pushed aside while the trade was good, never forgotten.

All this and more was going through Leaspida's mind as he gazed at the endless stream of paper that seemed to be breeding on his desk. Their small community numbered less than two hundred and yet it appeared to give more headaches than his father ever seemed to deal with back home. Home. The young royal elf tossed the latest piece of nonsense he had been reading onto the desk but it landed awkwardly and slipped gently to the floor, taking several other sheaves with it. He looked at the mess with irritation before reaching down and retrieving it.

The small village they had built for themselves rested comfortably within a wood in northern Curinlas, less than ten miles from the sea. Even here they weren't safe from the petty bureaucracy of the humans. Leaspida had always known that there would be problems – allowing this settlement had been one of them, but it had been overcome, as would all the others. Curinlas wanted to send more officials to oversee just what exactly was going on even though more than fifty had toured their small community in the last month alone! As an elf, Leaspida was well aware that these inspections were to remind the elves just who was in charge and it rankled with him, but as leader he had to remain above such feelings and work towards closer cooperation. All the same … he tutted, pushed back his chair and walked over to the window.

The huts that the elves lived in were simple affairs and yet all displayed the beautiful craftselfship and attention to detail that made all elf goods so highly desired by the other races of Eurasia. As leader, Leaspida could have ordered a more ornate dwelling for himself but he had been astute enough to realise the effect this would have had on morale, which was never good to start with. So his home also doubled as his office and contained only three rooms, the same as all the others. One room for sleeping and privacy, one room to be with one's family and the last room to welcome guests. Nearly all elf homes were built on this simple principle and it was considered distasteful for even the richest elf to violate this unspoken rule. Leaspida thought of the palace he had grown up in and the multitude of rooms it had contained; there are always exceptions he mused, a lesson the humans would do well to learn.

This group worked making weapons for Curinlas' military in the shape of bows, both longbow and hunting bow. Each bow was crafted from a single piece of wood, cut and shaped by hand using tools that often as not had been in an elf's family for centuries. Once the shape was defined, the artisan could spend as many hours on embossing it as he had on making it, and once finished these bows were supreme works of art. Individual arrows alone could take up to five hours to create, the feathers attached with love and a subtle blend of magic.

Try telling any of this to the humans! Oh for sure the lords and the mighty were pleased beyond measure to be able to boast the ownership of an elven longbow which could have taken more than a month to create but the military were a completely different matter. They demanded machines of war produced by the hundred, not individual works of art that a man would treasure for the rest of his days. Leaspida shuddered as he remembered the human general who had sneered in contempt as he turned over the first bow handed to him by the elves. Out loud he said, for all to hear, that when he wanted something to hang on his mantelpiece he would ask, but until then could they get on with making weapons!

The look on the faces of his people as he had tried to explain the ways of the humans and that if they were to stay then they would have to bend like the grass not break like the trees! Elves who had made less than a hundred bows in their lifetime were now asked to mass produce that many in a year. The women and children were put to work making arrows by the thousand, but nothing seemed to make the humans happy. They took what was produced, left payment and demands for the following month's order.

Truly if I stay amongst these barbarians for the rest of my days I will not understand them, thought Leaspida to himself as he stood silently at the window, watching life in his small community. Windows in elven abodes were merely empty holes that allowed nature in, and Leaspida revelled in the feel of the light breeze on his face. He never enjoyed visiting humans: standing on cold stone floors, with stone walls and glassed windows was akin to being locked in a tomb as far as he was concerned. He much preferred trading outside, but even this was usually denied him by the humans.

So much work to do, so many problems to solve. So many more that would still be there tomorrow! Leaspida gave a soft chuckle as he imagined his father's stern words of rebuke if he had heard such things from his son. When you come to a decision you must stick to it, not complain that it is hard or that people hate you for it. Leadership was not meant to make you friends, it was meant to safeguard the future.

The second son of the elf king was just about to return to his desk when movement on the track that led to their village caught his attention. Rounding the corner and walking purposefully towards them came two figures, a human and an elf. Leaspida was certain that no visits were scheduled for this day and he pondered what could be occurring. He watched as they came closer, gathering a small crowd of onlookers that made no attempt to stop them, but fell into step behind them, their eyes going to the window where Leaspida stood.

Leaspida's eyebrows arched as he recognised Denegtacus and then knitted together in concern as he tried to figure out what he was doing here in the middle of nowhere and with a human boy in tow.

Denegtacus stopped in front of Leaspida's window and gave a nod of greeting. Chard hung back a little, all too aware of the eyes that burned into him.

'Well?' asked the old elf. 'Aren't you coming out to say hello?'

9

Leaspida practically tripped over himself in his haste, stammering apologies and welcomes in equal measure. Denegtacus raised his hand to quieten him, then the two elves embraced.

'It has been too long, old friend!' said the king's second son with a broad grin.

'Many months that's for sure,' replied the enchanter. 'It might even have been longer but for your father's wishes.'

Leaspida's eyes narrowed for just the briefest of moments but he masked it well. 'You have been sent by my father? I told him and I'll tell you, we are staying here and that is the end of the matter!'

Denegtacus gave a rueful smile and shook his head. 'No, Leaspida, that is not why I am here, but we shall speak of that in due course. My reasons concern the human you see in my company and your father's attitude towards him.'

The elf glanced at the human only perfunctorily. He was young, he was ugly like all humans, and smelled terribly like all humans, what more was there to know? 'I can well imagine what the king would say about any human but I do not understand what this has to do with me.'

'It concerns your whole community. Gather them in the meeting area and we shall talk to all.'

Leaspida nodded and called on his people to assemble between the large elms. Bare minutes later every elf that called the settlement home was sat or stood in a wide circle around

Leaspida, Denegtacus and Chard, their glances shifting from one to the next, wild speculations as to the reason for their presence already sweeping through the crowd.

The young royal bowed his head slightly to show that he accepted Denegtacus' lead and would defer to him during the meeting.

Denegtacus inclined his own head in response and turned to look at all the elves gathered around him. Their faces were welcoming, honest, inquisitive, so long as they were looking at him. Once their gazes drifted to Chard it was a different matter, for although they accepted humans as a part of the new life they were crafting, his being there among their homes was something else.

The enchanter took in all of this and groaned wearily on the inside. The village he could see was shoddy by elven standards, the houses quickly built and lacking in much of the adornment that would be standard back in Bulair, but when compared to human settlements they were veritable works of art. Tree branches had been loving shaped by magic to form the walls and roofs of their homes in such a way that no human could hope to replicate. Although the majority of the buildings were on ground level, walkways criss-crossed above them linking many dwellings that were built among the boughs of the trees themselves. If truth be told, Denegtacus was impressed that so much had been achieved so quickly: the better traits of the humans must be rubbing off, he mused silently. However, praise was something that would have to be mixed with a fair portion of disdain if he was to get through to these people.

'My friends,' he began softly, his voice carrying, 'you know who I am and I am sure you are wondering what has brought me to your new home. No doubt you are worrying that this is some plan of the king's to coax his son and the rest of you back to Bulair, but this is not the case, although the Creator himself knows why you chose to live among humans!'

His joke got the polite laughter it warranted but none sought to interrupt.

'No, the king has resigned himself to a new world order that sees elf and human mixing freely in trade, peacefully, and despite the fact he cannot bring himself to say it publicly, I know that secretly he is pleased with the progress you have made. Talk of the king brings me to the first sad piece of news that I must share with you for I cannot keep it secret and nor would I wish to if I could. King Theaspida has declared me an outlaw and banished me from his realm for treason.'

The gasp that accompanied this statement would have made Chard smile but he knew better than to risk bringing his teacher's wrath down upon him and so he merely averted his stare and thought of other things.

Denegtacus allowed the tension and noise to build for a moment before raising his voice and quelling the gossip. 'He has done this for good reason and I do not blame him, but he is wrong! Theaspida is a good king, one of the finest I have known, but he has not embraced the future with the vision that you have shown, which is why I am here. I disagree with him and in my anger I almost turned against him, but he is my king and I his subject and I will have none cast aspersions on him. If I hear elves preach against him I shall strike them down, if I see treason in your hearts I shall cause that heart to stop beating!' Denegtacus' anger was half staged and half genuine – he truly meant the words he spoke and only wished he had had the foresight to say them to the king rather than his son.

'He would be proud if he could see your village and how you keep the elven way of life going when faced with trials at every corner. How easy it would be to slip into bad habits, the habits of the humans!'

Leaspida nodded sagely as his followers cheered both Denegtacus and himself.

Once more Denegtacus watched the mood of the crowd.

He almost had them, now it was time for harsh reality. 'Yet something troubles me. You have been here in this settlement for months but I see no school of magic, no temple to the Creator, no central government building with a regular link back to Bulair. Subjects of the Forest you were and Subjects of the Forest you remain, no matter that you no longer sleep under its protective canopy! So where are the cornerstones of elven society, why in the half hour I have been here has no one, save his son, asked me of the king's health? I shall tell you why, because you are too busy for it, just like the humans that you are beginning to resemble!'

Leaspida rose to his feet. 'My lord, you do us an injustice!'

'Perhaps,' replied Denegtacus, 'but I say it for your own benefit. If you are to remain true to your heritage then you must keep that legacy alive, it must be a part of you, not something you dust off whenever you want to feel superior to the humans. Never can the elf be separated from magic, nor magic from the land, for they are all one and the same thing. Should one wither then all will one day wither. Magic binds us to the land in a way that no human can ever understand; ignore it at your peril. Without magical knowledge passing seamlessly from one generation to the next, our whole way of life is put at risk. Do you really want to live in a world where elf and magic become disjointed? Where the elf no longer hears the whisper of the wind through the trees and, in it, the spirits of his ancestors? Such a people already exist and we call them human!'

The crowd were already cheering and many were on their feet as Denegtacus reached the end of his oratory. Several went forward and bowed deeply before the legendary enchanter, some asking for blessing, others just to voice their loyalty to the land and to the king.

Leaspida ultimately managed to restore order and the elves returned to the circle around the three, although they were now a great deal closer than before and the mood greatly more invigorated.

'My lord Denegtacus, I believe I speak for all here when I say that all your words are spoken in truth and that we shall act upon them immediately. I shall write to my father this night on your behalf and have this absurd misunderstanding between you resolved if it is in my power to do so.' A low murmur of assent rippled around the young royal but he pressed on. 'Also, the school of magic has long been a task we have put off and put off, but by the Creator I swear that tomorrow all children of school age will continue with their tutoring, which moving here has interrupted.'

'I thought you lived among humans?' enquired Denegtacus. 'What's wrong with today?'

The elves laughed at the joke, a few repeated it to their fellows, remarking once more that the human condition seemed to be one of constant haste.

Leaspida chuckled as well. 'Very droll, my lord. Very well, the children will receive their first instruction tonight and we would be honoured if you would do it yourself, ancient one, just until the schoolmaster has time to dig out his books.'

Denegtacus inclined his head with the briefest smile. 'I would be the one honoured. There is much to be said for the noble calling of teaching and none of us ever reaches the stage where we have nothing left to learn.'

The elven leader sensed that there was one other major issue that had to be resolved and that it would be wise to do it while the mood was good. Such was the outlook of the elves, it had been possible for him to totally screen Chard out of his mind when talking to Denegtacus but now his eyes fell on the human and it was all he could do to stop the corners of his mouth curling into a look of distaste.

'What of the human, my lord?' he asked loudly, and every pair of eyes turned to stare at Chard, who stared at the ground rather than face the endless sea of hostile expressions.

Denegtacus looked sideways at Chard and then at the young royal elf. 'He is my student and as such he goes where I go. He has entered the *tirocinium* and will remain at my side until I decide he has proved his worth as an apprentice of magic or failed. Is there any here who questions my right as a magi to tutor him?'

He turned a very slow circle, eyeing any who dared meet his look until they glanced away and he was once more face to face with Leaspida. For just a tiny moment the old elf really thought Leaspida was going to argue with him – too much of his father in him, he reflected – but instead he nodded slowly.

'Can I assume you will take responsibility for it?'

Denegtacus could have laughed aloud given a different set of circumstances. Here was an elf, considered forward-looking by all, living on human territory and trading quite freely, who still referred to them as objects not people.

'He will reside inside the dormitory of the school once it is built, until then he will stay alongside me.'

Leaspida knew what Denegtacus meant; the old elf as a visitor of importance would stay with him and so would the human. He had the space since he had not yet taken a wife, but all the same it was a shrewd move by the enchanter. It would send a clear signal to the whole community that the boy was here to stay and that he had been accepted by the king's son himself.

His duty was clear and he raised a guiding hand and pointed his new guests towards the door to his home. Denegtacus went first and Leaspida followed closely, leaving Chard to trail in their wake, the eyes of every elf boring into his back as he tried to make sure that he didn't trip over his own feet.

'Well my wily old friend,' began Leaspida once they were settled inside. 'You have certainly not lost your gift for surprises! There were more than few shocked elves out there I can tell you.'

'One of them was you,' replied Denegtacus, taking a small sip of wine from the goblet Leaspida handed him.

'Indeed it was.' The elf had hold of another goblet intended for the human but something inside of him rebelled at the thought of an elf of royal blood serving drinks to a human who looked like he had fallen in every puddle in northern Curinlas. He stared hard at the human who returned his gaze balefully. There was something about this man that rankled the elf, even more than most of his kind did, but he concealed it with a supreme effort and handed Chard the drink, which he took without a word of thanks.

'The grapes that make that wine grow only in the extreme south of Bulair. They say that when they are picked you can see the mountains that border the dwarf lands. The sun shining on the snow is meant to be a pleasant sight.' Leaspida had not yet taken his eyes from Chard, who continued to look back at him with an expression which teetered on insolence. Did not this child realise what it cost him to allow him into the village, let alone his home?

'Does that improve the taste in some way?' asked Chard.

'No,' replied Leaspida unhurriedly. 'I do not believe so. Why?'

Chard shrugged and took a large mouthful of the drink. 'I just wondered why you mentioned it.'

Leaspida shook his head with a snort of derision. How could you explain culture to barbarians? You couldn't, yet it never ceased to amaze him just how much humans did not understand. They thought the world was there for their entertainment and it sickened him. Seating himself opposite Denegtacus he resolved to ignore the human as much as was physically possible when someone is a guest in your home.

Over the next hour or so the prince and the enchanter chatted amiably of things past and of things to come and neither of them addressed a single remark to Chard, who allowed his mind to wander around the room while keeping half an ear open in case of anything important. In due course Denegtacus decided that the children should be assembled and that the first lesson in magic should commence. Leaspida agreed and shortly afterwards the old enchanter found himself looking at forty young elfin faces and one human one.

They were assembled under the stars in the open, just outside the village perimeter, and sat in an arc before the living legend that was L'tusian. Except that there was a very clear gap between most of them and Chard, who had taken his seat first and was now on the extreme left of the group, six feet from the nearest elf. Denegtacus smiled inwardly. The young human was not going to have an easy time of it, but then who did? Events would develop, he decided to see how.

'Children of the Creator, I have gathered you here tonight to hear my words on magic. There will be plenty of time for books and practice tomorrow but for now I want you to do something far harder, and that is to *listen.* I don't just mean with your ears, I mean with your soul, for that is where magic must come from if it is to be used as the Creator intended.' He paused just long enough to send a glowing ball of light from his outstretched palm into the air, where it hung some fifteen feet up, allowing them all to see quite clearly in the gathering gloom. 'A simple spell, one of the first that any elf learns to master and yet one of the most important. Why? Because you are sending light out into the darkness. Does it matter that outside of its glow the darkness is as strong as it was before the spell? No, for when faced with lighting the darkness, always remain focused on the light and never the dark.' Again he paused and stared hard at the assembled youths. 'Show me your lights, my children. Send them dancing among the stars!'

At once the children rose to their feet and shortly

afterwards the whole night sky seemed to be alive with dancing globes of light of many different colours. Some swooped and dived, others chased their friends to the sound of laughter while others soared as high as their creators could send them before plummeting back to earth in a blaze of glory.

Chard had stood with all the others and watched the spectacle carefully, but did not send up his own light to mingle with the others. Denegtacus wandered over to him and Chard gave a short bow.

'Why do you not join in?'

'May I ask my own question, master?' replied Chard evenly. Denegtacus nodded and Chard continued. 'What exactly am I meant to be learning here tonight? You know of my power and that this, this …' he waved his hand upwards, his self-control almost leaving him. 'This *show* is beneath me. I can do so much more.'

'You think these children cannot?' said Denegtacus with a smile.

'I merely wish to be allowed to show you what I am capable of, master. When I joined you I did not expect to be tutored alongside forty others!'

'You will learn a lot from simply being among them, Chard, not just magic.'

'But …'

'Send up your light, Chard,' said Denegtacus with another half smile that did not reach his eyes.

Chard looked up and pointed. The magic erupting from his outstretched fingers in one explosion of light and sound. The spell coalesced into a red ball of flame some hundred feet up where it seemed to hover for just a second before hurtling towards the nearest magical light. The two spells clashed, with Chard's appearing to swallow the smaller white light and then, without a pause, it went on to the next. Within a minute, all the lights had been chased, caught and swallowed by Chard's, with the exception of Denegtacus's, which now hung motionlessly above the group with Chard's some distance to the right. The rest of the children were staring at the human and the old elf in silence, waiting for whatever would happen next. None of their spells had been able to avoid Chard's or overcome it, and now only the master's remained. They wanted him to put the upstart human in his place.

Denegtacus looked around him at the expectant faces. They irritated him almost as much as Chard's show of bravado and with a wave of his hand he sent them scurrying back to the village and out of earshot.

Alone he spoke quietly to Chard. 'Do you think that little demonstration won you any friends, Chard?'

'I do not want their friendship, master; I simply want them to acknowledge that I am the best.'

'Why?'

'Because …' and he tailed off.

Denegtacus patted Chard on the arm. 'It was meant to be a bit of fun, Chard, just a bit of fun.' The old elf turned and walked away, leaving Chard alone. Above him, both the magical lights faded away and the area sank into darkness.

The next evening, Chard recounted the events of his first school day and his new teacher, a middle-aged elf called Usididies, to Denegtacus who was sat at his desk writing slowly and deliberately onto a piece of parchment, apparently giving Chard little attention. The apprentice was controlling his emotions with great effort, his fear of angering his master greater than his own rage. He was explaining the demeaning and petty magic he was forced to do, magic he had mastered years earlier. He was furious at being tutored by a man who knew less than his pupil and the all-pervading air of hatred that the rest of the class felt towards their unwanted human guest. Not that this particularly bothered him, but the snide comments could cause some lack of concentration.

Denegtacus listened to all of this and more as he continued to write. The work he was focusing on this decade was bees and, as always, he consigned everything he did to paper so that others who came looking would not have to cover the same ground. These ten-yearly tasks had begun a thousand years earlier in a bid to expound the knowledge of the world. It was his ambition to write a thesis on everything that interested him, but he knew that the list of subjects he had written had taken him more than a year and the probability of him covering even a tenth of them was minimal. But he pressed on all the same.

He remembered his first topic, the elfin royal family, which had taken twenty years and filled an entire shelf of its own. He had had to be hard on himself after that, making certain that he did not spend more than the allotted time on any one topic, but he found it so difficult. Seeming only to have scratched at the surface of a topic when the ten years were up, he was forced to go on to the next item on his list. Still, he had made many discoveries during his studies and he looked forward to the day when he would be able to discuss his findings with a suitable pupil; hopefully the one sat to his left, complaining about nothing. Perhaps when Chard was of a suitable level he would be able to entrust some of the research to him, yet somehow Denegtacus doubted it. Chard was clever and extremely able but he was no scholar. The old elf considered the look of horror on the apprentice's face if he was instructed to spend the next decade studying bees. Not for Chard the quiet life of a man devoted to the pursuit of knowledge. Chard was driven by power and ambition. In itself, Denegtacus knew that this was not a problem and could be an asset, but he also knew that it would have to be strictly controlled.

The old elf crossed the final 't' but still did not turn to face the human. The boy was clearly angry and making a good show of holding it and arguing cogently that he thought his schooling was a waste of time. There was a bit too much self-pity and whining at times, but then he was still young. Denegtacus noticed the ink stain on his finger and sighed inwardly. Placing the quill into its holder, making sure he had wiped any excess from it, he cleared his throat.

'You want to leave the school?' he asked abruptly.

Chard nodded curtly. 'I believe I would learn more from being with you than I would from being with them.'

Denegtacus inclined his head slightly. 'Evidently, but that is not the point. You are not just there to learn magic, Chard, you are there to learn about the ways of the elves and to become a part of this community.'

'I do not want ...' began Chard hotly.

'What you want is immaterial to me and all the others here,' interrupted Denegtacus in a calm voice. 'You have no conception as to what it is costing Leaspida to allow you to be here and you will repay his hospitality by learning to become less crass in your dealings with us elves. If you could achieve that in a year or two it would be wonderful, however, I believe with someone like you it may take considerably longer.'

'Someone like me?' sneered Chard. 'How easy for you to dismiss me, master. I have had my fill of communities to last me a lifetime. I was unwelcome with the humans and I am unwelcome here. I fail to see why I should struggle to get them to accept me when they never will.'

'That's the spirit, Chard!' said Denegtacus with a grin, and he slapped the boy on the shoulder. Chard automatically flinched and pulled away but the elf retained his grip on him and Chard discovered that he was unable to move. The elf's eyes burned with passion and apprehension filled Chard. He stopped his struggle and waited for the blow which did not come.

'Some of the elves will never accept the sight of a human

walking freely among them, that is the way of things. But some will learn that the races can live peacefully and that it benefits us all in the long run.' The elf released the human and brushed his shoulder where he had held him, his face still showing nothing but benign friendship. 'That is your first assignment for me. When you have achieved it, then we will go on to the next.'

'But … but that could take years! I could fail … I could…' spluttered Chard.

Denegtacus smile broadened. 'True.'

'Why are you doing this to me, master?' begged Chard. 'All I want is to learn at your side. To master enchantment, to become a great magic user, the greatest wizard ever! Why are you …' he broke down and stifled a sob. However, he regained his composure in mere seconds, to Denegtacus' surprise, and stared at the elf with cold, hard eyes. 'You seek to break me with impossible demands! I shall not fail, ever! I will do as you ask and live here as part of this village.'

'And so begins your mastery of enchantment, Chard. Enchantment is not just magic, young novice; it is much more than that. It is about understanding and just maybe you have taken your first step today in yours. You will return to the school tomorrow and you will listen and participate and show your teacher respect. We both know you are already a greater wizard than he, but that is not why you are there. Do not forget it!'

The elf's smile evaporated and with a curt wave of his hand he sent Chard from him. Chard bowed low and went to his bed to sleep and prepare for the next day. He knew the elves hated him and he did not blame them, nor did he care. Now he had something to focus his energies on, and he would succeed. How hard could it be to manipulate these fools into thinking he was actually concerned about them? Each night he knew that he would have a chance to speak with his master and he would make sure that every time he would have some progress to report to him.

Chard lay down on his bed and closed his eyes. He would be here for a long time, he understood that, but he was certain that eventually Denegtacus would begin his real training and not just this mind game nonsense.

The young human did not realise it, but this one task he had been set would occupy him for the next one hundred and eight years.

10

Chard walked through the village towards his home, nodding to one or two of the elves as he went. He strode purposefully, confidently, a far cry from the man who had first turned up all those years ago, trailing in Denegtacus' wake like some sort of errant child. After more than a century with the elves, Chard liked to think of this village as his home, for it had certainly left its mark upon him. An average human could expect to live to sixty, more if they were lucky. Chard was more than double that with the outward appearance of a man in his middle twenties. Perhaps the longevity of the elves was contagious, he mused silently to himself. Some of the human ways had certainly rubbed off on them, after all.

It was that time of day when the sun was just beginning to dip behind the horizon, people's thoughts turned to home and the comforts of a hot meal and the company of family. But not tonight. Tonight most of the two thousand members of the community were assembling in the main hall to be addressed by Leaspida. Disturbing news which affected all elves throughout the continent had come to the village, brought by the many human contacts that were a daily part of life these days.

By the time Chard eased his way into the hall, it was already nearly full. Row upon row of elves sat talking to one another, all but ignoring Denegtacus and Leaspida who were stood together on the raised dais at the far end having a conversation of their own, each of them casting an occasional glance at the elves who had come to hear what they had to say. Chard caught his teacher's eye and nodded slightly, pleased as always that the nod was returned by the great elf who then went back to his dialogue.

Chard shuffled to one side of the doorway, apologised to the elf whose way he had blocked, and found a handy piece of wall to lean against. For the next quarter of an hour or so, he watched as the last remaining seats were taken and then any available standing places filled up. Occasionally he smiled or passed the time of day with an elf, but none stayed very long to talk with the exception of a child from his class who was trying to explain why it would be impossible for him to have the homework done for tomorrow as Chard had ordered.

Chard listened and patted the elf on his head. He squatted down to talk to him directly. 'Gerniella, I want that work ready for tomorrow as I told you earlier today. Remember, magic requires work and attention to detail.'

'But, master,' began the youngster, 'mother will make me go to bed after tea; there is no time before the morning.'

Chard stood up and smiled. 'You're meant to be learning to be a wizard, think of a way. Or I'll turn you into a mouse and feed you to the school snake!' He added with a laugh.

The child grinned and ducked Chard's pretended smack.

'We don't have a school snake,' he said as he moved away.

'Of course we do!' called Chard. 'Why do you think there are so few children in the class these days? I used to just leave them as mice but they nibbled away at the books!'

Teaching the village children had been his own idea some twenty years earlier, one to which Denegtacus had responded eagerly, Leaspida less so, but he had relented under pressure. Initially it had proved troublesome to get the elves to allow their children to be taught magic by a human, but Chard's presence over the years had set him in good stead, particularly his detailed knowledge of herbal remedies and woodland flora.

In his first class there had been seven children. Now there were more than a hundred of varying ages that he did his best to see at least twice a week. Time was never an issue for the long-lived elves and spending fifty years or more at school twice a week was nothing out of the ordinary. It was his role as a teacher which had done more to seal his place in the village than anything else he had done in the previous eighty years. He still occasionally worked as a doctor, dispensing medicines but mostly advice to the elves who preferred to keep this part of their lives to themselves.

Chard watched Gerniella as he sat down with his mother and siblings. A nice child but one who lacked all but the most basic of understandings of magic. Such was the way of elves, they were born with innate magic and used it all their lives, yet few really bothered to study in a serious way. Chard wondered silently, not for the first time, what they could achieve if they really applied themselves to magic. Perhaps a whole army of enchanters? He smiled to himself and decided not to raise the point with Denegtacus at their nightly meeting.

The time had arrived and Chard heard Leaspida call for quiet, which came almost instantly for all were keen to know just what had transpired in recent weeks.

'Thank you all for coming,' began the elven leader. 'I will get straight to the point for I know many of you already know something and it is my intention to try and clear up some of the wilder rumours that are at present circulating.' He glanced around at the sea of expectant faces. 'Several elf communities on the Isle of Rittan have been attacked by the dwarves, casualties are unknown at present but they are high according to reports from the survivors.' A sudden rush of noise greeted the words and he waited until the worst of it had died away. The news was not fresh as such but to have it confirmed by the king's son somehow made it all the more immediate.

'We have always known that the dwarves were our historic enemies but the sheer treachery of these cowardly attacks shocks even me. On one occasion, the dwarves rode into a village apparently to trade with our brethren before slaughtering them without mercy! Not a word of a declaration of war! No reasons given! Just wholesale murder of women, children and the elderly.'

A roar of sound from the normally reserved elves shook the building as many of them got to their feet and made shouted demands for immediate vengeance. Their leader stood impassively for a moment and then raised his hands to indicate silence.

'No one is more outraged than I, my friends, but we cannot be too hasty.'

Chard shook his head as he watched and listened. The elf malaise of waiting was still endemic despite their decades of interaction with humans. What would be required to make the elves act instantly he pondered; nothing short of an act of God in all probability.

'No elf on the continent has been harmed by the dwarves, the trouble has so far been confined to Rittan, but doubtless it is only a mater of time before their violence reaches us even here,' said Leaspida with venom.

The sheer idiocy of what he was hearing was mildly surprising to Chard. He knew that Curinlas would not tolerate any breach of its borders by the newly independent Lish-Kar and the dwarves would never provoke such a major power by attacking the elves settled inside human borders. The objective was clearly Rittan itself which was a much softer target, but Leaspida was whipping his followers into a state of panic with every sentence he uttered.

'It is my intention to speak this very evening with my father the king. I have no doubt that he will authorise us to cross the

Curinlas Channel to aid our brethren.' Leaspida glared hard around the hall. Never had he felt as angry as he did now, not even when confronted with his father's short sightedness all those years ago. The dwarves were threatening all that he, and others, had spent decades building outside of the forest. To put up with humans and their pettiness had been bad enough! But now, just when things were beginning to settle down, their world was under attack by a race that had contributed nothing to the world save death and destruction! The dwarves were no better than goblins, who could at least be excused their savagery since it was their way and they knew no other.

'Once the king has given us his assent, it is my intention that we shall head to the port of Ruinlasha to the north of here where we shall book passage to Rittan. All of us, men, women and children. Our lives here in Curinlas are ended but we shall rebuild them on the new elf home of Rittan!' Leaspida smiled broadly and allowed himself to bask momentarily in the applause. However, he was no human, soaked to the soul with ambition and vanity, and he continued. 'This place we have lived in these last few years has never really been our home, despite the softly spoken words of the humans who only want us for the goods we can manufacture for them. I say we build a new elf motherland on Rittan! One that is for elves and elves alone and if that means the deaths of the dwarves who pollute it at the moment, then so be it.'

Not a single elf remained seated at these words. The sound inside the hall was deafening and Chard shook his head imperceptibly. His eyes fell on his mentor who had stayed silent throughout the proceedings and was staring at nothing on the floor. Chard knew that Denegtacus was not averse to violence but he wondered just what advice he had been giving to the prince in recent days. Somehow Chard could not see the old enchanter agreeing to this and yet he also knew that if it came to war, he would not like to be a dwarf.

*   *   *

Chard as always stayed quiet and unobtrusive in the background but his eyes and ears were open. Leaspida was stood behind his desk; Denegtacus was slouched comfortably opposite him, watching his body language which was taut and nervous.

'It is only natural to feel some apprehension at speaking to your father about such matters, particularly after such a long gap,' said Denegtacus carefully.

'Despite everything, it is this that worries me more than the fate befalling our family on Rittan! Is that very bad of me?'

The older elf smiled. 'It shows that you are elf and have your flaws as do we all.'

'I know that it will be particularly difficult for you, my friend, and I cannot thank you enough for, well, everything really. This piece of magic is most welcome at this time.' Leaspida sighed and slumped into his chair and ran his fingers though his long blond hair. 'I have a deep foreboding regarding this, Denegtacus. What am I to do should my father react in the way that you seem to think?'

'We have had this conversation, Leaspida. You know what you have to do.'

The elf slammed his fist down heavily onto the table top, an uncharacteristic outburst of passion to which even Chard raised an eyebrow. 'Does that mean I have to like it? You are talking of an irrevocable spilt with Bulair! I don't know if I have the strength for such a move. My father is a stubborn elf, cantankerous even, but he is still king and he still rules all elves, regardless of where they live.'

'Even me,' said Denegtacus softly, but Chard was unsure whether or not Leaspida heard him.

Leaspida drummed his fingers on the desk and then laughed out loud, a forced, joyless sound. 'We are putting off what needs to be done for no good reason. Let us proceed.'

Denegtacus inclined his head and pushed himself slowly to his feet. Over the years, Chard had noted a distinct lack of theatrics that accompanied the old elf's magic, which he failed to understand. When you had mastery over such power, what was the point unless you could flaunt it for all to see?

The air shifted slightly, the molecules becoming visible and then swirling into a myriad of colours as the magic pulled at them, twisted them, extended them. The patterns swirled into an oval shape and gradually the mass of colour began to clear.

Chard had seen these doorways opened before, had even attempted it for himself but had not been able to master it. It was one of the many pieces of magic that he had pressed Denegtacus to teach him and just another of those things that the elf had told him would have to wait until he deemed him ready. The fury that this built up inside the human had to be carefully guarded at all times. Outwardly, Chard was nothing except the model student who accepted all of his tutor's instructions without comment.

From his position, Chard was able to see into the doorway and the place it opened onto. The elf king stared expressionlessly from behind the grand table in the main palace eating hall. The last century barely seemed to have made an impression on his features, save a few lines around the mouth and eyes that had not been there before.

Leaspida had been in written communication with his father all the time and had been to Bulair several times in the early years to see him, but had not made the journey at all in the last five decades. The prince also knew that his father and Denegtacus had not spoken since the enchanter had left the forest. Chard watched as both men studiously avoided looking at one another and groaned inwardly. Stubborn old fools the pair of them, but he had no time for that now.

'Father,' began Leaspida. 'It is good to see you again and looking so well. Is mother well?'

'She's fine,' replied the king woodenly.

Leaspida glanced nervously at Denegtacus who said and did nothing. Nervously he licked his lips and pressed on. 'Correspondence would have taken too long over such an important issue and so I hope you do not mind the intrusion of this magic into your home?'

The king leaned forward and folded his arms on the table. 'Since when did whatever I mind matter to you?'

Leaspida was genuinely shocked by his father's attitude and could find no reason for it. He opened his mouth and then closed it as he hastily rethought his arguments.

'Stop gaping at me like a fool!' snapped Theaspida. 'Speak what is on your mind, you usually do.'

'Very well, father,' added Leaspida slowly. 'You know of the attacks in Rittan and the deaths of our fellow elves?'

The king nodded curtly and waved his hand for his son to proceed.

'It is my intention to take my people to Rittan and aid our friends in their war. I do not need your permission, father; I simply thought that I should ask you.'

'Quite right, boy, you do not need my permission, I wonder what the real reason for this is!' The colour was building in Theaspida's cheeks as the argument began to spiral out of control.

'It is my hope to cross the sea and make landfall on the coast of the new elf stronghold that is being forged. A place known as the Westernwood. I assume that is where you will be sending the bulk of the army and where we will be safest until we have formulated a plan of attack.'

'You assume wrong,' said the king in a worryingly quiet voice.

'What do ...?'

'I remember when it began,' interrupted Theaspida. 'Out in the night like thieves they went. Making a laughing stock of their own king, appointed by the Creator to look over his people! The people pointed and I could hear their sniggers at the old fool who could not stop even his own son from deserting the motherland. I endured it; I endured it all because I foolishly believed that it could be for the best. Your mother convinced me that I should even bless your leaving as if it was something to be proud of instead of a curse and a shame.' The king surged to his feet and pointed angrily at his son. 'Now they come creeping back! Like foxes into the henhouse! Begging for help and demanding that elf blood should be spilt to help them!'

'I made no demands!' shouted Leaspida.

Theaspida roared with anger. 'Never interrupt me, boy! I will not see a single elf lay down his life to help the likes of you! Go to Rittan; go to the devil if you wish! But you will not take any of my people with you. My true people that is.'

Leaspida slumped back into his chair, the sheer enormity of what was happening all around him too much to take in.

'Now I shall take my leave of you. Have your pet wizard close this doorway so my wife may be spared having to look upon her failure of a son.'

The king turned his back on his son and walked out of sight. Nothing moved within the doorway and it slowly drifted apart as Denegtacus released the magic binding it.

Silence reigned within Leaspida's home as all three present thought over what had transpired in the last few minutes.

Leaspida cleared his throat and made a show of settling himself comfortably in his chair. He turned his face to the left so that he could look directly at the enchanter. Understanding passed between them and the older elf nodded.

'It is time to put our plans into effect. We leave within the month. I want us in the Westernwood before midsummer's day.'

Denegtacus stood up and caught his student's attention,

and Chard moved silently to his side. 'It will be as you say,' he said before adding, 'my king.'

Leaspida stiffened in his chair and then waved his hand; dismissing them.

When he was alone, the new king of the island elves, as they would later become known, placed his head in his hands.

'That could have gone better,' said Chard drily as they walked through the evening air towards the home they shared.

'You think this is funny?' snapped Denegtacus angrily. 'Such things are almost a daily occurrence among humans I know, but with elves, where family and brotherhood still means something, it is cause for great distress!'

Chard bit back an angry retort, something he had been doing for longer than he cared to remember. 'My apologies, master. I was trying to make light of a difficult situation. It is a way humans have for dealing with problems.'

Denegtacus waved his hand at the door of their home as they approached which swung open and allowed them to pass before shutting itself behind them.

Chard was moderately taken aback by such a display of magic. Usually his tutor was angered by those who used magic without good reason, thinking it a waste of a talent given to them by the Creator to be used wisely. Prudently, Chard decided not to press the point and awaited his master's instructions.

Denegtacus paced briefly across the main room of the small house he and Chard had constructed. They had built it less than a year after joining Leaspida and the others. It was solidly built of wood with a thatched roof and consisted of the normal three rooms: one each where they could have their privacy and one that they shared. It had taken mere hours to build as Chard harnessed his magic to send the timbers in to place under the guidance of his master.

Even in the main room, Denegtacus' work papers spilled haphazardly across bookshelves and table tops. Where they all materialised from, Chard wasn't sure, but one day soon after they had moved in, the old elf had returned to his work and these papers had appeared. Chard assumed he had returned to Bulair to collect them but Denegtacus made no mention of it and Chard knew better than to press him on such things.

'I always knew he was short sighted but even I didn't …' Denegtacus tailed off.

Chard risked a question. 'What do you think I should do to be of assistance, master? I have no family to care for here and I believe …'

Denegtacus gestured for Chard to be quiet and he duly obeyed. The old elf stopped pacing and let go of a large breath. Clearly he had come to some decision and now that it had been made, he would make sure that it happened.

'The port just to the north, you go there quite a lot I understand?'

Chard nodded.

'When the company of us elves gets too much for you and you feel the need to sate your human desires in wayside brothels?'

Chard shrugged insolently. 'It is better to acknowledge your drives than to suppress them. I am human.'

The elf looked as if he would pursue this old argument but thought better of it and waved the point away. 'Whatever, Chard, your whoremongering and drinking is immaterial to me. Go to the port and secure us ships for travel to Rittan. You know where we are headed; we don't need a ferry across the Channel but rather all the way to the Westernwood. You think you can do this without incident? Or do I need to hold your hand for you?'

'What do I use for money?' asked Chard, the insults bouncing off his hard exterior like raindrops. He knew most of this anger was not intended for him and it hardly bothered him even if it was.

Denegtacus walked into his own room and reappeared a few moments later clutching a small bag tied up with string which he handed to Chard. Chard did not bother to look in it. By its weight alone he knew he was holding a small fortune in gold.

'We will meet you in thirty days outside Ruinlasha. I don't want to take two thousand elves through such a place; find somewhere where we can board in safety and away from the smell of the town.' He glared hard at the human. 'Once this is all over and if you have distinguished yourself, we shall address the question of your training.'

Chard grinned and bowed low to hide it as best he could. 'Thank you, master.'

'Go,' said Denegtacus curtly and Chard hurried out into the gathering gloom of the night.

Outside Chard walked briskly through the village, barely able to think straight. It was the very last time he would be making this walk but the thought had little impact on him. His mind was swamped with the promise of real magic and the enchantment that Denegtacus would show to him if he proved himself. Well, he would. Ships were easy and the dwarves would rue the day they raised their axes to elves. After that, Denegtacus could do nothing else but keep his promise.

The village was not completely dark. Lamps glowed brightly along the paths, hanging from handy branches to light the way for those in need. A sound to Chard's left drew his eyes lazily; he was not expecting trouble and reacted slowly to it when he saw it.

The child ran up to him and released the spell. The magical dragon, less than six inches from snout to tail, flew around his head, breathing fire that threatened to singe his eyebrows. Momentarily startled he jumped back, before releasing his own spell. A second dragon appeared, golden-red in colour and some ten times bigger than the first. It chased the smaller dragon before swallowing it in one large gulp.

Formositas clapped her hands and squealed with delight as the new dragon flew in a series of intricate arcs, leaving a trail of light wherever it went. Suddenly it raced high into the sky and burst into a shower of silver coloured sparks that fell slowly back to earth.

At the age of twenty-two, Formositas was the youngest of Leaspida's four children and, as one of three girls, a very low-ranking princess. Even so, she had her own private elfin tutor as it would not be proper for her to be educated by a human. Despite her years, she had the appearance of a human child of about seven, which was quite normal for an elf. Childhood lasted many times longer for an elf and their growth was also much slower.

Chard picked her up and swung her round, making her squeal all the more. Her long red hair flew wildly in all directions and reluctantly Chard put her down, pushing the unruly locks away from her eyes.

'Again!' she called.

Chard smiled. The child was beautiful even for an elf and her angular features were clear even in this light, her green eyes sparkling with mischief. 'Now now princess, you know you shouldn't be out at this time. What would your mother say?'

The child pouted. 'Don't care. They don't even notice if I'm there or not. They won't even let me play with the other children in your school! It's not fair!' She stamped her foot and crossed her arms across her chest.

Chard smiled but was wise enough not to let the child see this. 'Come on, Formositas, I'll take you home before you get us both into trouble.' Taking hold of the child's hand he began the short walk.

'Did you like my dragon, Mr Chard?' she asked, gazing up.

Chard grinned down at her. 'It was marvellous. I really thought it was going to bite my nose off!'

She grinned happily. 'I'm glad you showed me how to do it. I wish father would let me spend more time with you. You're a much better teacher than that horrid old servant.'

'Well, that's true,' confessed Chard.

He knocked on the door which was opened almost at once by Leaspida's servant. The king's servant now, Chard supposed, although he said nothing.

'Found this one wandering,' said Chard with a smile.

'Again,' muttered the servant. 'Inside young lady.'

Formositas danced across the doorway. 'Night Mr Chard.'

'Goodnight, princess,' called Chard, but the door was already closed.

Even the servants were rude to him. No, not rude, they simply didn't think of him at all. Chard sighed. He wasn't going to let such thoughts bother him tonight. Denegtacus had made him a promise and Chard was determined that he would hold the old elf to it. Idly he wondered if Gerniella would do the homework.

11

The port of Ruinlasha hadn't changed much in all the years that Chard had been visiting. It was a relatively, small place; the main northern port of Curinlas was some miles further eastwards up the coast where the stretch of water between Curinlas and Rittan was at its narrowest. The navy had several ships stationed there; Chard had visited a couple of times but had found it better to frequent places where fewer questions were asked, such as Ruinlasha.

Technically there was a town gate that had to be passed in order to get into Ruinlasha. In reality the town overspill had seen the wall used for building houses and the whole place was little more than an overgrown fishing village. The plentiful supply of fresh food had seen the population increase but as yet the imperial government had not seen fit to station a garrison there as was proper once the number of people went past ten thousand. There was a city militia which consisted of a dozen men, most of whom were ex-military, but generally they were not required. Curinlas was a law-abiding place and any infraction of the multitude of rules the state laid down was treated harshly.

Chard mulled over all he had learned about this area of Curinlas over the decades as he wandered unopposed through the sprawling lanes and made his way to the dockside. The empire had been in decline in recent years, ill-advised expansion into Rittan had brought it into direct conflict with just about every other race on the continent. War was expensive and losing even more so. The land Curinlas had seized in Rittan had been lost almost immediately as the dwarves, goblins and humans who were already squabbling over her turned on the newcomers. Rather than pull out gracefully, the empire had committed too many troops and resources into a war that none of her generals had been able to win. There were some humans in Rittan who claimed an affiliation to Curinlas but they said it quietly and in the security of their homes. Curinlas, for her part, had tried to put the Rittan wars out of her mind as she struggled to hold territory against dwarven expansion far to the south.

Still, despite everything, Curinlas was still the number one power in Eurasia and its navy was immense despite losses inflicted by the sailors of Tordos. A ferry to the Westernwood was unlikely to offer Chard any real problems and he had the best part of a month to enjoy the delights of the town without interruption from the elves. It did him good to mix with humans every now and again: he could drink, gamble and rut without feeling guilty, for he had never met a human who judged anyone on such things. Simply put, they did not care what you did, as long as you had the money to pay for it. At this thought, Chard hefted the gold on the inside of his robes, its weight having a cathartic effect on him and he grinned.

The days drifted by in a pleasantly uneventful way for Chard. He had found six ships that would take the elves to Westernwood on the date specified within a week of arriving. It would be quite a little armada that sailed off to pastures new. Technically, only five of the captains had been persuaded by his money – the last had had to have his mind twisted into place by magic, but needs must. In theory there was no need for any of this. He and Denegtacus had the magic to take all of them wherever they wanted to go in the blinking of an eye but Leaspida had said no. Not that the elf distrusted the magic, rather he did not want the elves to become slaves to enchantment and lose the ability to fend for themselves if ever it should not be there. For someone as independent minded as Chard, the elf's position was easy to understand.

With his work complete he had been free to play cards for as long as he wished. He did not even cheat when he played, using magic would somehow cheapen the experience. Instead he gambled as did the others, he watched faces and played the odds and, more times than not, he won. Chard was an exceptional poker player and was well known in most of the dockside gambling dens. His appearance could send lesser players to the exit.

Tonight had been an above-average win for Chard and that was something out of the ordinary which should be celebrated. Leaving the table more than a hundred silver pennies up, he was in a gracious mood. Money was spent like water. It had no real importance to him for he knew that even if he was penniless there was always a way for a man of his talents to get by. He bought round after round of drinks and treated himself to two whores an hour apart; he was getting older after all. Both girls he tipped heavily and wandered out into the night with nothing to show for his earlier victory except a fading feeling of well-being and a burgeoning hangover.

Chard tottered unsteadily down the road and paused to relieve himself in an alley. He gazed around unfocused as the steady stream continued to flow. It was nearer dawn than midnight and Chard struggled to remember where he was staying that night.

The blow took him completely by surprise and he was pitched from his feet to land heavily on the ground. Blood leaked from a cut on his forehead and pain roared across the back of his skull where he had been struck. With disgust he could feel the urine he had just got rid off soaking into his robes and he tried to push himself clear. Another blow connected savagely with his back and this time he cried out in pain. He rocked over onto his side to see what was going on.

Two men loomed above him, their features completely obscured in the dark since the only light came from a street lamp some distance away. Chard lost count of how many blows rained down on him and as he sought his magic the very real fear that these fools could kill him raced across his alcohol-sodden mind. Another heavy punch cracked his skull and any thought of magic drifted away, along with consciousness.

When Chard woke he realised he was being carried and he turned his head blearily to see who had a hold of him. On either side he was supported by militia men who were grunting with the effort of carrying the dead weight. The light of the sun was hurting his eyes, but even as the thought occurred the sun vanished as the three men entered a building and Chard found himself deposited unceremoniously in a chair which creaked threateningly with his weight.

He lifted his head and tried to look at the man behind the desk. The two cells behind him, Chard tried to put out of his mind.

'Someone did a right number on this one, Captain,' said a voice from behind Chard, who assumed it came from one of the two men who had carried him in. 'He's pretty beat up but he'll live. Found him down King's Way.'

The officer regarded Chard who was now touching various parts of his anatomy tenderly and trying to work out his own diagnoses. Captain Reggis didn't much care for drunkards. People didn't like having to step over bloodstained bodies that stank of piss on their way to work in the morning.

'Public drunkenness carries a five silver penny fine, ten days in jail with ten lashes if you can't pay.'

Chard tried to speak but his jaw ached too much and his throat was dry.

Reggis poured some water into a glass and passed it across the desk. Chard took it and drank it all in one, managing a muted 'thank you'.

'Well?' pressed Reggis. 'Can you afford the fine?'

Chard nodded. 'I can afford it.'

'Ain't got any money on him, Captain,' interjected one of the militia men. 'Whoever beat him up took it, if he had any in the first place. Looks like a vagrant to me.'

'Smells like one too,' said the second man.

Chard ignored it all and didn't even turn round.

Reggis shook his head. 'Look at his clothes. They might be dirty and covered in blood but they're expensive, well made.' He rubbed his chin. 'You're not a vagrant are you, son? What were you doing down the King's Way and who did you upset to end up in that state?'

Chard shook his head wearily and instantly regretted it.

'It wasn't a request, son,' said Reggis. 'I'm responsible for order in this town and drunken fights on the streets look bad on the reports.'

'I was playing cards,' said Chard slowly.

Reggis smiled thinly. 'Took too much from someone who took offence?'

Chard concurred with the tiniest of nods.

'Want to press charges?'

Chard glanced at the captain. 'No, I'll deal with it myself.'

'Now I'm not sure about that,' replied Reggis amiably. 'I think I'll come back with you and collect the fine and then see you out of the town.'

Chard forced himself to his feet and immediately felt hands grip his shoulders, not hard but with the distinct impression that they could be used forcibly if necessary.

'Make it easy on yourself,' continued Reggis. 'I don't want trouble from whatever friends you have. Pay the fine and get out.'

By now, enough of Chard's focus had returned and he

could feel the raw energy of magic bubbling just beneath the surface of his being. It was a comforting sensation, one he had grown accustomed to over the years, and the thought of being vulnerable had frightened him more than he even cared to admit to himself.

'I shall pay the fine because frankly I deserve to for allowing myself to be bested by a couple of fools. But do not test my patience further, *son*,' he added caustically. 'I was old before your grandfather was born and I shall be here when your grandchildren are long gone!' He glanced over each shoulder in turn and both the men restraining him let go with a startled gasp as pain lanced their hands.

Reaching outwards, Chard snapped his fingers and his purse materialised. From it he withdrew a large golden coin which he slapped down on the desk.

'I take it that covers your inconvenience!'

Reggis made no move to pick up the coin and tried to calm an unfamiliar sensation of terror that had gripped his whole body. This man would kill him without a second's hesitation, he knew this with a cold certainty, and he found himself nodding and grinning like a fool.

Chard walked from the building and out into the streets. Within moments he was out of sight and making his way to the room he had rented. None of the men he had left behind made any move to follow him.

The three militia men released breaths that none of them knew they'd been holding.

'I sure as shit wouldn't want to have him after me!' said one of the two men who had carried Chard in.

'Reckon we should try and stop him?' asked the second man quietly and without enthusiasm. 'People don't like bodies on the streets.'

Reggis stared hard at his men. 'I hope to God that I never lay eyes on that man again!' he said with feeling. 'When he's done what he has to do, I doubt he'll stick around.' He waved his men away and picked up the coin. He was holding more money than he had ever seen in his life before. It was heavy, and represented somewhere in the region of four years' pay. There was no way he could explain having this much money, the authorities would assume it was the result of criminal activity, take it off him and bestow some kind of punishment on him.

'To hell with that!' he muttered to himself. Two minutes later the ex-captain of the militia was making his way south to a new life with four years' wages in his pocket.

There was no point in being deliberately foolish about what needed to be done. Chard waited until his last night in Ruinlasha before he approached the two men who had so humiliated him. Finding them was no problem, his magic allowing him to watch his prey for several days before he decided to strike.

He sipped at his water delicately as he watched the group of card players across the alehouse. There were six of them and Chard knew all of them by sight, not a single player of any worth among them. A simple spell meant that none of them recognised him and he sat quietly, enjoying the game.

Originally he had simply intended to approach them, remind them who he was and dispense them. But he realised that this lacked a certain panache that Chard demanded of himself. So he had constructed a second plan, one which he hoped would provide much more amusement. Releasing the magic, he sat back to watch.

As one of the men dealt with a practised whip of his wrist, a second card suddenly fell from his shirt sleeve. With genuine astonishment he stared at it but that surprise was quickly replaced with alarm as he sensed the drop in temperature around him. The five other members of the game had not taken their eyes from the card, a black ace, since its appearance. The seconds began to draw out, tight with tension.

What happened next was so fast that even Chard did not know what to look at. Concealed knives surfaced in fluid and well practised moves. Insults and threats were not needed, not for men such as these. Furniture was sent flying in all directions as the dealer stepped back to give himself room and others leapt for him. Slashing blades, cries of pain and splashes of blood painted a gruesome tableau before Chard, who merely smiled sardonically and continued to drink his water unhurriedly.

Within three minutes, both of Chard's attackers were dead. One of a slit throat and the other of multiple stab wounds to his chest and stomach. Of the four other men, one was dead, one seriously wounded while the remaining two both carried light wounds. These two made good their escapes leaving the fallen men to bleed on the floor in a heap of broken furniture.

Those people who were drinking in the alehouse did not stop to see if the fallen required help. Five minutes after the start of the brawl, Chard was alone save for the alehouse's owner, one of his employees and the remnants of the fight. The two men hastily began moving the bodies from the premises out into the back alleys, probably for removal as soon as possible. No one wanted to explain three corpses to the militia, who believed punishment of crime was enough, the right perpetrator secondary. While they were gone, Chard watched as the wounded man died. He thought briefly that he was relatively innocent and had simply been gambling with the wrong people but dismissed the idea almost at once. Judge a man by the company he keeps.

Chard left the alehouse and returned to his lodgings. The whole sorry episode had certainly taught him a lesson and one he would not forget. As for the men who had just died,

Chard couldn't have recalled their faces for all the gold in Curinlas.

Denegtacus had stayed in his chair when the human had walked in, a contrived piece of bad manners and one that was beneath him, but today he was giving in to petulance.

The human had the same look of faraway disdain that spoke of arrogance and the unspoken displeasure of having to deal with mere elves that Denegtacus had come to recognise and loathe in all of Curinlas' officials. The visits of such men were everyday occurrences but this visit was slightly more irksome than the others, if that were possible, given the petty nature of it.

Once the decision to uproot to Rittan had been made, Leaspida had informed the local human authorities, just for the sake of politeness. He had not been surprised when this was met with diplomatic anger and frustration as Curinlas saw a source of excellent, cheap merchandise sailing off into the distance. This present visit, on the very morning that the elves were leaving their home for the sea and uncertainty, was timed for maximum inconvenience.

The human diplomat walked slowly around the near empty shell of Leaspida's home, his footsteps clipping on the floorboards. He glanced down at Denegtacus but managed to put him out of his mind almost instantly, a decrepit old fool who meant nothing to him, and instead rounded on Leaspida.

'You know how much our imperial government has appreciated all that you have done for us over the years and we deeply regret this sudden departure.'

'It would be a lot more sudden,' said Denegtacus irately, 'if we were actually able to get on with it!'

Leaspida made a silent appeal to the old elf to be quiet and cut in quickly. 'We have enjoyed and been thankful for all of

Curinlas' aid but when our kith and kin are under attack in Rittan, well, what would you do?'

'Quite,' replied the diplomat staring hard at Denegtacus. The man appeared to come to a decision and turned his back on the enchanter and focused on Leaspida. 'The imperial government feels that some small recompense for our bother at your leaving should be in order. Purely to aid our continued good working relationship once you return safely,' he added, with the smallest of bows.

Leaspida felt his own annoyance building but tried desperately to swallow it down. Denegtacus however, felt no such restraint and surged to his feet. Magic struck the official and lifted him from his feet. The man screamed, more in alarm than pain, as he felt himself carried through the air by the unseen force. Against the door he smashed, which flew open upon impact, and he was sent sprawling into the dirt outside.

He struggled to rise but stopped when he saw the old elf before him. The elf's face was a picture of fury and murderous intent. The diplomat was on all fours and closed his eyes; the emotion he saw in that stare, too much.

Leaspida touched Denegtacus gently on his arm. 'My friend,' he murmured softly. 'There is no need for this.'

The anger flared one last time and then receded to a level that allowed the elf to speak. 'Know that the only reason you live is because I am acquiescing to a request from my king! If I see you again, or any of your kind tries to interfere with our journey, I will destroy them, regardless of what my liege says. Do you understand me, human?'

The official nodded hastily and made no effort to stand. A grimace was forced onto his face which might just have been an attempt at a smile. 'I … I meant …'

'I care nothing for what you meant!' shouted Denegtacus. At once he spun on his heel and walked away from the spread-eagled official. Leaspida knew better than to comment on the situation and pushed it from his mind, concentrating on the journey ahead, rather than human interferences.

Denegtacus was stood at the window of Leaspida's house, the same place that the young royal had stood when Denegtacus and Chard had first approached all those years ago. Leaspida studied the back of the old elf's head and wondered, not for the first time, just what went on inside it. Denegtacus was an elf but this was tempered by a broader understanding of the world. Even so, his desire to see the elves strong and independent could sometimes lead to … over-reaction, mused Leaspida.

'What's it like to live forever?' asked the king suddenly.

Denegtacus glanced over his shoulder. 'I haven't lived forever.'

Leaspida smiled. A typical Denegtacus answer. For a fleeting second he felt a pang of empathy with Chard who had suffered it for longer than anyone. 'You know what I meant, Denegtacus.'

'You see the same nonsense over and over again. History is like eating rich food; it repeats on you. That,' and he waved outside the window where the official was rapidly departing down the track, 'is the sort of thing I got tired of a thousand years ago.'

'We are ready to leave.'

Denegtacus swung round and gestured for Leaspida to go first through the door. 'Let's be on our way then, my boy, no point hanging round here.'

The journey to the rendezvous spot Chard had chosen was uneventful. The elves moved swiftly through pleasant countryside, scouts spread along the entire route to keep guard, a precaution that Leaspida had been sure was unnecessary and one that he had insisted upon anyway.

Occasionally they spotted the odd human, most of them kept out of the way of so many well-armed elves. A few raised their hands in greeting, but none made any attempt to engage the elves in conversation or slow their progress.

It was midday when the elves reached the coast. The plan had been well explained and they split into the six sections automatically and waited to see how they would reach the ships which they could see bobbing a quarter of a mile offshore. Leaspida left his family to speak to Denegtacus who was taking in the scene with barely concealed irritation.

Leaspida glanced over the chalk-white cliff which sloped steeply before settling into a more gradual slope which would take them to the sea. To elves, used to living in trees, it offered numerous ways down, none of which would prove a problem to any but the infirm who had already been singled out for magical assistance in any case. The king's eyes scanned the cliffs, moved across the beach and out to sea. The six ships Chard had selected were there and Leaspida was momentarily shocked at the sheer size of the craft. Originally built many years earlier, the ships were military transports that ferried huge amounts of men and supplies across the narrow channel that separated Curinlas from Rittan. After Curinlas had pulled her troops out of Rittan the ships had been sold to private entrepreneurs who used them for varying purposes. Not today though; today they would carry nearly three thousand elves to their new homes in the Westernwood.

'The ships are some distance from us, my friend, people are asking how we shall reach them.'

Denegtacus glanced at his king but said nothing. His eyes were drawn to movement on the beach. Noticing the enchanter's stare, Leaspida followed it. He could see Chard standing at the edge of the water, his arms folded neatly inside the voluminous sleeves of his black robes.

'Start bringing our people down,' instructed Denegtacus. 'I'll speak to Chard.'

Chard bowed as his teacher approached but remained silent in the face of the obvious hostility that emanated from the elf.

Denegtacus watched as the elves made their way down the cliffs. He gave no indication that he had even noticed the human's presence until several minutes had passed and he finally spoke.

'What is your plan then, boy?'

Chard bowed once again. 'The ships are as close to the shore as they can comfortably get master. The jetties at Ruinlasha would have allowed us to embark normally but you ...'

Denegtacus interrupted him. 'Don't lecture me, boy, Ruinlasha is no place for elves. We both know that it'll take hours to ferry everyone back and forth. Time that would be better served making our way to Rittan so that we can help our brethren.'

'I have in mind a piece of magic that will allow us to embark somewhat quicker but I felt I should run it past you before I proceeded. I believe it requires enchantment, the power over the elements themselves.'

Denegtacus listened in silence as Chard told him what he intended. When he had finished the elf scratched thoughtfully at his ear. 'Get on with it then,' he said finally.

Chard watched as the elf began to move away from him, towards Leaspida who was stood some distance away. 'Don't I need your help, master?' called Chard. 'I thought ...'

'You think too much sometimes, Chard,' replied Denegtacus as he walked back towards the human, Leaspida beside him.

Chard nodded slowly and then turned to face the sea, his arms reaching out, fingers pointed.

'Well, human,' said Leaspida. 'How do we reach the ships? I see no craft ready to take us there.'

Chard ignored the question until he had finished working

the magic. The elves were well tuned-in to magic and all of them had felt the power being cast around them, Leaspida included.

Chard looked at Leaspida and then at the sea. 'We walk, your majesty.'

Leaspida looked at the sea and then at Chard and back again. 'Such a feat would require more magical talent than most of our comrades possess.'

'True,' said Chard. 'Which is why my magic has done all the work for them.'

With that, he walked into the sea. Yet he didn't. His feet made small splashing sounds as he walked across the top of the water. When he was a short way from the shore he stopped. 'The water will support us all, Leaspida, this is the power of enchantment.'

The elf king glanced at Denegtacus but he was staring at his pupil and did not appear to notice. Chard continued on his way, never once looking back until he had reached the ship he was due to sail with. He watched as the elves walked across the tops of the waves, held there by his power alone. For a fleeting moment he considered what it would be like to end the spell and watch the chaos as they were cast into the sea.

When the elves reached the sides of the ships another surge of magic lifted them effortlessly into the air and deposited them safely onto the decks of the waiting ships. The elves were more used to magic than the human sailors but even they were shocked at the display of might Chard had crafted and they scuttled quickly to their temporary homes in the cabins the humans had set aside for them.

The humans had not particularly looked forward to this venture, despite the fact they were all being paid heavily over the odds to ensure speed and comfort. Dealings with elves were still unusual and ancient enmities ran deep. The sight of magic silenced them all and stilled thoughts of duplicity.

All six of the captains now shared one thought: to get these elves to Rittan as quickly as possible and off their ships.

As the last of the elves boarded the last of the ships, the human sailors swarmed into activity, ready for departure. Denegtacus made his way through the press of bodies until he found Chard leaning against the portside rail, staring back at Curinlas.

'A following wind, Chard, keep it even and constant. The humans tell me they don't like strong gales so go careful.'

Chard stood up straight as he looked at his teacher. Not a word of praise for his first true piece of enchantment, which had worked perfectly. Instead, a demand for a second piece of enchantment and one that Chard wasn't even sure how to do.

'Perhaps some guide master, as to how ...'

Denegtacus waved his hand irritably. 'Feel the elements, Chard, all around you. Know your place among them. Recognise them and then command them. I cannot teach you such things, boy; I can only tell you where to look to find the answers for yourself.'

It was as if a veil had been lifted from Chard's eyes. All at once he knew that the secret was that there was no secret. Denegtacus had not been refusing to teach him; it was simply that he couldn't teach him. Either he was meant to be an enchanter or he wasn't. Chard felt the surge of power that this knowledge gave him. The old elf had merely been keeping an eye on him all these years, seeing how his talent progressed. Chard glanced at Denegtacus with new-found admiration for the power that the elf's body possessed. He found it shocking that such energy could be contained within such a thing! From now on there was nothing, *nothing* that was beyond him. He and Denegtacus were practically equals, the only thing separating them was Denegtacus' experience.

Turning his head upwards he smiled at the heavens. The

clouds drifting lazily to the northwest, the blueness of the sky, he could change it all at will. Forcing his mind into the air itself he began to turn it. He felt the resistance of nature and almost laughed at the notion that even she had free will any more. Everything on the planet was subject to him, nothing was outside his control! The wind suddenly roared in a massive arc as Chard forced it to change direction, the suddenness momentarily taking him by surprise. The ship lurched violently beneath his feet as it practically left the water as the surge of air hit it.

The screams of the passengers and crew he ignored completely as he felt the burning gaze of Denegtacus upon him. Quickly he adjusted the magic and the wind slowed to the correct level and direction. Except for a few ominous creaks from the timbers of the ships and the soft cries of an infant or two, all was as it should be. Only now did he turn to face Denegtacus, whose eyes were cold and hard. The human refused to be stared down and returned the intense look steadily.

'Control, Chard,' said Denegtacus eventually. 'Learn it … soon.'

'Master,' replied Chard with a nod. He did not bow and promised himself that he never would again.

12

The journey was quick and without excitement, except for the fact that they continued in the right direction no matter which way the wind apparently blew from. The sailors were even less talkative around Chard than they were around the elves. A few of the elves succumbed to seasickness but this was easily treated by conventional means and there was no need for magic. The ships docked at the new elven port which had been built specially for the supplies that the residents of Westernwood were expecting any time soon. Leaspida took immediate charge and decided that he would not dissuade them of that particular notion until later, when things were more settled.

Chard lounged against a handy tree overlooking the new port. The ships had already turned and headed back to Curinlas and the elves were busy making temporary shelters and organising food. Denegtacus had disappeared with Leaspida and several other high ranking elves and hadn't been seen since. The activity was already moving away from the coast and further inland where areas had been set aside for the development of a new elf city among the trees, which would be the capital of a new elf state in Westernwood.

Chard knew there were a thousand things he could be doing to help but none of them particularly appealed. The elves worked quite quickly and efficiently when pressed and would undoubtedly be fine without his aid. Instead he summoned the magic within and soared physically into the air, the sudden lurch making his stomach heave. Rising quickly, soon the wood was far below him. The air was cold and so another piece of magic was necessary to keep him warm. He could see for miles in all directions and on a whim decided to have at look at the enemy for himself. Denegtacus wouldn't approve, but then he never did.

Crossing Westernwood in minutes, he soon hit the plains of central Rittan where most of the mixed population of the island lived. Small pockets of humans could be seen all over, interspersed with dwarf, elf and even the odd goblin community. There was no real area where one species held dominance over all the others but it was clear to Chard that by sheer weight of numbers alone, the humans would eventually colonise all of Rittan. The elf villages were showing some movement westwards as they retreated from the dwarf attacks. Those on the far side of the island had been abandoned and Chard could see long lines of refugees, desperately trying to make their way to Westernwood but from his height he could see that most of them would eventually come into contact with dwarves who would slaughter them in the open.

A decision was made in Chard's mind and he swung in a wide lazy arc before drifting down to earth. He was closer to the eastern side of Rittan and had spied a small group of elves moving ever westwards. Rittan was a generally flat country but it was heavily wooded and they were unaware of a dwarven cavalry company several miles to the north of them which was headed their way.

Chard approached the lead figure in the column and for the first time got a good view of the elves. There were roughly fifty of them, mostly women and children with fifteen males guarding the flanks. The elf raised his hand and the column stopped. Fear and nerves were already drawn as tight as the bowstring which had a notched arrow pointed at Chard's chest.

'Who are you?' asked the elf, his tone harsh and suspicious.

'My name is hardly the pressing issue for you at the moment,' replied Chard calmly. He nodded at the now four arrows that were aimed at him. 'There really is no need for that; I am here to help you.'

The elf snorted derisively. 'As if a human would ever go out of his way to help an elf!'

One of the other elves whispered something in the leader's ear and he inclined his head thoughtfully. Chard's expression shifted a little as boredom began to overtake him.

'Any more of your kind round about?' the leader asked suddenly. 'You distracting us for your friends to sneak up behind us?'

Chard sighed theatrically and wandered forward.

'Keep back!' ordered the elf, the tension in his voice translated to the slight wobble on the bow he held.

Chard waved his hand irritably without breaking stride and the arrows turned into dust. The colour drained out of the elf's face and he began to move backwards, not even thinking of drawing his sword.

The human put his arm round the elf and smiled. 'I really am here to help you. Understand?'

The elf nodded dumbly.

'There are a hundred dwarf cavalry about ten minutes away who are intent on murdering you all. I assume they are a part of the same army that destroyed your village.'

'How do you know about that?' asked the elf, his curiosity getting the better of his fear.

'Because I am fighting for the elves against the dwarves and I assumed they were the reason you are on the move and your numbers are so depleted.' Chard beamed happily at the bemused expression on the elf's face.

'Who …?'

Chard waved the point away. 'Later. For now, gather your people over there.' He pointed to a slightly thicker glade of trees a hundred yards away. 'And I shall deal with the dwarf problem for you.'

Without conscious thought, the elf found himself obeying and within moments Chard was alone on the track. The enchanter pulled his hood up, tucked his hands out of sight within his sleeves and stood patiently. His heart rate increased and he found himself relishing the confrontation that was inevitable.

The horses were heard only seconds before he saw the soldiers. They rode into view in good order, six abreast and with the lord of the company at the front and marginally to the left, as was traditional. The lord looked much the same as all the other soldiers, although his armour was clearly of superior quality. He held up his hand and his dwarves drew rein. He rode forward with the first three sections who fanned out to surround the human who had not, as yet, looked up.

'Who are you?' said the dwarf lord, the second person to ask that of Chard in minutes, his voice gruff, his hand resting on the handle of his battle axe.

'Look at this,' said Chard quietly. He held up an ant he had found and which was crawling along his finger. 'Do you think this creature knows the peril it is in?'

The dwarf glanced at his captain who returned the look with a shrug.

Despite everything, the dwarf actually replied. 'I don't know human, why don't you ask it?'

Chard nodded thoughtfully, as if the point hadn't occurred to him. He was silent for just a second and then glanced up at the mounted dwarf. 'I told him, but ants cannot understand individuality, he thinks I am threatening his nest.'

The dwarf shook his head with a small laugh. 'Humans!' he exclaimed to the merriment of his troops. 'Come, we have wasted enough time here already. The elves cannot be far.'

He wheeled his horse and prepared to return to his troop, the others doing likewise.

'You see, I have squashed it, taking away its life and it never realised the danger, even at the last.' Chard wiped the remains of the ant on his robes.

Something in his tone made the dwarf look back. The human smiled and suddenly he knew. His hand pulled clear his axe and he drew breath to call out his command, but neither action came to anything as a white-hot bolt of pure energy struck him between the eyes. It burst through the back of his skull in a bloody explosion of brain and bone, his body pitching from the saddle to land with a dull thud upon the dry earth.

His troops recovered quickly, and those who had accompanied their leader rounded on Chard instantly. The enchanter despatched them all with blasts of magic without once moving his feet. Body after body began to pile up around him but Chard ignored it all. In less than a minute all eighteen of the dwarves who had ridden forward with their lord lay dead. The rest had edged forward but they stayed where they were, stunned into immobility.

He turned his head to look at those who remained and, stepping over the bodies, began to walk very slowly towards them. When he was a matter of yards from the dwarves he spoke. 'Well? Are you prepared to die fighting or are you all cowards who came looking for women and children and instead found nothing but death!'

At his words, many of the dwarves kicked their mounts forward and screamed battle cries. Chard's hands swept up and red lightning flew from his fingertips, decimating the ranks of the dwarves. Blood and flesh flew in all directions as the magic tore apart the frail, mortal forms of his enemies. The press of horse and bodies meant that most of the dwarves were unable to charge at Chard, even had they been possessed to do so. In moments, the carnage caused those at the back of the column to turn and flee. Chard did not spare them a second thought as he continued to pick off any dwarf he could see.

Finally Chard realised he was alone, a carpet of dead dwarves and horses before him. He smiled at the sight, a turning point in the Dwarf War, of that he was certain. A flash of irritation at having allowed at least forty of the dwarves to escape crossed his mind but he pushed it aside. They would be able to spread the terror of what they had witnessed and be forced to admit that they had fled from just one man after seeing their lord cut down.

Spinning on his heel he walked briskly away, his mood good and a spring in his step. Finding the elves he had helped he waited until their leader approached him cautiously, the elf's eyes wary and afraid.

'That was ...' he said, and ground to a halt. He stared at the mass of corpses in two distinct groups and shook his head.

'I know,' said Chard with false modesty and an exaggerated bow. 'Have no fear, with me on your side, this war will soon be over, the enemy routed.'

'Who are you?' the elf asked, stressing every word.

'I am death for your enemies,' replied Chard. Snapping his fingers, the magic instantly whisked him away and returned him to the sky where he made a leisurely return to Westernwood.

The elf, left behind, scratched his head. At nearly two hundred and fifty he was one of the oldest elves who had decided to make his way in the world outside Bulair, and now he was once more questioning that decision. The stench of blood and death was already assaulting his nostrils and it repelled him. He looked back over his shoulder at the elves who were his responsibility and then again at the dead dwarves. It really was no contest, a few dwarves against the children of the Creator, how could he be anything other than relieved at their sudden rescue? Yet … there was something about the human that worried him. No, not worried, *terrified* him. He sighed and tried to push the events from his mind, focusing instead on the task that still confronted him which was to cross Rittan to the safety of Westernwood. With a final glance at the body-littered ground, he walked back to his people.

Chard ambled through the groups of elves, chatting here and there but never stopping. A feeling of tiredness due to the exertions of the day was overtaking him and he began to wonder where he would spend the coming night. His feet were unconsciously leading him to Denegtacus. After more than a century together, they had a bond that went deep and he could sense the old elf wherever he was and was certain that this was reciprocated.

One of the elf homes was nestled comfortably among the branches of a solid Rittan oak. He knew Denegtacus was inside and with little effort he rose through the air, slipping neatly between the arms of the tree until he landed on a narrow walkway that connected this abode with another in the next tree. As he gazed at the collection of something like twenty dwellings that he could see, he paused. All were beautifully crafted by magic, love and skill so that they were practically indistinguishable from the trees that supported them. Perhaps the elves would do better if they could learn to destroy with as much passion as they created, then this business with the dwarves would be ended in no time.

He opened the door and walked inside, then drew up sharply as he saw the picture before him. It took just a second for him to realise that it wasn't actually inside the room but was a projection of something from far away. Denegtacus was sat at his desk, the clutter of books and paper strewn across it as ever. An image of how this stuff accumulated so quickly and how he managed to drag it halfway around Eurasia with him crossed Chard's mind but he pushed it away. He was L'tusian, and could do anything he so desired.

An oval window of magic hung in the air and Chard gazed at it. Bodies of elves were everywhere, perhaps fifty of them. All of them had been hideously mutilated, possibly before death, it was impossible to tell. Most of them had been burnt as well, the age-old punishment for meddling in sorcery, and understanding jolted Chard's mind. Denegtacus' eyes were burning into him, and the anger emanating from him was palpable in the air.

'I … I … ' stammered Chard.

Denegtacus rose to his feet. 'Spare me, boy!' he shouted. 'Fifty-two dead elves and all because of you!'

Chard reeled back as the elf rounded on him. His master jabbed a gnarled finger into his ribs, punctuating every word with another prod. 'You left them to die! You could have helped them but you were too busy congratulating yourself on your magic. Look at them!' He gripped the front of Chard's robes and forced his eyes onto the images of the dead elves. 'All of them were tortured and burnt alive! Women and children! Look at them!' he bellowed, his anger threatening to tip over into a berserk rage.

'The dwarves were in rout when I left, they were galloping away, I saw them.' Chard's voice tailed away as he took in the horror of the pictures before him. 'They came back …'

Denegtacus pushed Chard away from him and turned his back. 'An astounding piece of deduction!' he sneered. 'Thanks to you we have lost more elves and our enemy is now even more ruthless than it was before. Until today, the dwarves usually fought within the rules of war. Now though, they think we have turned to sorcery and will not take the risk of allowing any of our people to survive. Congratulations, Chard.' The elf slumped into his chair. 'You have just signed the death warrant of the Creator alone knows how many elves.'

Chard continued to stare at the image until Denegtacus ended the spell and it faded to nothing. The human shook his head and walked to the window. He leaned on the sill and gazed out at nothing and everything.

'I'm sorry,' he began, but Denegtacus interrupted him.

'Don't, Chard, don't apologise as if that will grant you absolution.'

'I don't want absolution!' said Chard with feeling. 'I truly am sorry that I left my enemies to live. It is a mistake that I will not repeat again.'

Denegtacus snorted derisively. 'Such sentiments are worse than your initial error, Chard. You should have been working out how to keep the elves safe, not how to kill the dwarves.'

Chard turned from the window and held his master's stare. 'If the dwarves were dead, the elves would be alive now.'

'Possibly, Chard, but that is hardly the point.'

Chard was exasperated. 'Then what is the point? You abuse me for leaving the enemy alive and for the deaths of the elves and now for thinking of killing the enemy! How many ways do you want to have it?'

'Remember where you are, boy,' hissed Denegtacus through clenched teeth. 'Your first thought was not for the sadness and loss of our brethren but for murder. What does that tell you of the state of your soul?'

'My soul is my concern! Those dwarves were soldiers intent on slaughter, all their deaths would have been an irrelevance when compared to saving those elves.'

Denegtacus shook his head. 'No, you cannot think that way! Ends and means are not the same thing. Instead of patting yourself on your back, you should have been using your powers to get them to safety. The end would've been the same and the means would not have required murder!'

'How can you call it murder? We are at war!' said Chard with a mixture of incredulity and anger.

The elf waved the point aside. 'Don't play with semantics, Chard, it isn't the issue.'

'It seems to me,' began Chard with conscious rudeness, 'that debates with you often rely on semantics being the only issue.'

'Get out, and you will ask permission of me before you think of leaving on another of your little trips!'

Chard inclined his head and spun on his heel, resisting the almost overwhelming urge to slam the door behind him. Once outside he took several large breaths and almost immediately began to feel better. The patter of approaching footsteps made him look up to see Formositas scampering towards him. She flung her arms around his legs and smiled at his face, such a long way up.

The human grinned and struggled to untangle himself from the child. Every time he wheedled one leg free she would grab it again all the tighter while squealing with laughter. The laughter soon started Chard off as well and eventually he collapsed onto the walkway, the young child jumping on his stomach in victory.

'You win, Sitas!' shouted Chard, although the child responded by merely jumping harder. 'Mercy!' cried Chard and swept her up in his arms, magic propelling him effortlessly back to his feet.

'Take me flying, Mr Chard,' said the princess with a grin.

He wagged a finger under her nose in mock admonishment. 'I got such a telling off from your tutor the last time I did that. We can't have a young lady of royal blood exposed to danger can we?'

'Don't care!' pouted Formositas. 'I want to go flying, the world looks lovely when you can look down at it, like a quilt.'

Chard nodded in agreement. The world truly did look lovely from the sky and without further argument they soared into the air.

* * *

Denegtacus and Leaspida sat at either end of a large, oval table around which sat another dozen elves, representatives from all the Trees that made up the population of Westernwood. Over the last three years they had masterminded a quite breathtaking feat of logistics in the construction of a new elf society within the safety of Westernwood. A new city had been constructed and was growing every day. Newport had grown from a bay that had seen Leaspida arrive with his people to a major port bringing in valuable food and commodities from abroad as well as acting as the central fishing port of the nation. Every elf in Rittan had finally been brought under the protective canopy of Westernwood and away from the savagery of the dwarves.

Westernwood had been divided into twelve regions with each leader of a Tree given governance over one of them. They in turn reported to Leaspida and all had the same advice for him this time.

'The time has come, my lord,' said Verbera, protector of the Tree of Oak, thumping his hand down on the magnificent table as his pent up anger sought some way of manifesting itself. 'Break out from this self-imposed prison and give the dwarves the war they want!'

Leaspida ran his fingers through his hair. His position as king meant that he in effect could overrule all of the elves sat around him, but he was well aware that his delays over the last twelve months meant that further procrastination could well jeopardise his standing and could lead to the elves actually disobeying his orders. For a fleeting second he understood just what he had put his own father through.

The silence was just beginning to stretch out into the uncomfortable when Leaspida cleared his throat and leaned forward, his elbows resting on the polished surface. 'I agree,' was all he said, but the effect was instantaneous. The elves roared their approval in a quite unelf-like way. 'For too long the dwarves have had it their own way. Now we shall show them of what the Children of the Creator are capable.' The elf king surveyed those assembled around him. He knew all their strengths and weaknesses and had chosen the best elves for each task that his plan demanded. He allowed the noise to continue for a short moment as the elves relieved themselves of tension, the thought of coming battle raising the blood.

Leaspida gestured for quiet, which fell instantly. 'For three years, Denegtacus has shielded this land from direct invasion from the dwarves, but they remain camped on our borders, attacking those who leave and disrupting supplies. They are a plague and an affront to the Creator and will soon be dealt a blow the likes of which will last through the ages as a warning of what happens to those who inflict violence upon elves!' The king took a breath and allowed his breathing to slow. He hadn't meant to get quite so emotional but he was angry and it did no harm for his subjects to see from time to time that he was flesh and blood like them.

'This morning,' continued Leaspida in an even tone, 'Denegtacus removed the spell guarding the Wood. Not because I asked him to but because there is no longer any need for it.'

'Then the borders are open?' asked the elf Fortis, protector of the Tree of Maple.

Leaspida glanced at him and then around the table. Several of the other elves were shaking their heads. Fortis was well known and respected for his courage but he lacked the sharper qualities of leadership and his mind was more suited to war than peace.

'No brother, the borders are not open.' Leaspida stopped and hoped that he could spare the elf the embarrassment of having to actually explain what had happened and that the penny would drop of its own accord. Fortunately for all of the elves, Fortis realised and his face cracked into a grin.

'The land knows!' he said.

Leaspida nodded in acknowledgement.

Fortis tapped the table repeatedly with his hand, his grin widening. 'So Westernwood truly is the home of the elf.' Standing, he lifted his glass of wine to Leaspida. The other eleven elves followed suit and allowed Fortis to make the toast. 'Elves, I give you King Leaspida of Westernwood. Today, he and the land have become one!'

Leaspida sipped his drink and the others followed his lead and sat themselves down. All had felt the change in the atmosphere around the table. Seven of the elves present had come to Westernwood several years earlier than Leaspida and the other five and had never really been comfortable to call it home. In the last three years the changes had been enormous, the most vital one being that now they had a king. The land knew this and had accepted Leaspida as its guardian. As the king was duty bound to look after the land, then so too would the land look after the elves. The magical properties of the elf homeland of Bulair were well established, and now it seemed that here in Westernwood the same was true.

'I endorse your sentiments, Fortis, but now we must continue with business,' said Leaspida smoothly. He handed each elf a selection of maps and instructions and allowed them a moment to flick through the sheaf of papers.

'The counterattack is scheduled for one month's time, the first day of summer. Any comments on your orders, you may come and discuss them with me.' Pushing his chair back he rose to his feet, the other elves standing as one. 'One month,' he repeated quietly. The leaders of the twelve trees bowed and left their king alone.

Chard was pleased that Leaspida had relented and allowed him to teach his daughter. The school was a pleasure to run; the extraordinary innate ability of the elves was an almost constant source of inspiration to Chard who loved magic as he loved nothing else in his life. However, there were so few elves who studied it with the drive and persistence that it demanded. The children drifted in and out of school whenever they had nothing else to do, and sometimes he did not see certain students for months at a time. He was well aware that time was something elves had in abundance, as did he, thanks to magic, but his human roots made him impatient and it infuriated him to see talent going to waste as the elf offspring came and went with blatant disregard for his timetable.

All except Formositas. She was a delight to teach and to have around the school. She revelled in her new-found freedom and spent more and more time at the school, soaking up Chard's words, her magic growing daily. Her natural talent was above average and with Chard's help she now boasted an impressive level of ability. Chard was certain that outside of Denegtacus and himself she was probably in the top five magic users in the Westernwood and at such a tender age too.

Chard had started opening the school more regularly, wandering in a few hours after dawn, kidding himself that he was there for other reasons than to be a personal tutor to a royal princess. As soon as he arrived and began to busy himself with some pointless task, Formositas would appear, her green eyes peeking mischievously around the door to see if she could catch Chard with his back to her so that she could try out a spell.

Despite the fact that he was well aware of her presence, every now and again Chard would allow the child to attempt her magic. Lightning bolts, flames and dragons had all leapt from the girl's hand, only for Chard to spin around with impossible speed and block the spell. It didn't matter that she had never landed a blow against her teacher; she enjoyed the game far too much to be bothered about things like that.

Chard glanced out the window of the school at the elves going about their duties. Nearly all the males who would be taking part in the battle had left. Those few who remained would be taken to the edge of the Wood by Chard's magic. This was the task that Denegtacus had assigned him in the greatest battle that had ever been fought on the soil of Rittan. Him! An enchanter! No better than a damn horse!

He let out a sigh which attracted the attention of his protégé. Formositas looked up from the task that Chard had set for her. 'What's the matter, Mr Chard?' she asked with genuine concern.

'Nothing, Sitas, I was just pondering on the war.'

'I don't want father to fight,' she said softly. 'I sometimes dream that he won't be coming back.'

Chard recalled when Leaspida had left some two weeks earlier. His children were all too young to accompany him to a battlefield and Formositas hadn't really understood why her father had to leave. The tears had pulled at Chard in a way he had found surprising but he had disguised it as he did all his other emotions. It had not gone unnoticed that when Leaspida had left, it was to Chard and not her mother that the little princess had run for comfort. Unsure what to do, Chard had embraced the little girl until the tears had stopped before scooping her up and returning her to the queen. All those present glared until the queen had nodded to a servant to take the child from the enchanter. It was extremely unseemly for a child of royal blood to be touched by another elf, let alone a human! Chard bowed low and backed away as quickly as he dared, then slipped into the school, the one place he felt comfortable.

'Your father is an important elf,' said Chard with a smile. 'He has to do many things and some of them are dangerous, but Denegtacus is there and he won't allow any harm to come to him.' Ruffling her unruly red hair, which was brushed and styled each morning by a servant only for it to become dishevelled within moments of her leaving the house, he hoped she believed him. 'OK, Sitas?'

She smiled and nodded before returning to her work. Formositas was shaping a rose with her magic, one of the most intricate pieces of the craft that Chard had attempted to teach her. He glanced at the flower and raised his eyebrows slightly as he saw the delicate petals taking shape, but said nothing. In silence he watched for nearly half an hour until finally the princess looked up at him and handed him the flower.

Chard accepted it and turned it over in his hands, marvelling at the ability the child had displayed. The colour was perhaps a fraction too bright and the scent was too sweet, but these were quibbling details when compared to the overall standard.

'Do you like it, Mr Chard?' she asked nervously.

Chard stared hard at the girl but could not hold onto the serious face and grinned. 'It is beautiful, Sitas. The craftsmanship is exquisite, better than any other I have seen since I began my teaching.'

'Truly?'

'Truly,' repeated Chard gently.

'I made it for you,' said Formositas. 'I'm glad you like it.'

As he was about to reply, Chard sensed the magic in the air and closed his mouth.

'What's the matter?' asked Formositas.

Chard did not reply but straightened his back and turned around. The oval window of magic was directly before him and he could see the head and shoulders of his master.

'It is time!' snapped Denegtacus and instantly his image vanished.

Chard sighed and glanced back at his student. He held out the rose to her but she shook her head. 'I made it for you, Mr Chard, don't you remember?'

The human gave a tired smile and attached the rose to his

robes. ‘School’s finished for the moment, Sitas,’ he said wearily. ‘Your teacher has other errands for now.’

The little girl stood up and hugged him. ‘You’ll come back won’t you, Mr Chard?’

Putting his hand on her head, he nodded. Turning from the child, he made his way outside to gather the final few troops that his magic would whisk to the battlefield.

13

The elves gathered around their king to listen to his words of encouragement before the blood-letting began. At some length he spoke, stirring their courage and their urge to kill. His words were what the elves wanted to hear: blood and death for their enemies who had visited such destruction upon fellow elves for so many unanswered years, keeping them caged up in Westernwood when it had been their desire to roam which had seen them come to Rittan in the first place. The power of the elf had grown and now the dwarves would feel it for themselves as vengeance was brought down upon them.

Chard was barely listening to the words as he leaned against the trunk of a handy tree. Such speeches meant very little to him and from the demeanour of some of the elves he had observed since his arrival the previous day, they needed restraining, not encouraging, to kill. When the battle began, the carnage was likely to be horrifying since dwarves were renowned for fighting on regardless of lost causes. Any dwarf regiment that surrendered or fled the field had its officers executed and the ranks of soldiers were decimated as punishment by the dwarf leadership. No quarter would be offered or accepted and he expected to be busy.

The human's eyes drifted to the building that was to be his place of work during the battle. It was long and slim, elegantly crafted, and there was no roof. The hospital was deliberately made so that it could accommodate long rows of beds and afford mortally wounded elves one last look at the trees and the sky before they passed over to the other side. Chard did not relish the prospect of using his vast skills merely to patch up wounded elves when he believed they would be far better employed in causing death to the dwarves, but in this Denegtacus was implacable.

The early morning light was slowly penetrating the thick canopy of leaves above him and Chard tilted his head to catch the soft, golden rays. He recalled the argument that he had had with his master the previous evening. Chard almost thought the old elf was joking when he had been informed of his duties, before remembering that it had been some time since Chard had heard a joke from the enchanter.

'We have here the two greatest magic users in the world and you are going to allow them to fight without our aid?' said Chard, making sure that he kept his tone polite.

Denegtacus glared at the human. 'Still you do not understand. We could wipe the dwarves out tomorrow and what would that achieve?'

'A victory?' replied Chard, lifting his eyebrows slightly.

'But not for the elves, for us! Where is the honour in that! The elf is proud and noble and does not need to resort to magic when courage and steel will achieve the same.'

Chard was stumped. The master and the rest of the elves mourned the loss of a single elf in any circumstances and yet here he was, arguing against Chard's proposal that would save hundreds, if not thousands, of elf lives. 'But how many elf lives will be lost?' queried Chard in genuine astonishment.

Denegtacus had sighed and stared unseeing at the distant stars. When he responded his voice was softer. 'That grieves me, Chard, more than you could ever know. Together we could destroy the dwarves and save all those elf families the pain of losing a loved one. Save those who will die in pain and discomfort. We could do all of that and more, but what would we lose?' He glanced at his pupil, wanting to hear the correct answer.

Chard regarded the question thoughtfully. As so often when debating with Denegtacus, his reply would need to be based at least partly upon what the old elf wanted to hear rather than what Chard truly believed. 'They will come to rely on us. They will lose the independence that they have striven for since leaving Bulair. It is all a part of their need to prove to the world that they are a nation, just as strong as Bulair, and if we were to win this war tomorrow, the whole world would belittle the achievement saying that the elves hide behind the robes of enchanters, like frightened children peeking out from behind their mother's skirts.'

Denegtacus nodded in agreement. 'All that you say is true, Chard, and I will tell you something. I argued long and hard with Leaspida that he should allow you to fight alongside the elves but he overruled me.'

'You spoke up for me?' The elf nodded slowly in reply. 'I should have liked to have worked my magic against the dwarves.' Something inside Chard made him add mischievously, 'You could have gone against his will.'

Denegtacus chuckled quietly. 'I think I have had enough of angering my sovereign to last me several lifetimes! No, he is king and he must be obeyed, even if his orders do not sit well with me.'

'So will you help me in the hospital?' asked Chard.

The elf shook his head. 'No, I will stand alongside the king and make ... suggestions while making certain that no harm befalls him.'

'He will not be happy if he realises you are casting a shield around him. You know what Leaspida is like. He will want to face the same dangers as his subjects. It is one of things which make his people love him.'

Denegtacus moved away from Chard, imparting one final

comment as he walked. 'Which is why I shall neglect to tell him.'

Jerking himself back to the present, Chard realised that his daydream had lasted longer than he thought and that Leaspida had finished. Troops were making their way through the trees to their positions, discipline was tight and Chard could feel the tension and suppressed excitement that emanated from the elves. *Not so different from humans after all!* he mused thoughtfully.

The elves slipped between the trees like ghosts, with barely a sound to be heard, while others scaled the boughs quickly, to be lost from sight in moments. At times such as these, Chard found it easy to be impressed by the elves. Slow to act on occasion, they were totally focused once a decision had been made, yet they retained a grace and style that would elude humans. Briefly he imagined the sight of a human army making its way through the trees and the cacophony of noise that would accompany it, the image bringing a fleeting smile to his face.

The dwarf army was camped a half mile from the edge of the trees, scouts keeping a sharp eye on the silent, green guardians of the elves. As soon as the first elves had broken cover, the alarm had sounded and thousands of troops swung into prepared positions. There were a thousand cavalry on either flank and seven thousand infantry making up the bulk of the army in the centre.

Leaspida cast a professional eye over the dwarf army. The cavalry all carried shields and long swords and were protected by a variety of differing styles of armour, although all of them had at least helms and breastplates. The infantry were armed either with axes or short swords and some carried both. Many had shields but Leaspida noted grimly that some did not, and these would have to pick them up from the bodies of the fallen – of which, he vowed, there would be plenty. Having studied war for many years, he was well aware of the strengths and weaknesses of the dwarven approach to fighting. On the mainland, the humans relied on the phalanx and massed cavalry but dwarves preferred to battle alone, challenging individuals and proving their own personal worth. Which was why the Curinlish phalanx had crushed the dwarves fifty years earlier when they had strayed across the border. A unit that fought together could destroy an army of individuals.

Still, there were nine thousand enemies to be faced when they had a mere four thousand five hundred, but Leaspida was unconcerned. Nine thousand or ninety thousand, it would make no difference to the outcome. The charge would take at least thirty seconds for the horses, three or four minutes for the infantry. He glanced at his own troops who were plunging arrow after arrow into the soil before them as women carried more quivers behind them, ready to replenish the supply for the warriors.

Seven groups of five hundred archers apiece. One hundred elves wide, five ranks deep with each elf firing one arrow every six seconds. The maths itself was enough to instil confidence in the elf king. The enemy would have to face a hail of death long before they could bring their own weapons to bear. Maximum range for the legendary elf longbow was four hundred yards although the stopping power was greatly reduced at such extremes. Between a hundred and fifty and two hundred and fifty, the weapon was at its most deadly.

He did not look at the trees behind him but sensed the presence of the eighth group of five hundred archers, hidden amongst the leaves, invisible to the enemy but there to plug any gap, stop any incursion that by a freak of war could breach his lines. As for the last five hundred? Leaspida smiled. The dwarves would soon find out.

'Rather a lot of them aren't there?' said Leaspida over his shoulder.

Denegtacus nodded grimly before realising that the king couldn't see him. 'There will be less very soon, my lord.'

Leaspida chuckled without humour. 'Amongst our side as well.'

'This is not a game of children we play, it is one of death. They have dug their graves,' Denegtacus said passionately, waving an angry arm at the dwarves. 'It is our duty to fill them in!'

The king showed his ascent but did not reply. The sun was warm on his face, it was going to be a hot day and the stench of death was likely to rise sooner rather than later.

'I would have liked to have prepared defences,' said Denegtacus. 'Spikes, trenches and broken glass would slow any charge.'

'Elves do not need to hide behind such things, L'tusian, they are for humans who lack honour,' replied Leaspida.

Denegtacus did not trust himself to reply. It was such things that had made humans the masters of the continent and the elves would do well to learn some of their better habits from them. In their own way, Leaspida and the others were just as stuck in the past as Theaspida and those who had remained in Bulair. It irked him that he would watch elves die needlessly today but Leaspida had become obsessed with proving himself to the world and his father, and Denegtacus had decided to allow this battle. Once the young king had seen the reality of war, it was unlikely that he would regard it with quite the same level of romance. Battles were for winning, not glory. Humans understood this, why couldn't elves?

The roar of sound from the dwarves shook Denegtacus out of his reverie. Thousands of soldiers were banging weapons against shields and screaming promises of death to their enemies. The sound carried easily across the short distance that separated the two sides and Denegtacus sensed all down the line the younger elves' nerves beginning to stretch.

'Courage,' he whispered, magic carrying the word to all ears.

'Are the sections in place?' asked Leaspida.

Denegtacus closed his eyes momentarily. 'They are, my lord. All is as we planned.'

Across the open grasslands the dwarves were moving forward at a steady pace, steeling themselves for the race across the killing fields. At four hundred yards a bugle sounded and the cavalry kicked into a gallop, the infantry picking up their speed as best they could. The battle cries had stopped: air was needed to power them as quickly as possible to the elf lines.

'Volley fire!' roared Leaspida, picking up his own bow and notching an arrow.

Instantly the first arrows were loosed to be followed six seconds later by the second. It was said that the best elven archers could have six arrows in flight before the first had hit its target and Denegtacus watched as this was proved to be deadly accurate.

Many of the arrows were turned aside by armour or shields or struck the horses in non-fatal areas, but many hit home. The first screams of the dying and wounded began, but the charge did not falter.

'Cavalry, three hundred yards!' bellowed Leaspida, and the elves adjusted the angle of flight for their arrows. There was no need to aim, so closely packed were the enemy, and as they closed to two hundred yards the stopping power of the longbow began to take serious effect. Of the two thousand dwarf cavalry who began the charge on the flanks, some twenty seconds later there were less than eight hundred still mounted. Casualties among the poorly armoured horses were much higher than among the dwarves and those whose mounts had died under them were forced to continue on foot. However, of the twelve hundred unseated riders, only three hundred lay dead or dying, and the remnants were still making their way towards the elves.

The distance continued to narrow but Leaspida remained calm as the mounted dwarves bore down on the line. The elves discarded their bows and drew light sabres, closing ranks to try to hold the charge. From his position in the second company from the left, Leaspida watched as the dwarf cavalry smashed into the elves in the next company, those on the extreme left of the line. Travelling at thirty miles an hour the powerful animals scattered elves in all directions but the press of bodies soon halted them. Unable to manoeuvre in the confined space, the hundred or so dwarves who had made it as far as their enemy were soon pulled from their mounts and despatched with cold efficiency by the vastly superior force they now faced.

The king whispered a comment to L'tusian who immediately vanished from sight only to reappear scant seconds later. 'The cavalry on our right have wheeled away and regrouped out of range, the dwarf who leads them cannot be quite as suicidal as the one who led the charge on the left.'

Leaspida swore and commented that he had rather hoped that he would have been.

Almost immediately, Leaspida had to put such thoughts from his mind as the dwarf infantry was now less than fifty yards away. 'For the Motherland!' he screamed and led the counter-charge, sabre held high. With a roar, the entire elf line broke ranks and swarmed out to engage the dwarves.

The two sides collided with a fury, the smash of steel on steel, the cries of the dying, the screams of bloodlust from those victorious in their duels. Leaspida ducked an axe swing that would have decapitated him and lunged out with his own blade, the sword biting deep into his attacker's groin, severing the main artery and sending blood spurting from the gaping wound.

Drawing back the blade he blocked another attack, this time from a dwarf carrying a broadsword, one of the unhorsed he supposed. The length of the weapon aided the dwarf but although strong, the wielder lacked skill, using it as he may have done an axe, hacking and not thrusting. Leaspida stepped inside the huge arc of the sword and slashed his slightly curved blade across the dwarf's throat. Blood fountained from the jugular, sending gouts of crimson across the elf's face. He swung round seeking a fresh target only to see his intended victim pitched from his feet by an arrow through his chest. The king risked a glance back at the trees and gave silent thanks to the unseen elves who were picking off the enemy with unfaltering accuracy.

All down the line, similar events were being played out. The lightly armoured elves were suffering appalling injuries and within moments Chard found himself busier than he could ever recall being. In his life he had treated many diseases and wounds but never the wanton destruction of a body that was placed before him now. Elves screamed in agony and pleaded with him for aid but Chard quickly came to realise that it was those who did not call out who most needed his attention. He placed his hand on the severed arm of a wounded elf, the blood flow ceasing at his touch. Building his will, he sent it into the elf, forcing his body to replenish the lost blood at a rate far in excess of normality. The arm itself could also be re-grown by magic but that would take time and the cries of anguish all around him reminded Chard that he did not have enough to spare straight away.

Moving as fast as he could through the hospital, Chard treated the wounded. He cleansed dirty cuts, healed torn arteries and flesh by the power of his magic and even found the time to reattach the almost completely severed arm of one unfortunate elf. However, even with his powers he was unable to save them all and those with brain and heart injuries died, usually before they even got to the hospital, although even the dead were accorded the dignity of a bed, the sheet pulled up over their faces.

For more than two hours he worked as he had never done before, enraged at the waste of life and the pain, pleased that he was able to help those who would otherwise have died. At one point he angrily drew the sheet over the face of an elf who had died just as Chard had reached him, the blood loss too great. A few seconds earlier, thought Chard to himself, and this elf would have lived! For a fleeting instant he contemplated going to the battlefield and ending the destruction personally, but dismissed it. Denegtacus would send for him if he was needed and would not appreciate having his orders disobeyed. Sighing, he returned to his seemingly unending task.

Back at the front, Denegtacus sensed the decisive moment had arrived and sent the message to Verbera, protector of the Tree of Oak, who commanded the five hundred elf cavalry hidden just to the south of the battle. Verbera had been sat astride his horse with the patience of an elf but once called he raised his sword and waved his troops forward.

Some minutes later, the scene of carnage that was the Battle of the Westernwood hove into sight. The elves and dwarves were intermingled in a bloody dance of death, the stench of open bowels and the screams of the dying drifted lazily across the open ground. Without a pause, the elf cavalry fanned out and moved from the canter to the gallop. The remaining dwarf cavalry attempted to intercept the charge but were brushed aside by the momentum of the elves who then smashed like a hammer into the unprotected rear of the dwarf army.

The tide turned almost instantly: where before the outcome had been delicately balanced, it now became a rout. Pockets of dwarves began to close ranks to form fighting squares but they were small and isolated and were soon hacked to pieces by the elves. There was no call, or offer, to surrender and the killing continued until every dwarf had been dispatched.

The elves were elated as the victory became evident but this was tempered by the realisation of the cost of it. Elf losses on the battlefield alone numbered over twelve hundred with several hundred more wounded. The figures were bound to rise once casualties back at the hospital were taken into consideration, but for the dwarves the scale of the defeat was almost unimaginable. Nine thousand lay dead on the field of battle, over half of whom had been cut down before they had even reached the elf lines. A carpet of dead stretched across the battlefield and already the carrion birds were beginning to settle, pecking at unresisting flesh.

'I have to get away from here!' hissed Leaspida to Denegtacus.

The older elf gripped the king's arm like iron, forcing their eyes to lock together. 'Do not even think it!' he replied through gritted teeth. 'You believe you are the only one to be sickened by the sight that lies before us! You must speak to your warriors and tell them how proud of them you are! Give words of comfort to the families of the dead and embrace the living.'

The king began to shake his head, 'I cannot …'

'You must,' said Denegtacus more calmly, releasing his hold. 'It is your duty.'

Leaspida forced himself to look round. Many of the elves were searching for loved ones or gathering the bodies of the fallen but equally there were any number of elves who were congregating around the king expectantly.

Clearing his throat, Leaspida spoke to the elves, his voice strong and clear, faltering when he mentioned the elf dead but rising as he promised similar treatment for those who would raise the sword against the elves. At the end, the elves roared their approval and chanted his name. Leaspida raised his sword and allowed it to catch the noonday sun.

Verbera rode up to the king and swung nimbly out of the saddle, the suppleness of the move belying his two hundred years. He bowed swiftly but a grin overtook his face as he waved at the dead. 'A great day, my lord!'

Leaspida stared at the field of the dead, arrows jutting from dwarf bodies, dismembered limbs and torn flesh. So many arrows stuck into the earth it looked like a field was growing them. He merely nodded in reply.

Verbera sighed and clasped the young king on the shoulder. 'It saddens me too, but what must be must be. The dwarves declared war on us, we had to defend ourselves and those of our brethren who fell here did so in defence of the Motherland. Their souls now rest with the Creator.'

'You are right,' said Leaspida, the tiredness in his voice very evident. 'I just wish that it could have been different.'

'I would like permission to use the dwarf horses that remain to ferry our dead back to the Wood where they can be given a proper, elven burial,' said Verbera, climbing back into the saddle.

'To the victor belong the spoils,' said Leaspida indifferently. Quiet for a moment he then added, 'The dwarves are to be buried as well. We will do this before we leave this place of death and build a simple monument to mark the spot.' He stared at Denegtacus, 'What is the name of the dwarf god? I should know but I cannot recall it.'

Denegtacus raised his eyebrows but answered the question. 'They call him Tanahis, my lord. Might I add that such a gesture is truly noble and worthy of you.'

Verbera almost looked as if he would interrupt and argue the point but he closed his mouth and very slowly nodded his assent. 'We are not like them,' he said. 'It is right that the dead should be honoured. It will be done, my lord.' Wheeling his horse away, he began to issue orders.

'Now can I leave this place?' asked Leaspida with a tired smile.

Denegtacus nodded, 'But there is one more visit that you must make.'

* * *

Although the battle was over, for Chard the work continued. There were many elves bringing those who needed treatment and others who used rudimentary magic or herb lore to treat the more minor wounds. But it was Chard who was everywhere, dispensing magic and advice to the elves around him in equal measure. When the flow of the injured finally abated and he was able to slump into a handy chair he was shocked to see that the sun was beginning to set, the first stars of the night showing against the deepening blue of the sky.

An elf approached Chard and passed him a goblet of cool water which Chard accepted with a forced smile. He sipped at the drink and leaned backwards in the chair, his head resting against the stone of the hospital wall. Within seconds he was asleep and although the horrors of the day were still fresh in his mind, exhaustion held them at bay.

Less than an hour later he was awoken by one of the elves, a female from the Tree of Pine whose husband had fought in the battle and died before Chard had been able to reach him. With a massive effort of will he roused himself and glanced first at the elfin hand on his arm and then at the sad, slanted eyes of the female whose name he could not recall.

'I'm sorry for waking you, Mr Chard,' she said softly.

Chard rubbed at his eyes. 'It is I who should be apologising to you for failing to save your husband. Please, what is it?'

She flicked a glance to the side and Chard followed it, seeing the king, Denegtacus and several of the leaders from the various Trees.

Fatigue forgotten, Chard rose quickly. 'My lords,' he began.

Leaspida held up his hand and Chard fell silent. Picking up a pitcher of wine and a glass, the king poured out a drink and silently handed it to the stunned human. Chard stared at it, the significance of the moment robbing him of his customary sharpness.

'They tell me that you did well here today, human,' said Leaspida.

'I had a lot of help, my lord,' replied Chard, still clutching the glass.

Leaspida walked passed Chard and looked out of the window at the early evening sky, his hands resting on the window sill. He looked every inch the king: his clothes were simple yet elegant, his features handsome but strong and he carried himself with a confidence of born nobility.

'What are the figures?'

Chard shook his head and gathered his thoughts quickly. 'There were four hundred and thirty-seven elves brought through here today. Of those, forty-one died on the way. Of the remainder, we managed to save all but sixteen. There are several who will require more treatment to replace missing limbs but most of them will be well enough to travel back to their homes within a day or two.'

'Your skills helped three hundred and eighty elves to live who might otherwise have died. For that, the whole elf nation thanks you … Chard.' He held the human's eyes for a while longer before spinning on his heel and leaving the building. As the king departed, the other elves bowed, just fractionally, to Chard and followed him out until only Denegtacus was left.

'I cannot remember him ever using my name before,' whispered Chard.

Denegtacus clamped his hand firmly onto his pupil's shoulder. 'I am proud of you, my boy, we all are. Drink your wine, you have earned it this day.'

Chard watched as his teacher left the building and finally took a large gulp of the wine. Like all elf vintages, it tasted divine, but Chard scarcely noticed it. His mind was afire with thoughts of what this day meant to him. The king himself had served him a drink and called him by name! After more than a century, Chard felt a level of acceptance among the elves that he would never have believed possible. The years of bitterness began to slip away from Chard as he stood there. Tears welled in his eyes but there was also a smile upon his lips. Having once vowed never to cry again, Chard wept silently as all around him elves who owed him their lives slept peacefully.

Denegtacus was sat at his desk, staring into the flames of the fire as the door to his home opened. He did not have to look round, or use magic, to know who it was. Only the king would dare barge into the home of the enchanter without knocking.

'There's wine if you want it,' said Denegtacus without looking round.

Leaspida helped himself and sat opposite the enchanter. The battle had been over for a month now and emissaries from the dwarves had formally agreed an end to the war. Leaspida had been generous with his terms, allowing the dwarves a sense of honour despite the catastrophic defeat they had suffered. Nearly half of the entire dwarf fighting strength in all of Rittan had perished on the slopes outside Westernwood and there were few dwarves who felt it necessary to continue with the war or had the resources with which to do it in any case. The dwarves had wanted the elves removed from Rittan but seeing them cooped up inside the Wood was almost as good. Seeing the monument built by the elves to their fallen comrades had also helped to mollify the more belligerent members of the dwarf hierarchy. The war was hastily being swept under the carpet of history.

Leaspida was well aware of all of this and it did not concern him in the slightest. Let the dwarves think what they would, the whole world had seen the mighty dwarven army humbled by the elves of Westernwood. If they entertained any further notions of attacking elves, he had promised to visit vengeance upon them, no matter where in Rittan they hid.

'What brings you to my home, my lord?' asked Denegtacus, the tiniest twinkle in his eye.

'You know damn well, enchanter, don't play innocent with me!'

'Chard has proved to be worthy of the trust I placed in him. His training is all but at an end. You yourself practically said as much,' he added amiably.

'I know what I said!' snapped Leaspida. He glared over the rim of the glass at the legendary elf, the eternal L'tusian. Sighing loudly he asked in a more conciliatory voice, 'Are you really going to go ahead with what you propose?'

Denegtacus met his king's gaze unblinkingly. 'Chard is the one, I am certain of it. He will replace me as L'tusian and the guardian of life. I have but one more piece of enchantment to show him.'

Leaspida shook his head, knowing that he had lost the argument but determined to go down fighting. 'The God Sword was never meant to fall into the hands of humanity, I do not understand why you can't see this. It was crafted for the use of elves and our defence, it angers me that you would hand it over to a human.'

'I am not handing it over to a human,' replied Denegtacus easily, rising slowly to his feet.

Leaspida's surprise was evident, his hopes dashed with the next sentence.

'I am giving it to L'tusian!'

'When?' asked Leaspida in a resigned tone.

'Fifty years, no more than a century for certain,' said Denegtacus, his eyes alight with passion and determination.

A century, thought Leaspida morosely, practically nothing in elf terms. With all his being he hoped that Denegtacus knew what he was doing.

14

Chard put down the scroll he was reading, or rather, the one he was failing to read, and gazed out of his window. He had constructed his own home some thirty years earlier, a fine but simple abode among the boughs of a sturdy oak overlooking Newport. He found that he enjoyed watching the sea and the tiny vessels that sailed upon her. The vastness of the ocean seemed to mock the insignificant ships that dared venture out, tempting them with promises of food, sending others to their watery doom. The enchanter smiled. He was getting poetic in his old age. At nearly two hundred years old, Chard would have been considered middle-aged by the elves yet his frail human body did not look a day over thirty.

Pushing himself out of his chair, he ambled to the window and perched on the open ledge, staring at nothing and everything. The last decades had been more wonderful than he had ever believed possible, with the elves treating him with something akin to friendship. Even those who refused to like him accepted his presence without comment. Now he was older than many of the elves in Westernwood and those who recalled his entry with Denegtacus were fast becoming a minority. The school was doing better than ever and attendance was now more regular for all children under eighty. Older children taught the basics to younger ones and he now had two other tutors to help him with the workload, one of whom was Formositas. Her magical talent was very great but even her studies had faded over the years, yet she had continued to attend the school regularly and had leapt at Chard's offer to become a tutor when she reached maturity. Leaspida had agreed, believing that it would be good for her to mix with the people until he had found a suitable husband for her.

Chard knew that her presence was not altogether as innocent as it would appear. He was well aware that she had been infatuated with him for years, and if the truth be told, he had done nothing to discourage her attentions. The princess had grown into a stunningly attractive young woman and Chard was painfully aware of the fact every time she was near him. Her red and brown hair tumbled alluringly around her face, framing her beauty. Lithe and supple, her figure drew admiring glances wherever she walked, even from those elves who knew that to be caught doing so would bring a deep shame upon them.

He shook his head and chuckled to himself. At the moment he was meant to be reading Denegtacus' plans for a new city in Rittan which he hoped could become the guide for all future development. Built on the great river of Tham'es on the eastern side of the country, it would be a truly independent settlement where all the races of the world would be able to come and go and trade in peace. The human looked at the title of the scroll which Denegtacus had decided would be the name of the new city: Tourne. It was a nice idea but Chard feared that it was simply a dream, and an unrealistic one at that.

The sudden appearance of Formositas at his window startled Chard so much that he slipped from the sill, stumbling to the floor, the screams of laughter from the princess ringing in his ears. Strangely, he did not get angry at such treatment but enjoyed the sound and making her laugh.

Lying on his back, he smiled as the princess hopped up onto the ledge and swung her legs through the window, to perch in the exact same position that until seconds earlier Chard had been occupying.

'Did I startle you, Mr Chard?' she asked sweetly.

Chard laughed gently. 'I think you've taken decades off my life, Sitas.' He propped himself up on his elbows but made no attempt to get up. As always, how she said his name he found particularly seductive. The stress on the word *mister*, the slight pause before adding his name. Chard wondered if she knew the effect she had on just about every male she came into contact with. Probably, he decided.

'You mean you might only live to be a thousand now?' she asked with mock horror.

'Was there any reason for this visit, or was it just to remind me of my mortality and taunt me a little?' responded Chard without rancour.

Slipping from the sill, Sitas walked into the house and sat on the edge of Chard's desk, directly behind where he now lay. His eyes followed her.

'Can't I come and see a friend?'

Chard gazed up at her, his eyes lingering on the smooth flesh of her legs which was covered by a short tunic of green, belted at the waist. Travelling further up her body he studied the outline of her breasts pushing against the cloth before realising what he was doing and tearing his stare away, forcing himself to look at her eyes.

She smiled, tilting her head to one side. 'Do you like what you see, Mr Chard?'

Rolling to his side, Chard got quickly to his feet and made a great show of brushing himself down, studiously avoiding her gaze. Colour raced to his face, burning his cheeks in shame. Like an awkward teenager in her presence, he was horrified to realise that she had been aware of his inspection all the time, choosing to be flattered by it, not mortified as was proper.

'You are a beautiful woman, my lady,' he said, the words stumbling out as he found that his tongue had apparently swelled and was in danger of falling out of his mouth. 'But it is not right that you should be here, unaccompanied.'

'It was fine in the past,' she replied, sliding from the desk and taking a small step towards him.

'You ... were ... a child then, and now ...' his voice tailed off.

'I am a woman?'

Chard closed his eyes as the princess took another step towards him. He could hear her breath and the soft footfalls of her approach. Her hand rested lightly on his chest and he flinched as if burnt, edging backwards.

'Don't ...' he whispered.

Without replying she once more laid her hand on him, her fingers tracing a figure of eight on the material of his robes. His eyes opened slowly, locking with the sparkling green orbs of the princess, entranced. She leaned into him, her face brushing against the side of his. A soft groan escaped Chard's mouth as desire began to overtake him.

'Do you want me to stop, Mr Chard?' she murmured into his ear, her lips pressing lightly to his skin.

It felt as if he had been struck with lightning and Chard literally sagged, his arms moving out without conscious thought. His hands rested on her hips, drawing her into his embrace. Tilting his head downwards, he sought out her mouth with his own. The kiss was brief, both of them pulling apart to hold one another with their eyes before plunging in once more, the second kiss becoming more passionate. Their tongues became entwined; hands began to explore each other's bodies.

Madness! screamed a voice inside Chard. The risk they were taking suddenly seemed to crash down upon the human's shoulders and he pulled back, pushing Sitas away gently. Holding her by the arms, he tried to avoid the expression of hurt and confusion that was upon her face but there was nowhere else to look.

'What's the matter, Chard?' she asked plaintively, her own hands reaching up to take a hold of his, their fingers interlocking.

'It is not right, Sitas,' said Chard slowly, every word drawn from his soul in agony. 'You are a princess and your marriage is to be arranged by the king. You and I both know that this can never be.'

'Then let us leave here and go somewhere where we can be together!'

'Sitas ...' said Chard, his voice choking up with emotion. 'I cannot, you cannot.'

'It's the magic isn't it?' said Sitas suddenly angry. 'You want Denegtacus to carry on teaching you and you won't risk it for me!'

'I don't give a damn about the magic!' said Chard, the intensity of his feeling shocking both of them. As soon as the words were out Chard realised that they were true. What was there left for him to learn? He knew he was the most powerful magi in the world. The thought was not arrogance but the result of a proper understanding of what it meant to be an enchanter.

As he opened his mouth a knock at the door interrupted him. They both turned to the sound and watched in horror as the door began to open. Few elves would intrude in such a way which meant that it was someone important. Leaping apart, Chard tried to get to the door before it opened all the way but he was far too late and drew up as Denegtacus strode into his home.

Guilt was plastered across his face and Chard glanced back at Sitas who was once more sat on the corner of his desk. 'Master, you are welcome to my home,' he said, facing his tutor once more.

Denegtacus took in the scene in a moment, his face curiously blank. Chard swallowed and tried to fill in the lull, aware even as he did so that he was probably digging his own grave. 'The princess and I were just going over some lesson notes from the school but it can wait, can't it?' he said, addressing the question over his shoulder to Sitas.

'For the time being,' said Sitas in a slightly mischievous tone.

Chard closed his eyes and began to pray but Denegtacus said nothing.

The princess walked passed Chard and Denegtacus to the door. 'Goodbye, Mr Chard. To you as well, Denegtacus.'

Denegtacus gave a small bow. 'My lady.' As he turned back to Chard, Sitas winked before leaving, the door closing gently but still managing to make a noise akin to the slamming of the lid on a tomb, or so it sounded to Chard. He turned away and practically fell into his chair behind the desk and poured himself a glass of wine, failing to add any water to it.

'Did you read my plan for the city of Tourne?' asked Denegtacus, sitting down opposite Chard and helping himself to a glass of water.

'I have not as yet finished it,' replied Chard, his thoughts still disjointed, his heart still hammering inside his chest as he thought of the events of the last few minutes. There was no way Denegtacus could be fooled, thought Chard morosely. All these years and effort and it was to count for nothing.

'Please do, Chard, I would appreciate your thoughts on it.'

By now, the human had begun to reassemble his fragmented brain. He stared at the profile of the elf who was gazing out of the window. Was it possible that Denegtacus hadn't leapt to the only conclusion that Chard had thought available?

'It's a truly wonderful vision and I think that most of the races could be persuaded as to the validity of such an operation. There is a real need for such a free trade area. It is not good for the continent when Curinlas controls so much of the commerce.'

Denegtacus nodded his agreement to Chard's sentiments. 'But you don't think it will happen?'

Chard rested his elbows on the desk and held the elf's eyes. Let him look into the window of my soul he thought. Let him see the secret I am holding! 'On the contrary, master, I think that it will happen because there is such a need for it to happen. Only the dwarves will be against it in the long run. All the other races will shout and complain while simultaneously making plans to become a part of it.' He took a small sip of his wine and started to regret not watering it first. 'Once it is established and successful, even the dwarves will begin to wonder what they are missing out on.'

Denegtacus nodded once again. 'You're right!' he said, slapping the desk. 'It could be the start of something new.'

Chard swirled his drink absently as he ran the conversation through his head, seeking any hidden meanings in what Denegtacus was saying. There were none he realised, the thought coming as a relief at first. As he mulled it over in his mind he became slightly more irritated. The elf had not suspected anything untoward because it was beyond his thinking to come up with it! Sitas was an elf and a royal princess and Chard was simply that: Chard. A human whose presence was suffered, not enjoyed by any elf, certainly not the daughter of a king. His anger began to grow but Chard hid it, as he had done so many times over the decades.

Denegtacus seemed genuinely cheered by their conversation, the brief encounter with Formositas already forgotten. 'How long has it been, Chard?' he asked suddenly.

Chard decided to top his glass up with water, the wine was a little too strong for his liking. 'I stopped counting after the first century,' he replied with a half smile.

'You have done well, my boy, I don't tell you often enough.' Denegtacus stirred his drink absently with his finger, sending ripples across the surface. 'Better than I did in any case,' he added ruefully.

'But then I had a teacher and you did not,' said Chard.

'True, but you have mastered in less than two hundred years ideas and power that even today I am still working on. Do not be modest, Chard, we both know that you are as great as I except for one thing.'

Chard was beginning to wonder exactly where this was going. 'One thing?' he repeated carefully.

'The God Sword,' answered Denegtacus with a grin. 'With it, L'tusian is not just an enchanter, he is an instrument of the Creator! Compared to the power it contains, you and I are like children blundering in the dark, playing at magic.'

The human was stunned. The God Sword! It was a fable, a myth, and yet here was Denegtacus throwing it into the conversation as if Chard had known the answer all along. 'I thought the sword was a story, allegorical.'

Denegtacus became more serious. 'No, Chard, the sword is real and has existed since the beginning of time. Crafted by the Creator as a tool for His servants. You, me and those yet to come.'

Looking at his hands, Chard saw that they were shaking, not in terror as they had been moments earlier, but in anticipation. 'I am no swordsman …' he said, the words stumbling out.

'Do you think I am? No, no, my boy. The sword does not need to be wielded skilfully but with righteousness. It will cut anything, block any attack without conscious thought from L'tusian.'

'You have it?' asked Chard, yearning in his tone.

Denegtacus raised his eyebrows, a twinkle coming to his eyes. 'As L'tusian it will be there when I reach for it, but do I have it hidden under my bed? No I do not.'

Chard thought about what Denegtacus was saying. As with everything, it was a test of some kind and he turned it over in his mind. 'It knows who its master is!' he said, the words coming quickly. 'Sweet God, it is sentient!'

'Quite so,' replied Denegtacus easily. He pushed himself to his feet and ambled to the door. 'Tomorrow Chard, you are to take over from me as L'tusian. Enjoy this last day of freedom for on the morrow you will have no free will. Everything that you do will be as L'tusian and trust me when I say this: the world will judge your every decision or indecision.'

Chard shook his head dumbly, the thoughts inside his head rendering him speechless. All those years of torment! All those years when he had been unsure of himself and the direction his life had taken him! His bitterness and resentment fell away from him and a grin spread across his face, lightening his features, making them infinitely more handsome. Glancing up he saw that Denegtacus had left and Chard fell back in the chair, his smile broad and genuine.

Leaspida had aged well in spirit but his body was much weakened. At nearly three hundred he was well aware that his time was coming to an end but there were few regrets. His eldest son would make a fine king when he had gone and only the previous year had himself become a father to a beautiful baby boy. Only his youngest daughter remained unmarried and Leaspida had finally found the right husband for her. It hadn't been easy, he thought to himself, her wilful nature was well known as was her friendship with the human. The second son of Comiter, Protector of the Tree of Yew, had been suggested and despite the fact that he was relatively low-ranking, it would seal the friendship of Comiter who had often voiced opposition to the king over matters of diplomacy and trade with the humans. Utilis was a good lad, if a little on the slow side, but his loyalty was without question. He would make a fine son-in-law.

The king was racked by a coughing fit and pressed his kerchief to his mouth to stifle the sound and not disturb his wife who lay resting in the next room. He had called on Denegtacus more than he cared to remember over the last ten years to mend the various parts of his body that were in the process of packing up on him. With the birth of his grandson, he had decided that he would do so no more. Now the growth in his chest was getting larger, slowly, oh so slowly, choking him to death.

When the fit had passed he took a sip from his water, trying not to notice that the silk of his kerchief was flecked with blood. Denegtacus had merely nodded when he had told him that he wasn't to use any more magic to save his life, which had irritated the old king. No protest, no demands to help him regardless, just mute acceptance. But when you had lived as long as Denegtacus, he supposed you got used to seeing your friends and kings die.

Sighing, Leaspida waited calmly for his daughter to make an appearance. He had sent for her more than half an hour ago and yet she had still not graced him with her presence. Still, now that she was to become a wife she would have to start conducting herself with a little more decorum as befitted a woman of royal blood.

A rap on the door interrupted his thoughts and the king called for the visitors to enter. One of his servants, an old retainer by the name of Decurio, walked in and bowed low. Announcing Formositas he left almost at once after a dismissive wave from Leaspida.

As always, Leaspida was pleased to see his beautiful little girl, so like her mother.

'Father,' said Sitas, kissing him lightly on the cheek.

He placed his weathered hands on her shoulders, giving her a gentle squeeze. 'You look more like your mother every day, sweet one,' he said with a smile.

'You tell me that every day, father!' she replied with a giggle. 'How pretty can one girl be?'

'I shall answer that when you stop getting any more so,'

responded the king mildly, sitting back gently. As he did so the bones of his shoulders cracked and he winced.

Sitas frowned. 'You must allow Denegtacus or Chard to have a look at you. It isn't right that a king creaks like an old floorboard every time he moves.'

Leaspida gave a thin smile. 'Such language to a king!' He breathed out slowly before drawing in more air. 'That is one of the things I wish to speak to you about. I was pleased when you offered to help at the school but I am told that you are spending more and more time with the human.'

'His name is Chard, father,' snapped Formositas.

'Irrelevant!' hissed Leaspida, his anger rising. 'It is not fitting that an elf of royal blood spend so much time with a human, alone as well. You must remember your position and conduct yourself accordingly.'

'Mr Chard is the perfect gentleman, you need not worry for my virtue.'

The king waved the point aside. 'His behaviour is not the issue. A daughter of mine should not be flaunting herself in such a manner in front of lesser races.'

Formositas found her anger combining with an unpleasant sensation of guilt. 'Lesser races?' she asked evenly.

'You know what I mean!' said Leaspida testily. 'Anyway,' he continued in a more conciliatory tone, 'it will soon be immaterial.'

Formositas went cold, dreading her father's next words and yet needing to hear them. 'Why?' she whispered.

'I have good news for you, my dear. Comiter has accepted our proposal of marriage between you and his son, Utilis.'

Formositas was aghast. 'Utilis! That gawking fool!' She stepped back from her father, her rage giving way to incredulity.

'That is no way to speak of the son of a protector!' snapped Leaspida. 'And your future husband,' he added.

'I will not marry such an elf!' cried Sitas, tears coming unbidden to her eyes.

The king stood up and moved to embrace his daughter but she moved back.

'My beautiful one! It is necessary that you marry this elf, you have always known that your marriage would be arranged. It is how things have always been done.'

'Really?' asked Sitas coldly. 'Was that how it was for you?'

Leaspida's face darkened, 'Remember who I am, child. You were not even born when I was facing turmoil the likes of which I hope you never have to endure! My choosing of my own wife was a symbol of a new beginning. My father, may the Creator grant him peace, was a good king and ruled wisely according to the will of our ancestors. If things had have been different I would gladly have married the woman of his choosing.'

'So easy to say,' sneered Formositas, 'so impossible to disprove! Things have changed father, we are different from our cousins in Bulair, we don't need to blindly follow every stupid tradition like they do! We can begin our own traditions! We can …'

'Silence!' roared the king, the sound startling his daughter. The effort was too much for the old elf and he staggered, grasping the edge of the desk to stop himself from collapsing. He waved Formositas away angrily as she moved towards him and took several breaths until the dizziness in his skull lessened and the pain in his chest passed.

'You will obey me in this,' he mumbled.

'I will not,' replied Sitas quietly.

Leaspida's eyes narrowed as he glared at his youngest child. Suddenly she did not seem quite as beautiful as he recalled, not as much like her mother, who always supported his decisions and advised competently, never emotionally. For just a moment, he empathised with his departed father but this was entirely different from then. He hadn't turned his back on millennia of tradition and shown such arrogance and disdain in front of the king as his daughter was now doing. Or had he? Closing his eyes, he recalled the events that had led to his leaving Bulair and he almost smiled. Perhaps he was wrong. Perhaps this was something he could allow. His thoughts were derailed as Formositas spoke.

'Anyway, I'm in love with another. A man who is worth a hundred of Utilis. And you will not stop me from being happy with Chard because he feels the same way.'

'Love is to be cherished,' began Leaspida but he drew up suddenly as he realised just what Formositas had said. Chard! All his previous thoughts of comparing his daughter's actions to his own crumbled into dust. Never had a king been shamed like this in all elf history. His own failings were highpoints when associated with the sentimental drivel his daughter was spouting.

'Chard!' bellowed Leaspida. 'No elf will allow herself to be sullied by a human while I am king! Especially not my own flesh and blood.' A hideous thought crossed his mind and he paled. 'Tell me that he hasn't … touched you,' he said.

Formositas had held her ground in the face of her father's anger, having expected it and prepared herself, but this was one question she hadn't considered and she paused.

Taking her silence as an admission of guilt Leaspida's rage hit a new level. Such was his wrath his voice actually became calm. 'My daughter is a whore!' he stated without emotion. 'You disgust me and are a traitor to your race.'

Sitas' hand slapped against Leaspida's face, rocking him. 'How dare you?' she screamed. 'Mr Chard has always conducted himself in the best of ways and my virginity is intact. 'I disgust you? I am ashamed to think that someone like you could have sired me!'

Leaspida rubbed his cheek thoughtfully. The situation was bad but redeemable if what she said was true, and such was the intensity of her words, he believed them. Reaching behind him he pulled a rope which rang a bell to attract his guards. Three elves marched into his room and saluted sharply. The king wondered if they had heard their argument but dismissed it; royal guards would never betray anything they happened to overhear and he trusted their discretion.

'See that the princess Formositas returns to her room and remains there. If she tries to escape, tie her to the bed.'

'Sire,' responded the elf who stood in the middle and took a firm grasp of the girl's arm.

Sitas attempted to struggle but it was useless and she found herself half dragged and half carried back to her private chambers. She had not bothered to speak to her father as he ordered her arrest, nor had she spoken to the soldiers who had so ignominiously dumped her on her bed. The one person whom she needed to communicate with was beyond her and she wondered what would become of him. Pushing her face into the pillow so that her sobs would be muffled, Sitas wept.

Chard had barely slept the previous night, his mind far too preoccupied with the forthcoming morning. Now that it had finally arrived he felt elated. His whole life had been one long journey towards this point and he would relish every second of it. Walking easily, his steps measured, he enjoyed the physical exertion as he made his way through the forest. Denegtacus had given no time or place but Chard knew all the same and strode deeper into the forest, guided unerringly to where his master waited.

Some two miles from the settlement, Chard came to the side of a stream which bubbled gently across the shale. It was clear of trees and the sun shone down on the glade, sparkling on the water, and Chard smiled. Everything here was perfect, it was an oasis of beauty that could have come from the

Creator's own garden. Stepping out of the woods, Chard glanced to his left and saw the elf who, after today, would no longer be called master.

Denegtacus was stood calmly by the side of the stream, next to a rock that was nearly half the size of the elf. He held a sword by the hilt in both hands, the tip of the blade resting on the ground before him, leaning forward slightly as if using it as a walking stick. His face was completely void of expression and had Chard been paying more attention this mask would have aroused his suspicions, but he was too caught up in the moment.

Chard forced himself to walk slowly over to the elf, trying to keep the grin from his face. The seriousness of the day could not detract from the boyish excitement he was feeling inside. As he drew close to Denegtacus, he found his eyes drawn to the magnificent sword the enchanter had clasped in his fingers. Elf weapons were works of art but compared to this they appeared to have been cobbled together by children.

'Master,' said Chard evenly.

Denegtacus was silent for a just an instant and in that second a feeling of disquiet hit Chard. Something was wrong and a sickening sensation gripped him, icy tendrils of fear surging through his stomach.

'Chard,' replied Denegtacus emotionlessly.

The elf walked slowly around Chard, who shuffled his feet to keep Denegtacus in his field of sight. 'This is the God Sword,' began Denegtacus, lifting the blade so that its tip came up to chest height, angled upwards and resting just an inch from Chard whose sense of dread was escalating. 'It is the single most important artefact on the planet, crafted solely for the use of L'tusian. No evil may sully it, no person with ill intent in their heart can even touch it. Only L'tusian can hold it and he becomes as one with the steel, his will merging with the force of the sword. At this time, Chard, nothing is unknown to me; all men's hearts lie open.'

Chard swallowed and licked his lips nervously. 'A truly marvellous thing, master,' he said, mainly for the sake of saying something, anything.

'Marvellous? Yes it is.' The elf swung the sword above his head and held it there like a knife, poised above Chard. The light of madness touched Denegtacus and in that split second, Chard saw death. With a scream, Denegtacus plunged the sword downwards. Stunned by the turn of events, Chard made no attempt to move or defend himself and waited with a detached sense of anticipation for the metal to plunge into his flesh.

At the last possible instant, Denegtacus wheeled to one side and the blade smashed into the rock, sending sparks in all directions as it bit deeply. When the elf released his hold on the sword, only the handle and a matter of inches of the blade were left jutting from the stone.

The elf staggered back and nearly fell, but regained his composure. Stepping up to Chard he pointed at the buried blade; 'Pull it out!' he hissed through clenched teeth.

Chard was incredulous to find that he was still alive and did not respond at once. Seconds drifted by but Denegtacus did not speak again and eventually Chard forced himself to look at the sword. 'Another test?'

'The last!' whispered Denegtacus, the passion not dissipated by the low volume.

Chard stepped up to the rock, stealing one last fleeting look at Denegtacus. And then he knew. There was no way he could remove the sword and Denegtacus was simply waiting for him to fail. Anger was beyond him, there was just a gut-wrenching sense of despondency that hit him like a punch. He reached out and grasped the hilt in both hands. A burning feeling hit him but he refused to let go and wrenched upwards with all his strength, gritting his teeth as he felt the flesh on the palms of his hands begin to blister and blacken.

Screaming in despair and agony, Chard released his hold on the sword which remained where Denegtacus had put it. Reeling away from the rock, he stared at his damaged hands in anguish. Collapsing to his knees he stifled a sob as nausea threatened to engulf him.

'I take back my gift, Chard!' shouted Denegtacus. 'Carry those wounds to remind you of what you have lost, what might have been!'

'Why?' screamed Chard.

'You ask why! Did I ever deny you your human desires Chard? Did I ever forbid your drinking, whoring and gambling? No, I indulged them and wasn't I the fool for thinking that you could overcome them on your own!'

Forcing himself back to his feet, Chard struggled to comprehend what Denegtacus was saying. Clearly he had committed a crime of some sort but he did not know what. 'What have I done?' he asked, the yearning to understand masking the pain.

'Formositas, Chard, the king's daughter. Did you really believe that you could have her? She is an elf and out of your reach simply by her species. But not only that, she has the blood of kings in her veins! Not only do you insult one family with your carnal urges, you slight the entire elf nation!'

Chard was shocked. To have come so close and now be castigated for something he hadn't done was too galling for words. 'I …' he began.

'Spare me more lies!' roared Denegtacus. 'Her marriage to Utilis was put in jeopardy by you, but thankfully the matter has been concealed and the ceremony is underway even as we speak.'

Over the years, Chard had experienced more anger than most but it was as nothing compared to what surged through his body at these words. His eyes flashed and his will surged. Realising the danger, Denegtacus prepared himself for the magical attack, shielding himself in protective spells. This was what he had always feared, a confrontation between the two most powerful magi, the consequences of which were likely to be terrible and unpredictable.

Chard's hand rose and he screamed in berserk fury. His fingers closed into a fist and he punched Denegtacus in the face, the skin around the elf's mouth splitting on impact, sending blood down his chin. Totally unprepared for a physical assault, the slender elf was pitched from his feet and dumped to the earth, stunned almost senseless.

The human towered over the fallen elf. 'You know nothing about which you speak! I am human and have needs and emotions. I allow myself to feel, you ... you have experienced nothing for centuries except your own smug sense of self-righteousness!' With another bellow of fury, Chard grabbed the front of Denegtacus' white robes and struck him again, the sound of breaking bone coming from the elf's cheek, blood spilling freely from his battered face.

'Yes I desire Sitas but because I love her, not because of what you call "carnal urges". Yet I held back because I knew it could never be and to hear you accuse me of ...' he shook his head. 'And to refuse me my destiny because you understand nothing of love and are as prejudiced as the rest of your bastard species sickens me!'

Chard slumped back from the semi-conscious elf and collapsed onto the grass, crossing his legs and staring at his, once more, ruined palms. He looked at the sword and laughed bitterly, without humour. In the space of a few minutes his entire life had come crashing down around his ears. How many times had the same thing happened?

'She wanted to be with me and I told her no,' said Chard quietly, talking more to himself than the fallen elf. 'I do not believe this marriage is what she wants so I shall ask her myself.' Standing, he glanced down at Denegtacus, a sneer distorting his features. Showing the elf his hands, Chard concentrated his magic. Slowly, the blackened skin began to heal itself until eventually it was once more fresh and healthy. 'There is nothing left for you to teach me, Denegtacus, it is good that I finally see it.'

Denegtacus lacked the strength to reply and could barely make out the words Chard was saying let alone see the pink, undamaged skin on his hands. Not for centuries had he been as weak as he was now. If Chard so decided he could kill him and the thought terrified the elf far more than he had ever dreamt possible. So many things left to do, so many elves that still needed him!

Looking at his former mentor, Chard understood the thoughts of the elf almost as if he was hearing them aloud. His eyes narrowed and he gave an almost imperceptible nod. 'Know that you live from this time forward only because I have allowed it!' Mustering his power, Chard vanished, leaving the elf bleeding and alone.

Having been built from the sturdiest Rittan oak, the door leading to the royal hall, where the celebration was taking place, might happily have remained standing for centuries. But against the unfettered might of an enchanter, it blew into splinters in the blink of an eye. Experienced in the ways of magic, the elves felt the power moments before the spell was unleashed but there was simply no time to cower or shield themselves from the explosion. Cries began as wounded elves fell to the debris-strewn floor, their blood leaking out to mingle with dust and overturned furniture.

Stepping through the door, Chard scanned the assembled gathering. His eyes were more than blank, they were empty, devoid of anything recognisably human. None went to help the injured, no voices answered pleas for help: the crowd's attention was firmly upon Chard.

'Who spread these lies about me?' he asked between gritted teeth.

At his words, all eyes turned to the king. Leaspida pushed back his chair and rose slightly. Guards were positioned all around the hall but Leaspida was under no illusions about the strength of their attacker and a shake of his head told them that Chard was not to be approached.

'You do not scare me, human, and your denials are worthless since my daughter has already told me of your clumsy, attempted seduction. I thank the Creator that she has already married this fine elf.' Leaspida gestured towards his new son-in-law who looked less than enthusiastic about being drawn into the conversation. 'Your overstayed welcome here in Westernwood has finally come to an end.'

Chard stared at the king with an unerring calm. 'You lie,' he said simply. It wasn't a question but a statement. 'I can see the guilt and terror written across your soul. Formositas would never say such a thing.'

'I didn't say that, Chard,' said Sitas as she pushed her way through the guards who had tried to hem her in once they understood the nature of the problem. One of them grabbed her by the wrist and she let out a small hiss of pain.

Chard's face didn't change as he cast his magic. The guard screamed in agony as the hand he had laid upon Sitas burst into flame. In moments it had burnt away to a bare stump leaving him moaning in pain and the smell of burning flesh lingering in the air.

'Never touch her,' said Chard. 'Ever.'

Sitas walked over to Chard, her once immaculate white dress covered in dust. No one made any attempt to stop her although some of the other guards cast worried glances at the king, unsure of what they should do.

'You didn't need to do that,' she admonished, 'he was only doing what he thought my father would want.'

With a shrug, Chard glanced at the elf he had just wounded. A new hand sprouted instantly, pink and unmarked from the ruin of his wrist. 'Say the word, princess, and it shall be as you say.'

Formositas tilted her head to one side. She knew the true meaning of Chard's words. If she told him to go, he would go, and if she told him to let the elves kill him, then he would die. At that moment she knew real power.

'I want to be with you!' she whispered softly.

Leaspida literally roared with anger and reached out to implore his youngest child to remember her duty, his face crimson with rage. 'Think of the dishonour!' he shouted, but it was to an empty space as they vanished.

15

Denegtacus pushed himself to his feet with a monumental effort of will. It seemed as though the world was trying to dislodge him as unpleasant feelings of nausea swept through his stomach and head. Grimacing, he spat vomit from his mouth and noticed that his robes were covered with flecks of foulness, and he tried unsuccessfully to wipe them away. Another, more powerful feeling of queasiness threatened to bring up more from his tortured stomach and he rested his hand on the stone. As it had done so many times over the centuries, the sword commanded his attention. Even looking at it seemed to calm his sickness and ease the wounds in his soul. Tentatively, he reached out his hand and took a hold of the God Sword. Immediately he felt its energy revitalise him and fresh strength flowed through his veins. The elf drew the sword slowly from the stone, staring at the blade. Always, when he held it to the light, it cast no shadow, for the God Sword gave evil no place to hide. Denegtacus hurled the sword high into the air. Travelling much faster than should have been possible the sword was soon lost from view as it vanished into the heavens. With one final glance upwards, Denegtacus made his way to Leaspida.

By the time he arrived at what should have been the midpoint of the wedding feast, the arguments as to what should be done had already gone beyond anything that most elves had ever witnessed before. Loss of control was considered an ugly, human, characteristic and to see the elves indulging in it brought a chill to Denegtacus' blood.

His arrival had at first gone unnoticed and so the enchanter was able to make it all the way to the royal table without comment. The sight of his king was yet another unpleasant shock in a day that had become full of them. Very few people knew just how ill Leaspida had become, but to look at him now, you could practically see the Ferryman waiting for his coin. Surrounded by most of the protectors of the trees, Leaspida seemed half the elf he had once been. Shoulders stooped and slumped in his chair, he nursed an untouched goblet of wine, turning it continuously in his hands.

'Give the king room!' roared Denegtacus, barging two elves out of the way. When things were bad, people liked to know that someone seemed still to be in charge.

At the sound of his voice, the crowd fell silent and parted before him. Leaspida glanced up briefly before returning what passed for his attention back to his wine.

'Everyone appears to have an opinion on the situation but me,' he murmured softly.

Denegtacus cast a look around the room, taking in the shattered door. 'Formositas?'

'Gone,' the king replied simply.

Denegtacus closed his eyes. Having known Chard for as long as he had, the elf was unsurprised by the theatrics of the magical display, but to actually kidnap a royal princess, surely even Chard wasn't arrogant enough to believe that he would get away with this crime!

'My lord, this abduction will not go unpunished …' began Denegtacus.

'Abduction?' interrupted Leaspida. 'If only it were so simple. Where were you when we needed you, Denegtacus? My daughter has gone to the human and turned her back on all that we elves hold dear. Only you could have stopped her and now she has gone.'

Denegtacus stiffened at the words but held his temper. If the truth be told, he agreed with the sentiment behind the words, he just didn't much care for it. 'She went voluntarily?'

Leaspida rose to his feet. Hands reached out to support him but he angrily slapped them aside. 'I should never have allowed this situation to arise in the first place. Had I not allowed humans to sully our territory, my daughter would still be here.'

'You cannot blame yourself,' said Denegtacus.

'Who said anything about blaming me?' His finger jabbed at Denegtacus. '*You* are the one who brought him here. You are the one who failed to see that he was ingratiating himself with my child. You are the one asking damn fool questions when you should have been here to see what occurred for yourself!'

'I know you have suffered a loss, Leaspida, but you forget to whom you speak!' shouted Denegtacus, oblivious to the shifting, nervous crowd.

'I am king here! My word is law! So here is another. From this moment those two are to know no peace. Wherever they go I want them found. If they crawl under a stone in the goblin mountains I want an elf ready to bring me their heads. If they burrow into the ground like dwarves, I want an elf waiting with a shovel to dig them out. Do you hear me, Denegtacus? Do you all hear me?' He waved madly at the assembled elves. 'Bring them to me!'

Denegtacus nodded curtly. 'Sire!' With that, he turned his back and left the hall.

Leaspida watched him go. 'Well?' he began. 'Follow our good Denegtacus' example why don't you! Leave! Find them!' The last part of his tirade brought on a coughing fit and he collapsed back into his chair. The queen placed her arms around him and held him close.

'They've taken my girl,' he sobbed.
She stroked the king's hair. 'I know.'

Chard lay comfortably on the ground, his head resting in Formositas' lap. The sky seemed bluer, the clouds whiter. Had he been able to, he would have shaken his head! Such nonsense he was deluding himself with. But it remained fun all the same.

'What are you smiling about?' asked Sitas, her hand pausing in its exploration of his hair.

Chard tilted his head back so he could see the upside-down features of Sitas staring back down at him. 'How even the wrong way up, your smile still looks like a smile.'

'You're becoming quite the poet in your old age. Whatever would people say if they could hear the mighty wizard!'

'Enchanter!' protested Chard.

'The mighty wizard,' continued Sitas, putting heavy emphasis on the word wizard. But she didn't get any further as Chard rolled out of her lap and then on top of her. They lay just staring at one another for a few moments.

'I believe we were about here ...' said Chard softly as he kissed her.

In his home, Denegtacus paced angrily back and forth. Rage needed to be kept in check, he knew this, since it discoloured your thinking and left you open to mistakes. However, it certainly gave you energy and desire to see through to the end what needed to be done.

That was the trouble. Oh the king had given him his orders but Denegtacus had been given a lot of orders by a lot of kings and he was the one who chose which ones he obeyed. Was it really in the interests of the elves to go looking for this couple? No one knew better than L'tusian that if

Chard decided that he didn't want to be found then there wasn't an elf alive who could find him.

Except one.

What if he did find them? Somehow, Denegtacus didn't see Chard handing himself over without any fuss for Leaspida to have him executed. No matter how angry the king had been, if anything were to happen to his daughter in the crossfire, it was unlikely that he would see this as good. Now that the ancient elf had had time to think, he was certain that it would be better for all if the two were simply forgotten and the whole matter put behind both the king as an individual and the elves as a nation.

Despite this being the best way to move forward, Denegtacus was under no illusions as to just how difficult this would be. The king would need convincing that the two lovers were dead and Chard would need convincing that no one was coming looking for him. Even if these two, rather troublesome, issues were resolved, it still didn't eliminate the factor of chance. The chance discovery of Chard by another elf or the chance that Chard would draw attention to himself after Denegtacus' lie to the king. Be all that as it may, as far as Denegtacus could see, the only real next step was for him to talk to Chard and hope that he would listen rather than react with violence.

A sigh exploded out of the frustrated elf. It was undoubtedly prudent for Denegtacus to wait before he spoke to Chard but that meant that there was the possibility, however slight, that someone else would stumble across the couple before he did.

'Run away and hide, Chard,' muttered Denegtacus to himself. 'Find some rock to crawl under and for the Creator's sake don't come back here.'

* * *

'So ...' said Sitas, elongating the sound. 'Where are we going?'

Managing to shrug while lying on his back with his head propped up against a tree wasn't easy but Chard succeeded. 'We have the whole world to choose from, princess. So long as I am with you, it doesn't really matter.'

'Aren't you sweet!' said Sitas with a smile. She paused, 'Anywhere?'

'Well, so long as it isn't too cold. Or wet,' he added as an afterthought. 'I mean, Westernwood was all well and good but it did rain a lot.'

Plonking herself unceremoniously in Chard's lap, Sitas grinned. 'I want an island.'

'An island?' asked Chard mildly. 'Did you have one in mind?'

'During lessons one time you showed me a map of the islands that lie off the coast of Bathenia. I want one of those. Not one of the really big ones obviously.'

'Obviously,' noted Chard drily.

'But not too small either. And I don't want to share it and I don't want people turning up without our permission. It should be just ours. Our own island,' she whispered, 'where we can be alone forever.'

Chard kissed her lightly on the lips. 'Sounds perfect.' For the second time in a matter of hours, they vanished into the air.

Time to elves was a very different experience than it was to humans. Knowing that you have centuries to complete a task brought with it a certain lack of urgency. Since Denegtacus knew that he had even longer if he so chose, he had left the journey to seek Chard and Formositas a lot longer than any human would have done.

The intervening months had not passed pleasantly. The

king refused to die despite becoming desperately sick and even the queen had begun to ail, most likely succumbing to the weight of work and worry that Leaspida's illness had placed upon her. On top of all the domestic issues that plagued Denegtacus, he had become aware of a massive build-up of arms in the east. Arrogolia was a war-torn, savage land that was at almost constant war with itself. Now though, the winds of change had blown through it and a new emperor was uniting the tribes into a country the size and strength of which the world had never seen before. They called him Khagen, or 'great king', and Denegtacus didn't like the sound of it one little bit. However, if there was one thing that could always be relied upon, it was that the emperors of the east tended to last only as long as it took their assassins to load their crossbows. No doubt this present difficulty would soon be resolved.

Pushing thoughts of arrogols from his mind, Denegtacus sent out his magic, seeking, as he had done all those years earlier, the man he had once thought was to replace him as L'tusian. Chard was a long way away, practically on the other side of the continent. Concentrating, Denegtacus soon narrowed down his search to the islands off the coast of Bathenia.

No matter. With the power of enchantment, distance meant nothing. Waving his hand, an oval of light materialised before him. Denegtacus did not even pause as he stepped through.

The hot summer sun shone down ferociously on this part of the continent. The force of it hit Denegtacus like a sledgehammer when compared to the incessant drizzle of Westernwood. A simple spell soon dispelled most of the unpleasantness and Denegtacus walked forwards purposefully in the direction that he knew Chard to be.

Less than a minute later, he reached him. He was sat on a rock overlooking the sea. Several fishing boats could be made out trawling in the distance. The sea was a brilliant blue and there was barely a fleck of white in the sky. All in all, it was about as perfect a place as you could ever hope to find.

'That's some view,' began Denegtacus as he sat down on another rock a few feet from Chard.

They shared the sight before them for a few moments. 'I felt you searching for me,' said Chard softly. 'After nearly a year, you decide to track me down. I had hoped that you'd leave us to live out our lives.'

Denegtacus glanced sideways at Chard. He has wearing a white tunic belted at the waist which reached to his knees and his skin had been tanned brown by the sun. It was clear that he had found his happiness and, having seen him, the old elf didn't doubt that Formositas would be equally as healthy.

'I have to congratulate you on the magic you've wrought here. This whole island has been hidden from the people surrounding you. Even those who had memory of it have forgotten its existence. Tell me, how do you stop people accidentally just washing up here?'

'Just a few underwater currents,' replied Chard, and he gestured to the sea.

Denegtacus nodded in acknowledgement but made no other comment.

'She's happy here, we both are,' continued Chard. 'My magic got us started, built us a home and all that, but over the months I've used it less and less. We really are trying to live as ordinarily as possible.'

'Other than owning your own private island.'

Chard exhaled and smiled. 'An island was nothing, had she asked for the whole world I would have given it to her.'

'Leaspida is still clinging on,' said Denegtacus, changing

the subject. 'I think it's only the thought of your death that keeps him alive. Terrible that an elf should sink so low.'

'Then tell him I'm dead. I don't care. We are not going back and we are certainly not going to let her deranged father keep us apart.'

The elf nodded slowly, thinking. 'I'm truly sorry how things turned out, Chard. If there was a way for all this to be put right ...'

'You speak as if things are not right,' interrupted Chard. 'If being L'tusian meant giving up Sitas, then I would say no. Although events overtook us somewhat, in the end, they worked out for the best.'

Coming to a decision, Denegtacus stood up. He made a brief show of brushing the front of his robes before he turned to his former pupil. 'Had I not seen you in person, I would never have believed that such a change in a person's outlook was possible. Your bitterness has left you, Chard, the shadow I once saw hanging over your soul seems to have disappeared. You are correct. It has turned out for the best. Two people are happy and I can continue as L'tusian until another comes to take my place. Leaspida is old and his hatred will not be enough to sustain him through another winter. When his son replaces him, I'm sure what occurred with you and Formositas will be glossed over and we can all move on.'

Chard didn't look at Denegtacus but he inclined his head. 'Thank you,' he said simply.

Without another word, Denegtacus stretched out his hand. There was the slightest of pauses as Chard's eyes swivelled to focus on it before his own reached out. Their eyes met as they shook and understanding passed between them.

'Denegtacus!' shouted a voice, its tone joyous.

At the sound of his name, the elf turned. The greeting that was forming on his lips died with a choking sound as he took in the sight that stood before him. Almost as if they had a will of their own, his eyes locked on the swollen belly of Formositas and refused to move.

'You'll give me a complex staring like that!' laughed the princess. 'Chard says it's due any day!'

Chard had sensed the change in the atmosphere, even if Sitas remained oblivious. Pushing himself to his feet he stood between the two elves. Breaking eye contact seemed to snap Denegtacus out of his stupor.

'How could you be so stupid!?' he bellowed, anger sending spittle flying from his mouth.

Perhaps at some point Chard would have flinched before Denegtacus' wrath but now he stood quite calmly. Without taking his gaze from the visitor, he spoke over his shoulder to Sitas. 'Wife, you should rest. You know how the heat makes your ankles swell.'

'Oh no, Chard,' protested Sitas. 'I'm not the same little girl that he thinks can be pushed around and intimidated as he may have done in the past. If there's arguing to be done, I shall fight my own corner!'

'I don't doubt it for a second,' replied Chard soothingly, 'but I do not want you to get excited unnecessarily. Once Denegtacus here has realised just how silly he's being, I'm sure he'll come and apologise to you.'

'Apologise! I knew you were blinded by lust Chard but I never thought you'd be stupid enough to actually father a child with her!'

'I fail to see what the problem is. We are more than ready to become parents. After all, I am several hundred years older than my father was when he had me.'

'And what a sterling job he did!' replied Denegtacus sarcastically. 'I know you, Chard, and I have a fair idea what sort of person you'd raise. That,' he began, pointing a finger to Formositas' stomach, 'is a problem for the entire Westernwood which will no doubt come back to haunt us all some point in the future.'

'It is my hope,' said Chard, still desperately trying to keep a lid on the building pressure in his head, 'that our child will see himself as a part of both cultures. If he …'

'Or she,' said Sitas automatically.

'Or she decides that they would like to see where their mother grew up, we shall explain the somewhat delicate nature …'

'Can you not hear yourself, boy?' snarled Denegtacus. 'You're speaking to L'tusian! I've seen it all and I just know how that will turn out! He'll grow up with the hate-addled heart of a human and cause no end of suffering to my people of the Wood. He'll think only of what he wants and give no thought at all to the bigger picture!'

Behind him, Chard sensed Sitas start to edge away. Some mothering instinct told her that her baby was in danger and she sought distance.

'Well I have lived long enough to know when action is needed in order to prevent problems further down the line.' Denegtacus stepped to one side and made to move towards the princess.

Chard's hand touched Denegtacus' chest, his fingers spread widely, the pressure he exerted minimal but all the same the elf came to a halt. 'No,' he said calmly.

'She will be unharmed, Chard, you will still be able to sate your lust upon her but that child will not be born. It is for the best.'

An almost serene sense of peace took hold of Chard and his voice showed no sign of anger. 'Better for whom? The elves? You? Or perhaps the child itself? You judge in advance of any crime and pronounce a sentence of death; hardly the actions of L'tusian.'

'You were always clever, Chard, I never disputed that!' snarled Denegtacus. 'But you wreaked enough havoc among the elves. The Creator alone knows what damage some bastard half-human could cause!'

'And if he does, then you will be able to take issue with him, but until that moment you will not deny my child the right to exist.'

Reaching up, Denegtacus knocked Chard's hand from his chest. 'Stand aside,' he ordered.

'I will not,' replied Chard steadily.

'If you think I will spare you because of past friendship, you have learnt nothing of what it means to be L'tusian.'

'Perhaps you are right, Denegtacus, because I would never have believed you capable of cold-blooded murder,' responded Chard, still in the same level tone.

'I've done worse, boy! L'tusian does what has to be done and is judged by no man! I answer only to the Creator and if I am wrong then my punishment will be far worse than anything you could conceive. For the last time, get out of my way.'

In a blur of movement, Chard's hands sprang up. Magical fire engulfed the elf who screamed in pain and rage. Defences blocked the worse of the damage but nonetheless the elf had sustained a serious hit. Pressing his advantage, Chard unleashed a white-hot bolt of lightning which struck the elf in the chest, sending him staggering. Denegtacus however, had fought many magical duels in his years and although stunned by the power and suddenness of the attack, he was far from beaten. Regaining his footing he sent a combination attack of spells, specifically designed to disorientate even the strongest mage. An ice bomb crashed against Chard's magical defences, simultaneously a fireball struck him and finally, a third spell was directed at his feet, shaking the very ground upon which he was stood, an attempt to distract his attention, a mistake few wizards made more than once in magical combat.

The counter-attack did indeed cost Chard but he retaliated swiftly. Magic, raw and pure, flew from him and cascaded around the elf. It clung to him, it dripped from him and where it touched, it burnt. With a yelp of pain, Denegtacus fell back, desperately close to the edge of the cliff. When he realised his danger, he moved away, casting a quick glance at the long fall to the sea.

The two mages stood glaring at one another. Having tested each other, they knew that they were perfectly matched in their abilities and that the battle could well last for some time. Denegtacus glanced at a burn on the back of his hand and instantly it healed; Chard brushed the torn and bloody front of his tunic which similarly repaired itself at his touch.

At some unspoken command, they walked forward until they were close enough to reach out and touch. Slowly, each stretched out his right arm, the palm of the hand facing their adversary. They manoeuvred until their hands were less than an inch apart and then an explosion of magic discharged from them.

Sparks of all colours flew from the clash. It soon became impossible to make out the two fighters as a magical hue surrounded them, distorting light and hurting the eyes of any who would dare look. For over two minutes they pushed their magic against the other, neither giving ground. Then, blood began to seep from Chard's nose. It ran, slowly at first, into his mouth, the taste it left behind unpleasant. Not for a second did Chard relent in the struggle, indeed it seemed to spur him on to greater efforts. Now it was Denegtacus who started to feel the strain. The flesh of his hand began to smoulder, wisps of smoke drifting lazily up past his eyes.

Each mage gave an animal-like roar and fell back. Blood was leaking from every orifice on Chard's face, even his eyes, leaving crimson trails like red tears. The elf's hand was a charred and ruined mess and as he looked at it, a drip of melted flesh fell from what remained of one of his fingers. Through gritted teeth, Denegtacus summoned his will to repair the damage but although his hand healed somewhat, the injury was still clear to see. Chard however, did nothing to stem the flow of blood; indeed it appeared to be getting worse.

A bolt of lightning struck Chard from above, the magically enhanced clouds avoiding his defences. It hit just above his left eye, tearing a chunk of flesh from his face and sending blood in all directions. He cried out in pain and staggered back further before losing his footing and falling to the ground. Clutching his hand to the wound did nothing to stem the loss of blood and Chard could feel his consciousness fading. Denegtacus began to walk slowly towards Chard, taking nothing for granted.

Sitas appeared between them, her expression a mix of fury and fear. She held out one hand to Chard, the other held up to stop the elf's advance. Denegtacus did not even break stride as his hand grabbed Sitas' wrist and twisted it savagely to one side while the other backhanded her across the face. The woman collapsed to the ground but was back up in an instant. As she moved to intervene again, she suddenly gave a sharp moan and fell to her knees. Something in the tone of the cry made both mages look at her. One looked with an expression you might have after stepping on a bug, the other with an anguish that banished all thoughts of defeat from his mind.

In one fluid movement, Chard was on his feet, his injuries healing themselves and magic blazing from his fingertips. Dark red bolts of magic hit Denegtacus square in the chest at close range sending him several steps back. With a howl of rage he continued his march towards Chard. Putting out both hands he touched the very ends of his hands to Chard's chest, sending all the power he had straight into him. The human's feet left the ground as Denegtacus' magic lifted him, held him, tortured him for long seconds. Then, with a dismissive wave, he sent Chard's limp body cartwheeling through the air to land in a battered heap which remained still.

This isn't happening! Cried a voice inside Sitas' head. Finding strength she never knew she had, she forced herself to her feet and staggered to where Chard lay. Blood was trickling down her inner thighs, pain constricted her insides and it was all she could do to stop herself from passing out. Kneeling down beside Chard she put two fingers into his throat and felt for the pulse. Relief flooded her when she found it and she gently slapped the side of his face to try to rouse him.

'Princess,' said Denegtacus softly, 'it is time.'

Gently, Sitas lowered Chard's head and made herself stand to confront the elf. 'Whatever you are going to do, please reconsider.'

Remorselessly, Denegtacus walked towards her and, hating herself for her fear, Sitas edged away. 'Do you want me to beg?' she screamed. 'If you want me to beg to save my unborn's life, I'll do it!'

'I take no joy in this, princess. Sometimes there are things that need to be done,' replied Denegtacus.

Finally her retreat had brought her to the very edge of the cliff. Briefly she turned her head to look at the long fall to the sea. Tears began to fall from her eyes, another cramp sent a spasm of pain through her and she fell to one knee.

Through sobs, Denegtacus heard only one word, 'Please', but it meant nothing to him. He reached out, ready to do what had to be done. Sitas took one final step back to avoid his touch and was gone. It was almost funny – one moment she was there, the next she was not. Denegtacus' hand stayed out as if he expected her to grab it, but all that remained was her scream of despair as she fell. A scream that because of the nature of sound and how it travelled, Denegtacus could still hear for a few seconds after her death.

16

Denegtacus laid the body down gently. His magic had repaired the damage inflicted by the rocks but even he could not give life. He glanced at Chard's unmoving body and shook his head sadly. How had it come to this? None of them really deserved what had happened, especially Formositas, but that child couldn't be born. At least that problem no longer existed. The elf looked out over the sea, the cold wind perhaps the reason for the tears in his eyes.

Chard's eyes snapped open. There was no hesitation, no listening to the screams of protest from his body as his injuries sent waves of pain through his battered form. In one movement, he stood and cast his gaze around, searching for what he already knew he would find. Only a matter of feet from him, he saw Denegtacus crouched beside the inert Sitas. It was so incredible a sight, so unlike the image he had of his vivacious wife that he almost laughed. Half walking, half staggering, he covered the short distance that separated them before collapsing onto his knees. For long moments he simply stared at Sitas' face, so peaceful, so still. Gently, he reached out and laid his hand on her forehead, flinching slightly at the unnatural coldness of it.

'How long?' he whispered, without looking at Denegtacus.

'A minute; no more than two. You came round fast, must

have a thick skull.' The words were spoken softly, with no intention to wound.

'People have said it …' the words trailed off and Chard lowered his head. Suddenly he jolted upright and swung to face Denegtacus, his hands gripping the old elf by the arms fiercely. 'We can bring them back!'

Denegtacus made no attempt to dislodge Chard's hold on him but he shook his head slowly.

'They are dead, Chard, they are beyond us.'

A fire seemed to be building within the human. 'No! This body is as nothing! They might not have crossed beyond our reach. The river, the journey, we can still follow.'

The elf had stopped shaking his head but gave no encouragement. 'The afterlife is somewhere we cannot go until it is our time.'

Chard grabbed Denegtacus by the front of his clothes. 'I'm not talking about Heaven; I'm talking about the journey. Her soul is still within reach and every second we waste arguing is one more she walks beyond our grasp. For the love of God, help me!'

Although he did not like to admit it, Denegtacus was intrigued by the possibility of what Chard was suggesting. It would take a lot of magic to open the gateway and he would have to do it alone. Reaching inside his robe, the elf pulled out a coin and flicked it to the human. 'Take this, it might be useful.'

Crossing the divide was not a step to be taken lightly, but Chard was right, the longer they waited the slimmer the chance of success. Spreading his arms, Denegtacus focused his energies and slowly a circle opened before him. Beads of sweat broke out on his forehead as, inch by inch, the circle expanded. It looked much as these things always did when doors were opened to cross distances, but this was not a physical boundary but one of the soul. Chard stared into the circle and saw nothing. Just a void, a blank space in the world. He reached out his hand and touched the surface of the circle. A chill raced up his arm and he snatched his hand back. Bright red welts were already appearing on the skin.

'Perhaps you might go faster!' snapped Denegtacus through gritted teeth.

Chard slipped the coin into a pocket and looked at Denegtacus. For a moment their eyes held one another's but no words were spoken. Without further pause, Chard dived through the hole …

… and landed hard onto unforgiving grey ground. Ash rose around him in a cloud and he coughed for several seconds. Forcing himself to his feet he cast his gaze about in all directions while wiping the worst of the dust from his clothes.

Grey land, grey sky and grey, bare trees, bent and twisted, stretched as far as the eye could see. Chard turned slowly but in such a bleak world it was hard to tell up from down let alone which way offered the best hope. Somewhere in the distance, he thought he saw movement and with no other options, hurried towards it.

It was hard to tell how long he had been holding this gateway open but Denegtacus was finding it increasingly difficult to maintain it. It was smaller since Chard had crossed and at this rate if he did not return within half an hour, the door would be gone. The thought struck Denegtacus immediately; would that be such a bad thing? Chard was trying to bring back a life that had run its course. There was a time to be born and a time to die and although Denegtacus had interfered a number of times, this seemed somehow different. Slowly he lowered his hands and instantly the gateway shrank to the size of a dinner plate. For a moment he hesitated but then waved his hand across the opening which sealed at his command. Staring straight ahead, Denegtacus' face was unreadable. Abruptly, he turned and walked away leaving the body of an elf princess alone in the dirt.

The movement turned out to be a procession of the dead. Grey figures shuffled towards some destination that they knew was out there, waiting for them. Up close, Chard could see that perhaps he had misjudged them, they were indeed greyish but features and even clothing were clear. All species, both sexes and all ages, they trooped silently forwards. Few even glanced at each other let alone at Chard as he approached. Now that he could see them, Chard had a direction to head in. He ran as fast as he could towards the front of the column that stretched out into the distance.

After running for several minutes, Chard reached the front of the procession. A figure dressed in a reddish-brown cloak was herding spirits onto a boat, using a pole to push them closer together in order to fit more on. Chard pushed his way through the throng to reach the waterline.

'Make way!' he roared. 'I must cross!'

The noise and the disturbance made only a few of the spirits glance his way, most totally ignored him. However, one figure turned round sharply at the sound of his voice.

The Ferryman stared at Chard, a look of mild surprise on his face. 'Well, well,' he said with a smile. 'What have we here?'

Chard held out the coin Denegtacus had given him, 'Formositas the elf passed recently. There's been a mistake and I have to bring her back.'

Charon didn't even look at the coin. 'That a fact?' he asked and rested some of his weight onto the pole he carried. 'Can't say there's ever been a mistake before. Still, first time for everything.'

'Sitas!' snapped Chard. 'Has she passed?'

'This is not your time, Chard,' replied Charon calmly, a thin smile still resting on his face. 'You do not belong here and I have work to do.' He turned and began gathering up the mooring rope, looping it around his arm.

'You think I'm playing?' bellowed Chard and grabbed Charon roughly, swinging him round to face him. 'I crossed the divide to be here and I don't expect you to stop me getting across this damn river. Now here,' Chard forced the coin into the ferryman's hand. 'Take the money and take me to the other side.'

'You have another coin for the journey back?' Charon asked mildly.

Comprehension passed across Chard's face and he slowly released his hold. 'Please,' he whispered, 'I'm begging you.'

Charon shook his head. 'Sorry, son, these things are nothing to do with me. I just work here.' He patted Chard softly on the shoulder. 'She must have been some woman.'

Chard rubbed his hand across his eyes. 'Yes,' he said quietly, 'she was.'

Sighing, Charon continued, 'I remember her, Chard. They've both been ferried.'

'Both?'

'Her and the boy. Shame when they're that young. This one didn't even get the chance to live, but like I said, these things have got nothing to do with me.'

'My son,' said Chard. 'Tell me what you want!' he shouted. 'I'll give you anything but you have to take me to them before it's too late.'

'It's already too late,' replied Charon with a certain amount of pity. 'No one leaves here, Chard. That's just the way it is.'

Charon clambered on board the boat and pushed the pole into the murky grey water. Inch by inch, the ferry started its journey across the river Styx. The passengers shuffled their feet, perhaps in anticipation of the afterlife that their deeds in life had granted them. Fog that had hung motionlessly above the water now began to swirl gently around the ferry as the boat passed through it. Soon the ferry was lost from sight, the only evidence of its passing a few ripples which soon settled.

Chard slumped to the ground, defeat etched into his very soul. The ferry would soon return and he could try again but he knew that it would be a waste of breath. Charon had no intention of taking him across and even if he did, it was certain that Sitas had found her way to the afterlife by now.

How long he sat like that, he did not know, but eventually he stirred himself. The ferry hadn't returned but the next group of passengers didn't appear to mind. The ghostly figures just stood and waited patiently. Staring out over the water, Chard smiled sadly to himself. 'Yes, she was,' he repeated softly.

As he was about to leave he heard a splash. Curious, he walked towards the sound. Close to the queue of the dead, he saw a man sat on a rock. He was holding a fishing rod, the line of which disappeared beneath the surface of the cloudy river. Dressed all in black he was also wearing a strange pair of glasses which were so dark they hid his eyes from view. Chard guessed he must be around fifty. He had a balding head and a little too much weight round the middle to be healthy.

'Nothing seems to be biting,' commented the man as Chard approached him.

'Not sure you'd want to catch anything that lived in that water anyway,' replied Chard.

The man chuckled. 'You're probably right.' Standing up he tossed the rod aside, ignoring the muffled splash it made as it landed in the water and slid beneath the surface.

'Who are you?' asked Chard. 'You don't look much like a fisherman.'

'Oh but I am,' he replied smoothly. 'A fisher of men you

might say,' and he laughed gently as if he had made a joke of some kind. 'You see, I knew you'd be here round about now and I wanted to help.'

Chard was suspicious but curiosity got the better of him. 'Very well, I'll take the bait. How did you know I'd be here and why do you want to help?'

'I sense lots of questions. Why don't we take a stroll along the river bank?' He gestured with one hand for Chard to accompany him. Shrugging, Chard followed; there really didn't seem any alternative.

'You're here to bring back your wife's soul to the land of the living, yes?' enquired the stranger.

Chard nodded. 'The Ferryman thinks it's too late. They've already passed beyond reach.'

The stranger kicked aimlessly at a loose pebble, sending dust billowing up as high as their waists. 'Yes and no.'

Such answers reminded Chard of his years debating with Denegtacus and did little to improve his temper. 'Yes and no?' he queried.

'Yes your wife is beyond your grasp and no your son is not.'

Chard halted and reached out to take a hold of the man's sleeve. The cloth felt odd beneath his fingers, it appeared to move almost as if it were alive. The stranger glanced at Chard's hand which he immediately removed.

'What do you mean?' he demanded.

'Sitas has gone to her afterlife. As an adult she knew where she was the moment her soul left the physical world. She had heard the stories and a part of her mind simply knew where she had to go and that there was no going back.' He continued along the bank, forcing Chard to scurry along behind like some errant child. 'So assuming she lived a good life, she is presently enjoying her just reward or some such nonsense. However, the child hadn't even escaped the womb before he died. At the moment his soul wanders the void, lost and confused, searching elusively for … well, something. An end to the journey perhaps? Who can say?'

'Then we must help him!' shouted Chard, hope, happiness and fear all present in his tone.

'Must we?' asked the stranger in an easy voice.

'Isn't that why you're here?' countered Chard irritably.

The stranger grinned. 'I suppose you've got me there.' He rounded on Chard, standing straight before him. 'There is something I need from you, Chard, and in order to get it I am willing to help you and your son.'

'You seem to know a lot about me,' began Chard warily, 'so how about you tell me who you are?'

'I have lots of names. You may pick the one you feel most comfortable using.'

The human nodded slowly. 'I also know that favours from you come at a high price and that you are not helping me out of the kindness of your heart. There is always a catch.'

'How about I tell you what I want first?' the stranger asked pleasantly. 'If you feel that it's something that you are uncomfortable with, I'll be off and leave you to try and figure out how you're going to get home now that Denegtacus has closed the gateway.'

Chard tried not to let the fear he felt at this news show on his face. 'I'd find a way.'

'Perhaps, you're very resourceful after all. That's why I have chosen you.'

Looking for a way out, Chard found none. 'What is it that you want?'

The stranger smiled broadly, 'There's a good chap! Now, I have a few of my people on the surface who are preparing an invasion of Eurasia from the east. None of them are even close to your intelligence and cunning and I want you to take charge. In particular, you're going to have to fend off magical interference from Denegtacus while the arrogols plunder the west.'

Chard stared at his feet before looking up. 'Denegtacus beat me once already today. I don't see how I could do as you ask.'

The stranger patted Chard in much the same way Charon had done earlier. 'You and Denegtacus know all about using gateways to cross distance and you even worked out how to use such knowledge to cross the divide. But, I can give you gateways to other worlds that you do not even know exist and weapons to battle even the mighty L'tusian.' As he spoke the name, Chard could hear the sneer in his voice but said nothing. 'With Denegtacus out of the way, the eastern armies would crush the west and usher in a new age.'

'If you are who I think you are,' said Chard carefully, 'why would you care who rules which bit of land?'

'Worship, Chard. That's what I want. Once the west is beaten and the Faith crushed, all living things will turn to me as their salvation. Followers who are obedient unto death and beyond! I shall rule the mortal world and break the Seals!'

'And in return you'll give me my son?' asked Chard.

For a moment it looked as if the stranger hadn't heard, he continued to stare off into the distance. Snapping himself out of it he stared at Chard before grinning. 'Quite. One boy means very little to me but is a lever for me to get my way. It'll cost me nothing to help you but I shall always have your servitude in return.'

Chard turned his head to stare across the river. 'So how do I get over there and more importantly, how do we both get out of here?'

'You give me your word to do as I wish?' asked the stranger. 'Swear upon your soul?'

Licking his dry lips, Chard knew that from this point on there would be no turning back. 'I swear it.'

*   *   *

Sitting once more in his small home in the forest, Denegtacus considered all that had happened since he had first met Chard. Leaving him sealed up in the divide was not a high point in the elf's life but, as with so many things that L'tusian did, the greater good mitigated some unpleasantness to individuals. He exhaled in disgust at his own rationalisation of what was a petty piece of evil. When the time came for his replacement to take over the role of L'tusian, he hoped that he wouldn't judge him too harshly. Gazing out of the window, the elf thought that this was unlikely since he judged himself guilty.

'Excellent,' replied the stranger. 'Without Charon to take you, you cannot cross the Styx, but I can.'

'Wait a minute …' began Chard.

'I will keep my side of the bargain, Chard. I always do. I'll take your son some *when* he will be safe.'

'Some when?' asked Chard. 'What does that mean?'

'A place in time where he will be allowed to grow, unharmed by your enemies.'

Shaking his head, Chard felt his anger rising. 'This is not what I thought I was agreeing to! I want my son!'

'How exactly do you plan on finding him? You have fallen at the first hurdle!' He waved a hand at the river. 'I can find him, get him out of here, give him a body and take him to a place where he will be safe!' The stranger poked a finger savagely in Chard's chest, sending him staggering several paces back. 'For all of this I ask merely that you'll keep one little elf out of my army's way!'

Regaining his footing, Chard stepped forward. 'Will I see him again?'

An odd smile played across the stranger's face. 'Oh yes. As long as there are people to speak, words of your meeting will echo through the ages. Of that, I assure you.'

'There are things you are hiding from me but I have no choice but to believe that you will keep your promise.'

'I always keep my promises, Chard. That's what my enemies forget.' He held out his hand.

Chard eyed the hand as if he could drag the information he needed from it. Hanging at his side, his own hand clenched and unclenched involuntarily. Making the decision, he shook the stranger's hand, locking stares.

'A wise choice, Chard.' As he spoke his left hand closed over the top of Chard's. Pain lanced through the flesh and Chard tried to pull his hand away. Held firmly in two hands, Chard was going nowhere. He could feel the skin on the back of his hand burning, melting, the smell of roasting flesh assailing his nostrils. Suddenly the stranger released his hold and Chard fell back, clutching his hand to his middle. 'Wear my mark with pride, Chard, it will open doors for you.'

Lifting his hand, Chard looked at it, biting back tears. The flesh had been seared by magic, leaving a burn that Chard knew would never heal. His eyes tried to ignore the damage to his body and instead locked onto the three sixes permanently affixed to the skin.

A voice called to him from some distance away. 'The pain will subside eventually,' said the stranger from the other side of the river. 'Well, mostly.' He touched his fingers to his forehead by way of goodbye.

'Wait!' screamed Chard, and he ran to the edge of the river.

'Wave to daddy!' said the stranger to the tiny child who stood beside him on the far bank.

Chard stared at the child and automatically raised his hand. The child copied the motion and was then led away by the stranger, both of them soon swallowed by the grey fog that never dissipated. For some time, Chard found himself simply looking at the empty space that they had occupied, unable to leave.

The choice he had made here today was irreversible, he knew that, and the knowledge that he was now bound to this side of the fight saddened him. In his heart he was certain he was not evil – oh, things had happened and there were things he was not proud of, but overall he hadn't deliberately tried to cause harm. It had been meeting Sitas that had changed him, sent him down a different path to the one his life had been headed. Denegtacus' intervention had been key of course, but it had been that beautiful elf princess who had really altered him. It seemed fitting that it was her death that would once more be the catalyst for change in his life.

A long breath escaped from Chard and he bowed his head, simultaneously itching at the damage to the back of his hand. Already the pain was fading to merely unpleasant but as long as he lived, it would never cease. Perhaps he could stay here, he mused silently to himself. It's not like anyone would come looking for him. Except one, and Chard had no desire to make him angry.

However, he had absolutely no idea how he was going to return to the world. Denegtacus really had played him for a fool, trapping him here for all eternity. At least he'd get to talk to him when the old elf finally upped and died. Chard gave a rueful smile; that might be some wait.

The itching was not getting any better and Chard scratched even harder. 'Open doors ...' he murmured quietly. Holding out his hand he channelled his magic through the numbers themselves. A soft red glow emitted from the digits, coalescing into a ball that hovered just before him. Through the mist he could just make out trees and a hillside. Stepping forward, he vanished, leaving behind the same grey world that he had entered.

17

Tens of thousands of men. Thousands of horses. Hundreds of wagons. They stretched as far as the eye could see in all directions. It had been months in the planning, one disaster after another, but finally, the arrogol war machine was rolling westwards. Khagen sat astride his horse and allowed himself the luxury of the thinnest of thin smiles. His empire already reached back to the mountains they called *ur-al* and as far south as the great inland sea. Now it would go west to the Wood of the elves and perhaps beyond! Such an achievement was greater than anything he could possibly have imagined mere years earlier, further proof that God was with him on this great crusade.

The only matter which displeased him was currently sat on a horse immediately to his right. Dressed all in black, his hood pulled so far forward that unless you were head on to him, you couldn't see his features, the magi had appeared a few days back and simply taken over many of the roles that his advisers had previously undertaken. He was efficient, cold, powerful; all the things that Khagen usually liked in a man. Yet, no one knew anything about him or where he had come from. It was without doubt that he was committed to the cause and got things done. When he had first walked into Khagen's presence, the emperor had simply ordered his death, annoyed at the upstart's interruption. In the next thirty seconds, the magi had sent seventeen of his finest warriors to their deaths without even moving a muscle. Once quiet reigned in the room, the magi had explained that he was there to help with the invasion and that if he had wanted to stop Khagen he would merely kill him this instant. After such a demonstration, no one felt inclined to voice opposition and so this human had entered Khagen's closest circle of advisers.

The main invasion would have to take place at walking speed but the major thrust of the army would cover as many miles as was possible every single day. Their horses would carry them deep into enemy territory, killing all who stood in their way, never allowing survivors time to pause or reorganise their defences. Such 'lightning war' had helped take Khagen from being the son of a farmer to emperor of the largest nation ever seen on the face of the planet.

'The western armies will fall like wheat before our Arrogolian scythes!'

The magi gave no indication that he was even listening to the emperor, and did not reply.

Khagen glanced over his shoulder to where the rest of his immediate followers waited patiently. 'Did you not hear what I said?' he roared.

'They heard you,' interrupted the magi, annoyance hanging on every syllable. 'Must you shout so loudly? It really is quite disagreeable.'

Unused to anyone telling him what he should or should not do, Khagen was unsure how to react. 'I was merely voicing what we were all thinking. What marvellous sport this will be! I particularly look forward to gutting me a few elves.' These words drew appreciative chuckles from the arrogols nearby.

The magi turned his head to look at the emperor. Chard's face was a picture of contempt with the sort of expression most people used when they realised they had trodden in something unpleasant. Having faced death many times in battle, Khagen did not frighten easily, but there was something in this human's eyes, something unnatural, that made even Khagen avert his gaze.

'Well, Mors,' continued Khagen, more from wanting to fill the silence than because he had anything to say, 'don't you have any words of encouragement for the troops?' He cast his gaze back and forth over the assembled multitude, pretending he had always meant to look away at that precise moment.

'No,' answered Chard, and kicked his horse forward. Khagen watched him go, all the time picturing the many varied deaths that he would like to inflict upon this insect once he had outlived his usefulness.

The first day they advanced sixteen miles on a thirty-mile front. Estimates of the dead were between three and four hundred, mainly farmers and their families. One border post had been destroyed but that had housed only three soldiers from the Imperial Legion of Rostian, all of whom were over fifty. Khagen hadn't lost a single man and was in good spirits, but they all lusted after a proper battle and the chance to show these westerners what the east had to offer.

At first, reports of the invasion were sketchy and uncoordinated. The king of Rostian then sent more scouts to see for themselves what all the trouble was about. It would take ten days to fully assess the extent of the catastrophe that was engulfing Eurasia, by which time the arrogols had advanced nearly a hundred miles into the plains of Rostian. A further ten days passed before the legions were assembled to do battle with the invaders, just outside the capital city of Lvov. In the space of six hours, the cream of Rostian's youth were butchered, virtually to a man. Those who tried to surrender were sacrificed on makeshift altars, those who fled were hunted down.

Khagen made himself comfortable in the newly-vacated

palace while they waited for the baggage train to catch up with them. Behind the invasion came even more troops with the supplies, widening the front, securing the rear. This was a war to conquer territory, not just kill the enemy, and the arrogols were making certain that the world knew that they were here to stay. However, speed was also of the essence and Khagen had given orders that the army was to be ready to move in seven days, always westwards.

Denegtacus had witnessed his fair share of man's inhumanity but even he was appalled by the brutalities the arrogols were showing to any and all who were unfortunate enough to fall into their clutches. Prisoners were nailed to trees and if they survived too long, their ribs were cracked open and their hearts removed.

The elf wandered unseen amongst the camp, listening to idle conversation and picking up the odd morsel of information. It was without doubt that he would have to intervene but the role of L'tusian was complex. People would want the chance to stand upon their own two feet and wage war on the enemy. Only when things were at their bleakest would they come to L'tusian, begging for his help. How many would die just because the leaders of nations wanted to play at soldiers? Once it was all over, he'd get the blame for not having helped sooner! The elf shook his head, the workings of the world never ceased to amaze him.

Eventually his meanderings took him further away from the camp. This area of Rostian was known for being flat, but there was a gentle slope just to the south that Denegtacus found himself drawn to. As he walked, the suspicion he felt continued to grow so that by the time he reached the top, he already knew what he would find.

'Hello, Chard,' he said amiably.

Chard was sat cross-legged on the grass, idly picking the

petals off a small flower. Without looking up he responded. 'It's Mors now.'

The elf shook his head, 'Calling yourself death is a little melodramatic don't you think?'

With a shrug, Chard climbed back to his feet. 'It's what they expect.'

'Since when did you start caring what arrogols think or want?'

Chard wiped down the front of his robes, even though they were immaculately clean. 'I guess since I was abandoned in the divide and had to be helped by a friend of theirs.'

'It was for the best,' replied Denegtacus smoothly.

These were the words that Chard had been expecting, but hearing them out loud did nothing to improve his temper. 'Better for whom?' he snarled menacingly. Without waiting for a response he continued; 'Do you know what I've always hated about you, Denegtacus?'

'Do tell,' said the elf mildly.

'How you always just seem to know what's "for the best". How there's never any doubt in your mind. No matter how evil your actions, you've always got some self-justification to back them up. It all sounds so plausible, it's only when I walk off and think about what you've actually done and how many people you've hurt or killed that it appears wrong! I really have to bow before a master deceiver.' And Chard bent in the middle with an exaggerated flourish. 'Killing the only person who ever truly mattered to me was just another day at the farm to you wasn't it?' He waved the point aside. 'Doesn't matter though does it? What's done is done. I found her body. You couldn't even be bothered to spare the time to bury her. I thought I was in the divide for only a matter of minutes but when I returned I discovered that several days had past. Do you know what happens to a body left out on a hillside during hot weather? The last image of my beautiful bride I have was of a maggot-infested corpse that every scavenger on the island had taken a bite from. Never mind, I'm sure you thought it was *for the best.*'

The elf had listened calmly to the outburst, and no trace of anger showed on his face. 'It must be nice to be able to blame me for so much, while avoiding your own culpability in events.' Something that Chard had said then filtered through to the elf. 'What exactly did you mean when you mentioned a friend of theirs? How did you escape the divide?'

'Haven't you figured it out yet?' sneered Chard. 'That mob down there is only the beginning. Eurasia is going to burn and I'm going to make sure that you go up with it!'

'Have you got any idea what you've done!' shouted Denegtacus, his previous composure deserting him. 'When you make a deal with … him … there's no going back! Whatever he promised you isn't worth your soul.'

'My soul?' replied Chard derisively. 'That's long gone. I don't really think he's getting much from the agreement. I however get to salvage half of what you took from me. My son lives, no thanks to you.'

'And have you seen him? Have you held him?' asked Denegtacus.

A flicker of doubt crossed Chard's face. 'I saw him. He was safe and I was promised that we shall meet soon.'

'You are a fool,' said Denegtacus, but the words were not spoken angrily but rather with a resigned fatalism. He reached out and placed his hand on Chard's shoulder. The human bowed his head. Noticing the mark on Chard's hand, the elf took a hold of it and turned it to the light for a better look. 'Nothing is worth this Chard, nothing.'

Pulling his hand free, Chard towered over the elf. 'You have no son, Denegtacus, I do. I would see a thousand worlds destroyed if it meant he would be safe. This,' and he held up his hand, 'is nothing.'

'I have already proved myself the stronger, Chard; will you make me do it again?'

'You think threats of death bother me?' Chard smiled without humour and began to walk back towards the arrogol camp. 'After all, I *am* death!' he called back over his shoulder.

Watching him go, Denegtacus considered killing him but pushed such thoughts aside. Obviously there would come a reckoning but the elf wanted there to be witnesses. It would be important that others saw evil defeated.

Even though he was an elf, when the time came for speed, Denegtacus could move quicker than anyone. In the space of two days he had travelled to every leader of every nation in Eurasia and informed them of the situation. Most had been sceptical but once he dragged them by magic to see for themselves, all became converts to the idea of stopping this invasion. Far harder for them to accept was the plan that the elf had put together to halt the arrogols.

Seated around a circular table, the leaders of the continent cast suspicious glances at one another and at the maps spread before them in equal measure. Never before had such a meeting taken place and they all felt the weight of responsibility pressing down on their shoulders. This, however, did not stop them from acting in the manner that Denegtacus would have predicted – self-serving and blinkered.

Although it was Denegtacus who had brought them together, he was trying to take a back seat in the discussions, but as time wore on and at least half of the people present had stormed off at one point or another, only for the enchanter to drag them back, he began to see that they would only do the right thing if someone made them.

'Every minute we argue here is another minute wasted!' shouted Artife, the new king of Rostian since his father's death at the swords of the arrogols.

'Much as it pains me to agree with him,' began King

Orstesses of Rostike, 'he's right. We simply have to reach agreement. There is too much at stake.'

'Funny how you agree,' sneered Gokkib, the only goblin present, 'since your shitty little nation is next!' He wrenched a leg from the roast goose before him and began to devour it noisily.

'As L'tusian tells us that we're all next, I fail to see your point!' snapped Orstesses. 'And chew with your damn mouth closed!'

The goblin smirked and opened his maw even wider.

'I think we're all in agreement that action must be taken,' said King Hebare of Curinlas, studiously ignoring the goblin's loud chewing. 'Surely we can see that.'

This was met by several voices all disagreeing, the tones becoming angry and frustrated.

Denegtacus slipped out of the door and exhaled deeply. The stubbornness and stupidity of these people! Despite seeing it for themselves, they still believed that the arrogols were a problem that would simply go away if they ignored it for long enough. Elves, goblins, dwarves, and humans; at that moment Denegtacus was tempted to let the arrogols do what they wanted and damn them all. But he knew that the driving force behind this invasion was not Khagen but something far worse. For that reason alone, he knew he had to go back and sort out this mess.

The door swung open forcibly and Sirilediar, king of Tordos stormed out, barely noticing the elf.

'Going somewhere?' asked Denegtacus quietly.

He swung round. 'I have better ways of spending my time that listening to a bunch of old women talk and talk. If it's all the same to you; I'm going home.'

All pretence that this meeting was for the peoples of Eurasia to sort things out for themselves evaporated instantly. Snarling with anger, the elf grabbed hold of the human who was over two feet taller and ninety pounds heavier than he was, and lifted him from the ground. Walking forward, he used the king as a battering ram and sent the door flying inwards in an explosion of wood. Inside, he hurled the dazed king back into his chair and turned to meet the stunned faces of the rest of the leaders. For long seconds he dared them to speak but when none volunteered any words, he decided it was time to get things moving.

'The continent faces a crisis the likes of which even I have never seen before and all you can do is squabble like children! This ends now!' None tried to interrupt him. 'I have marked on your maps in precise detail where and how we are going to turn back this attack. I have given you plenty of time to decide whose forces go where and you have failed! So,' and he made a considered effort to calm down, 'we go with my plan. At present rate of advance we have less than a month to organise. When you and your people are ready, I will transport you all to the site of the battle. Are there any questions?'

Silence reigned in the room until the youngest member of the conclave spoke. 'The plan is solid, L'tusian. The Bull's Horns is a tactic that has worked when faced with a numerically superior force.'

Denegtacus studied the casual demeanour of the speaker. Iskander of Bathenia had made himself king by killing all opposition to his appointment, including his own father, but he had shown outstanding leadership on the battlefield. His opinion might add something to the discussion.

'I sense a but?' said Denegtacus.

'*But* I feel my men would be better employed than simply making up part of the right flank.' He eased himself to his feet, commanding attention. 'Replace my force by slightly thinning the line in other areas or take them from the reserve. I shall lead my forty thousand into Arrogolia itself. It is the last thing they'll expect. I daresay we could find ways to make ourselves inconvenient to the enemy.'

Scratching at his chin, Denegtacus considered this and slowly nodded his head. 'If you run into difficulties, there won't be anyone to come to your aid.'

Iskander gave a grin. 'I seem to have managed to overcome any that I have come up against so far. They say the world ends somewhere in the far east of Arrogolia …' his words tailed off and the young king stared wistfully into space. 'The ends of the earth, hey L'tusian! I bet that's something to see.'

The elf licked his lips. Fewer men in the line was not ideal but if things looked bad, he could always intervene more directly. A move as bold as this might actually help swing things the west's way without L'tusian having to lend a hand. 'So be it. Are there any other points?'

'King Iskander refers to reserves, L'tusian,' began Hebare, 'yet according to this plan, there aren't any. What happens if the arrogols break through our lines?'

'Let me tell you something,' replied Denegtacus. 'In fact, let me tell you all something. There is to be no talk of defeat, no retreat, no surrender. This is the defining moment of our times, gentlemen, the moment that we shall all look back on as the single greatest achievement of our lives. In the shadow of Bulair, the peoples of the west will fight together as one and show the arrogols that to take on one is to take on all! It will be the start of peace in the west and of greater understanding between us. No more will ancient hatreds be the reason for current troubles, races will come together in the spirit of friendship to trade and bargain with one another. For this to happen we must join to turn back this horde from the east and chase them out of Eurasia forever.

'So, Hebare, there is no reserve because every man will be needed to hold the line and every man will be expected to do his duty. There will be no running because there is nowhere to run to. This invasion must be stopped.'

This speech was greeted by a series of nods from the

leaders. Iskander spoke for them all. 'Wise words as ever, L'tusian. Have no fear, the men will stand. The enemy shall not pass.'

A chill went up the old elf's spine when he heard the words, spoken with such finality. 'Do you hear us, Mors?' he bellowed, his voice getting louder with every word. 'They shall not pass!'

Balling the paper up, Khagen discarded the letter with barely suppressed rage. 'Bathenia has invaded Arrogolia!' he hissed through clenched teeth. 'Why is this happening?' The emperor of the east turned away from the hapless messenger and rounded on Chard. 'You never said anything about the west coming to my lands!'

'It's really quite a clever move,' said Chard with a touch of admiration. 'I must commend L'tusian on thinking of it when I see him.'

Khagen surged out of his chair and stood nose to nose with the magi. 'I'm not interested in their cleverness, I want to know why you didn't tell me this was about to happen and what you intend on doing about it!'

Chard blew gently into Khagen's face but the arrogol flew backwards to land in his chair as if he'd been punched. In one step, Chard was before the emperor and placed his hand on the arrogol's chest. Before he could utter a word, Khagen watched in horrified fascination as the magi's hand disappeared inside his flesh like he was made of nothing more substantial than fog.

'With one squeeze on your worthless heart, I could kill you,' said Chard with no more expression than if he'd been discussing the weather. 'L'tusian shields his plans from me in the same way I shield ours from him. How you and the military choose to respond to this inconvenience is up to you, but I have to be here. I have to stop L'tusian wiping out your invasion force with one flick of his wrist. If you ever question me again, I shall give your soul to the master and your shredded remains to the dogs.' He pulled out his hand, causing Khagen to spasm in pain and cough violently.

Chard regarded the emperor before turning and walking away. Khagen climbed gingerly back to his feet, his breath coming in ragged gasps. None close tried to help and the emperor could feel the respect he had earned over years slipping through his fingers like sand. 'Divert the reinforcements to the south,' he ordered. 'We'll take the west with what we have.'

For so many elves to be in the same place and all headed in the same direction was a rare event, but when L'tusian ordered you to assemble your army on the far eastern side of the wood, that's what you did. A standing joke among them was that there were two kinds of elf: those who questioned L'tusian and those who were alive.

Throughout the entire wood, thousands of elves travelled swiftly yet effortlessly through the dense vegetation. Chatting, laughing and bickering; it was all a release of tension since none were under any illusions as to the seriousness of the problem. Fighting alongside those who have been your enemies for generations was a difficult concept for the long-lived elves who viewed anything that happened in the previous thousand years as recent.

Two young elves from the Tree of Yew ambled alongside one another, chatting aimlessly. Both were less than eighty, barely old enough to be going to war, but they talked of victory with the confidence of youth. They carried longbows and two quivers of arrows as well as supplies for three days, but they moved quickly and assuredly.

Emmissis held out his long bow before him. 'See that?' he asked his companion.

Yussarriel grinned. 'You've mentioned it once or twice.'

'Going to get a few with this I reckon. Great grandfather gave it to me, said it never did him wrong whether he was hunting deer or goblin. My first proper longbow just in time for my first proper battle!' He grinned and clapped his hand down on his friend's shoulder, 'Don't get much better than this!'

All over the wood, all over Eurasia, similar scenes to this were being played out. Young men so convinced of their own immortality, marching jauntily off to a battle from which fewer than half would return.

18

The trees just seemed to go on and on. A sea of green that Khagen would enjoy watching burn. Before him ranged the might of the western armies. On his right, the enemy's left, he could see the standards of Curinlas, Slavia and the remnants of Rostike's forces. The other flank was a mix of humans from Tordos and goblins from their various territories and Holayew. The centre held the dwarves of Lish-Kar, a scattering of men from Rostian, more troops of Curinlas and various forces drawn from the Isle of Rittan. Cavalry and the cursed elves waited somewhere in the background.

Only Bathenia's flag was missing and Khagen swore under his breath as he thought of them. Iskander's forces had routed the troops sent to defeat him and were now marching largely unopposed through the vast tracks of southern Arrogolia. The man seemed unstoppable, like the Devil himself! It meant that he had had to send more of his soldiers back to the homeland to crush this insignificant human, further diminishing the resources he had available to him today.

On top of that, Mors had gone missing. Quite how his wizards would fair against L'tusian without Mors to help them was open to question. Still, they had sworn that they had the power to do so and Khagen had no choice but to believe them. The plan was simple: drive through the centre of the enemy's line and split them into two groups. From the back his men would then encircle the west's forces and obliterate any who would raise arms against the east.

All eyes were on the emperor and he savoured the moment. A light drizzle had fallen, softening the ground which rolled straight and flat for miles. In short, ideal cavalry terrain. Drawing his sword, he raised his arm smoothly. He held it there before dropping it swiftly. Several bugles sounded instantly and the front rows of arrogol horses began to trot towards the enemy. Khagen smiled. It would be a glorious victory and one that would live on through the ages. Nothing could stand before his armies, nothing.

Denegtacus had travelled the length and breadth of the lines the previous night, talking, giving encouragement, reminding the various races that success relied on them remembering who the real enemy was in this battle. More than once he had had to intervene to stop fights between individuals becoming full-scale battles. Now, as he watched the perfectly straight ranks of arrogol cavalry coming towards them, he couldn't help but be impressed.

Magic had elevated him twenty feet into the air at the rear of the western centre so that he could see what was occurring. Thousands of elves stood in front of him with quiver upon quiver of arrows at the ready. Many had been stuck into the ground by each archer's feet for easy reach making the earth look like some vast hedgehog. Those not killed by the arrows themselves would almost certainly succumb to blood poisoning from the dirty arrowheads.

The arrogol cavalry broke into a canter as they crossed five hundred yards. A few elves loosed their shafts but most held firm, waiting for the order.

'Steady, lads,' said Denegtacus quietly, yet all heard him.

As they crossed four hundred yards and kicked their horses into a gallop, Denegtacus screamed out the order to shoot. Thirty thousand elves loosed arrow after arrow, a quarter of a million in the first minute. Hundreds of horses and their riders fell, causing obstacles for the lines behind. Khagen however, was no fool and the ranks had been spaced correctly, giving the riders at the back time to change direction.

'Three hundred yards!' bellowed Denegtacus, causing the elves to change the distance since none were actually bothering to aim, instead relying on L'tusian to direct them.

So severe were the arrogol losses that many of the riders chose to wheel aside from their intended target and concentrate on the flanks instead. They smashed into the front lines of western infantry, scattering many, but were soon brought up by the press of bodies. Without infantry support, such an attack was doomed to fail and they found themselves being dragged from their saddles and dispatched coldly.

A faint ray of hope began to light the eyes of many from the west as they saw the attack falter. These easterners were not invincible and despite their seemingly endless numbers, they could be beaten! Then the first cries of despair went up as fingers began to point at something in the sky.

A shape was hurtling at breathtaking speed towards the Eurasian forces. A shape not seen for centuries and yet familiar. The dragon's roar echoed across the sky, its fiery breath tore through the ranks of Holayew's soldiers leaving a hundred dead in an instant as it swooped low over their heads. Soaring majestically into the sky it suddenly pivoted and dropped like a stone towards the shaken western soldiers. Its huge mouth opened and a bolt of lightning flashed out, striking into the densely packed ranks of men. Dozens were blasted to pieces, more thrown to the ground. A few elves shot arrows at the monster, but most missed and those that connected bounced harmlessly from its armoured sides.

Atop the beast, Chard allowed himself a smile. The sensation of riding this magnificent creature was simply incredible. The power, the magic, the feeling of invincibility. Wheeling it in the air, he ordered it to hover a hundred feet above the battlefield, making certain that all could see. Below, Chard could see that courage was already starting to desert some of the men in the line as they ran for the perceived safety of Bulair. His eyes sought out Denegtacus. When they locked onto each other, Chard grinned.

'Foolish boy!' hissed the old elf through clenched teeth. 'You don't understand what you've done!'

The dragon flapped its wings lazily. Its immense bulk was far too large for it to get airborne without recourse to its magic which it had in abundance. Dragons were creatures of magic in a way that fish are creatures of the sea; they simply couldn't exist without it. It let loose another blood-curdling screech which weakened the resolve of the allies still further.

Sensing the change in fortunes, Khagen ordered his vast lines of infantry forward as well as thousands more cavalry. They crossed the open ground between the two sides as fast as they could, their officers ignoring the losses from the heavy rain of arrows in their desire to engage at close quarters. The western forces drew swords and raced to meet the arrogols, assuming that fighting men was easier than fighting a dragon. In the shadow of the dragon, many men fell as their eyes were drawn upwards rather than towards the immediate danger of the arrogols.

The centre of the west's line began to bulge outwards, the ranks thinning as men were cut down or fled from the dragon. The Bull's Horns tactic meant that this bend was meant to happen and then the flanks would close around the back of the enemy, enveloping them. However, Denegtacus could plainly see that the line would break in minutes unless it was strengthened. If he ordered the elves to reinforce the centre he risked the dragon wiping them out with a few blasts of magic, yet if he didn't the day would be lost anyway.

For the first time in years, Denegtacus was racked by indecision. His gaze flicked across the battlefield and then up to where Chard sat on the dragon. They stared at one another, Chard fully aware of the problem that the elf faced. A smile spread across the human's face but he made no other move to intervene further in the battle.

'Damn you, boy!' whispered Denegtacus softly.

The screams of the dying and the wounded rang in his ears. With a roar of rage, L'tusian fired a bolt of lightning at the hovering dragon. It slammed into its chest sending it several feet further into the sky but other than that the attack seemed to have little effect.

'Did you know,' began Chard conversationally, 'in the world this magnificent creature inhabits, dragons have actually learned to feed off magic? Amazing really. If an enemy attacks it with magic, it absorbs it like a sponge and then uses that energy against its opponent. I have the master to thank for bringing it here, such magic is beyond even us.' Apparently bored, he looked down on the battle and shook his head. 'Your centre's looking very stretched. Best send in the elves.'

'So confident, Mors,' shouted L'tusian, 'but you forget one thing!' Raising his hand to the heavens, L'tusian called for the God Sword. Instantly the sword appeared in his grasp, shining like the sun itself. 'Elves!' bellowed L'tusian. 'Forward!' At the same time, the elf flew upwards, brandishing the sword in both hands. He covered the distance between them in a matter of seconds. The dragon tilted in the air as the elf swung the weapon in a scything arc. The tip of the sword sliced a tear in the thin membrane of its wing. The wound was slight but Mors ordered the dragon to land.

On the ground once more, L'tusian stood close to the dragon and its rider. Despite its intelligence, its magic and its strength, the overwhelming sensation coming from the beast was one of rage. Rage against all things that dared to breathe the same air as it did. Mors lifted his leg over the dragon's neck and slid smoothly down to the ground.

'I didn't forget. In fact, I was counting on it.' He patted the dragon absently as he spoke. 'You see, the master requires that sword and I have been tasked with retrieving it.'

L'tusian glanced at the dragon. Its outline seemed to have blurred since Mors had touched it. Within the shimmering, the elf could see that it was beginning to change shape. A blinding flare briefly illuminated the area and where there had been a dragon there was now a blue sword hanging a few inches from the ground.

Calmly, Mors placed his hand on the sword. In a flash, he swung round, the razor-sharp edge of the Dragon Sword opening a gash across L'tusian's upper right arm. The elf stepped back out of reach, his left hand closing on the wound to stop the blood. Glancing down he saw that the blood was already infected with maggots.

'Another neat trick,' said Mors pleasantly.

Gritting his teeth, L'tusian used his magic to clean and seal the injury. Lifting his sword, the two mages began to circle one another. Neither had had any training in the use of such a weapon, instead they both relied upon their magic and their sword's innate intelligence to both protect them and attack the other. Magically enhanced attacks were blisteringly fast. Thrust and counter thrust. All attacks were blocked, all moves anticipated. Long minutes went by and still neither had opened the other's defences.

Some distance away, the battle for Eurasia went on and on. Thousands upon thousands of young warriors hacking away at one another, each caught up in their own desperate battle for survival. The dead were piled up so deep in places that the defenders began to use them as barricades. Hundreds of arrows still rained down from archers on both sides. All pretence of a battle plan or of any organisation went out of the window as it became a bloodbath.

How long L'tusian and Mors hacked away at each other was uncertain, time seemed irrelevant. They stepped apart, both gasping for air. L'tusian leant heavily on his sword, his chest heaving, his skin caked in sweat. Mors remained resolutely upright, refusing to show his tiredness. Some part of him was distracted. He found his thoughts wandering to his son and the promise that had been given to him. Yes, he would see him again but there was no indication as to when that would be. For all Chard knew, the master may have been referring to their afterlives. There was no choice left to him, he had to obey. If the master wanted the sword then he'd get it for him, although he was intrigued as to the reason. All he had said was that it was the key to the struggle and then he had chuckled. Chard knew he was being used and that thought ate away at him. Deep down, he felt the need to rebel against the authority that was controlling him. Even if he killed L'tusian, what would there be for him? He hadn't been able to beat L'tusian with his magic on that hillside, and now he was relying on help from a dragon and the master.

Wearily, the two men walked towards one another. The elf watched the human's eyes carefully; something seemed to have changed. Perhaps he was more tired than he was letting on. Whatever, L'tusian had a job to do and he would allow nothing to sidetrack him. Lifting the sword slowly, it remained steady in his grasp. Mors made no attempt to lift his own; in fact he barely appeared to be looking at the elf. Instead, his eyes turned to focus on the battle.

Without a moment's hesitation, L'tusian ran Mors through. The God Sword slid smoothly through Mors' flesh. Wrenching it back, it came free in a spray of blood. Mors slumped to his knees, his face a picture of agony, but he kept hold of his sword. He lifted it slightly to show L'tusian.

Already it was flickering, its outline becoming faint and indistinct.

'Don't ... let ... it change!' he hissed through clenched teeth.

L'tusian raised the God Sword and brought it down on the midpoint of the Dragon Sword. It broke in half, black blood spewing out accompanied by a screech of pain. In mid-change, the dragon twisted and writhed on the ground, its blood bubbling and burning the soil wherever it touched. The elf tore his eyes from the death throes of the beast to look at Mors. Both of the human's hands were clutched to his stomach, blood sluicing between his fingers, and his eyes were closed tight.

L'tusian's face remained impassive. The suddenness of the ending of the duel did not appear to have unnerved or surprised him. Once more he raised the God Sword and swung it horizontally. Mors' head landed several yards away; his body slumped to the dirt. Walking over to the head, L'tusian picked it up by the hair and made his way back to the battle.

Chard opened his eyes. The master sat on the same rock as before, a fishing rod held casually in his hands.

'Never a dull moment when you work for me!' he said jovially, tossing the rod aside once more.

'I'm dead, aren't I?' asked Chard sadly.

'Oh, yes and no,' came the reply. 'Yes, old L'tusian is currently showing the arrogol emperor your severed head and setting the world to rights but no, you're not dead ... not completely.'

'I had no idea there were shades of grey in such things,' replied Chard drily.

'There are shades of grey in everything,' countered the master affably. Placing his arm around Chard's shoulder he walked him over to the queue of the dead waiting to be ferried.

Charon grinned as they approached. 'Didn't have to wait too long for a ferry ride after all, hey Chard? Never mind, son, that's how it goes sometimes.'

'I don't have a coin,' said Chard. 'Does that mean I can't cross?'

The Ferryman glanced at the master who stared back, a faint smile on his lips.

'Ordinarily it would, but as you're with … him … I can make an exception.'

As the ferry crossed the river, Chard turned to the master. 'You promised me I'd see my son.'

'And you promised to obey me. Looks like we've both been naughty. But unlike you, I was actually telling the truth. You will see your boy, just not now at this time.'

'How? I mean, I'm here!' Chard waved at the surroundings.

'This isn't the end for you, for us. There will be another chance for me to get that sword.'

The ferry gently bumped into the far bank and they disembarked. Chard glanced back to see Charon already pushing the craft back to the other bank. The Ferryman smiled and flicked a casual salute before being lost in the mist.

'Here.' The master picked up a black robe from the ground. 'Put this on.'

Chard took hold of the cloth which seemed to wriggle in his grasp. As he stared at the master he saw only his reflection in those strange black glasses he always wore. Chard hesitated.

'Surely you trust me? Haven't I always been there for you? Right from when you were conceived I kept watch on you. I followed your early life, ensuring that nothing too terrible happened to you. I made them despise you, it helped you grow strong.'

Memory of the dark that had haunted his dreams came back to Chard. Other memories of all those who had hated him. Shruna, the children, even Greevish. A lifetime ago. Without further pause, he put on the robes.

'And the hood,' said the master.

The robe was deep black, thick yet cold and clammy. The thought of the hood closing in on his face made Chard shiver, yet once more he obeyed. As soon as he flicked it up, pain even worse than the wound L'tusian had inflicted upon him tore through him. He opened his mouth to scream but nothing came out. He wanted to fall to the ground but he couldn't move. Then it was over, the abruptness of it making him stagger to one side.

'Do you like your new look?' asked the master, and he held up a mirror.

Chard peered into the surface and saw a human skeleton looking back at him, the eye sockets lit by a dread red glow. He fell back, away from the image, his hands coming up to cover the mirror. Skeletal hands peeked out from the sleeves of the robe and he knew that this was the fate of his entire body.

'You are one of the four riders,' intoned the master. 'My most important one in fact. A thousand years from now, I shall need your services again.'

'A thousand years?' said Chard incredulously.

'It'll fly by, just you wait and see!' And he thumped Chard on the back.

Chard reached out and slowly lifted the mirror, trying not to shudder as he took in his appearance. 'Today I am become death,' he murmured.

'The destroyer of worlds,' said the Devil.

L'tusian strode the battlefield in an almost blind bloodlust. Magical fire and lightning had killed hundreds of arrogols and dozens on his own side but he cared nothing for them. His white robes were now drenched in blood. Finally he reached Khagen and threw Mors' head at him. 'Take that back to Arrogolia!' he roared. 'Put it in some museum to remind your people what happens to those who come to the west while L'tusian is here to defend it!'

Khagen held the head at arm's length, his face betraying his fear. 'You're letting me live?'

'Go now, this very instant, and take your men with you! Any arrogol who does not leave Eurasia in the next hour will die!'

'My God, we must be twenty days from our border!' shouted Khagen. 'Have mercy!'

L'tusian waved his hand and a gateway the size of a city opened before the arrogol. 'One hour, not a second longer!'

Khagen looked at the elf and saw death. Quickly, he issued orders for the retreat and then rode straight into the gateway. Almost immediately, his retinue followed him and then more and more of the arrogols turned to flee as the news started to filter through the army. Weapons, supplies and the wounded were all abandoned as thousands streamed to the gateway.

The Eurasian forces watched in astonishment as their enemies turned to run and then vanished through the portal. Some continued to shoot arrows, some chased after them, others despatched the injured coldly. As the minutes ticked by, the battlefield began to quieten. When the hour was up, the gateway disappeared, leaving many thousand arrogols stranded. They continued to head east, pursued by western forces all the way.

Even before the final isolated skirmishes had finished, the carrion birds began to settle. Sharp beaks tore at unresisting flesh, the birds gorging themselves on the unexpected bounty. Those wounded and too weak to defend themselves had to endure the scavengers while still alive. For hundreds of yards, the ground had become a carpet of the dead and the dying.

Yussarriel the elf walked up to his friend. Both had managed to survive. 'Thought I'd give chase, see if I can't get me some more,' he said by way of introduction.

Emmissis barely glanced at his comrade. His eyes were locked on the field of the dead. Occasionally a hand would rise as if imploring for help and the moans of the dying were beginning to fade out. In one smooth motion, Emmissis brought his longbow up and then broke it in half across his knee. For a second he regarded the ruined weapon before throwing it down.

'Why the hell did you do that?' asked Yussarriel incredulously. 'That was a family heirloom!'

'You do what you want,' replied Emmissis. 'I'm going home.'

There was no real boundary between the arrogol lands and the western nations that bordered them, an oversight that L'tusian had decided to rectify. Following the arrogols through the portal, the elf watched the ragged stream of men move ever eastwards, back towards their homeland. He struggled with his desire to kill them all but the hour's wait had taken the edge off his fury and now he was once more in control of his emotions.

The battle had been won but at a cost the elf could scarcely comprehend. Just over half the men who had faced the arrogols were dead, countless more were wounded. As for the arrogol losses, the scale was so vast that L'tusian seriously doubted whether they'd ever recover from such a blow. Whatever happened in the east was not his problem – indeed, he hoped his actions would ensure that it would never again be his problem.

The God Sword was a thing of beauty and power. L'tusian

turned it slowly in his hand and marvelled at what he saw and what he felt simply by holding it. The magic it held was beyond his imagination and he was sad to think this would be the last time he would wield it. Pulling back his arm, he drove the blade deep into the ground. He let go and edged backwards but the sword continued to tunnel down.

An ominous rumbling started in the cavernous depths below his feet. A crack started to appear, opening wider and wider, racing both to the north and to the south. The ground was literally tearing itself apart and L'tusian hastily backed away. Amongst the choking dust a new mountain range was being born. A hundred million years of continental plate collision in the space of sixty seconds. The peaks were now already passing a thousand feet and still racing upwards. L'tusian watched for a moment longer before turning his back and walking purposefully westwards. An impenetrable barrier that would keep east and west apart for all time. For those Arrogols still on this side of the mountains, L'tusian did not give a second thought. They would be hunted down.

As the elf moved away, the mountains continued to grow.

EPILOGUE

As he glanced up, the clock ticked over to 20:18. There was the faint hum of air conditioning and the intermediate crackle of the public address system calling one doctor or another to one emergency or another. A strong smell of disinfectant assailed the nostrils with every step. The sombre looking man ignored it all as he made his way through the brightly lit corridors of the hospital towards his goal.

In his arms he carried a new-born infant, little more than an hour old, and he held him with surprising tenderness, while all the time his eyes, hidden behind dark glasses, scanned the various signs posted throughout the hospital.

Any people he met he skirted without breaking stride. Coming to a crossroad he swung a left, which would take him to the maternity suite. The child in his arms was asleep, or at least he had his eyes closed, it was immaterial to the man holding him. Eventually he reached a private room which contained a woman cradling her new son in her arms. The father was caught in traffic and had missed the birth due to its early arrival and speedy delivery. The man in the black suit knew that this would get the father into some trouble when he turned up.

Without a pause he opened the door with his free arm, stepped through and closed it again. The woman was tired and she looked up slowly, expecting to see a doctor or some other hospital employee. But then something very odd happened, she seemed to freeze in position. Her eyes were glazed, her mind blank.

The man placed the baby he held onto the bed. Standing straight, he removed his glasses. Red eyes stared hard at the scene before him. Reaching out he picked up the notes from the end of the woman's bed.

'Marie Monroe, Mrs,' he read aloud. 'Patient of Doctor Louisa Prestin.' It was the right woman, but then he had already known that and was merely being thorough. She was quite pretty in a human kind of way, but such things held little interest for him, he only maintained this appearance out of habit. Had he chosen to, he could have manifested himself in any form he wanted but somehow he seemed to like this one.

Also, despite what it looked like, he was not actually here. He existed in the underworld, a prisoner until the breaking of the Seals. What was stood here was merely a projection of his will.

The baby the woman was holding had a small tag around his wrist and he reached down and unclipped it. He looked at the label which read, 'Date of birth: 20 June 2016. Michael Monroe. Male. Three point four kilograms.' He smiled, an unattractive sight which displayed nothing of any real pleasure. Fastening the band around the baby he had brought with him, he settled the new child into the mother's arms.

The two children were practically identical, he had made certain of that and the half-elf features of the new Michael Monroe were so small as to be virtually unnoticeable. The fact that elves were a genetic offshoot of humanity made this piece of deception all the easier. There was no angling of the eyes, no pointing of the ears, he could pass for human anywhere and anywhen. Besides, no one in this time knew anything of elves.

He picked up the woman's own child and stared impassively at him. Having seen the future he knew that had he not intervened then this particular child would have grown up to study biology at Nottingham University. He would die in the nuclear war of 2036 after volunteering to fight. He would father no children and that would be that.

However, for this child there was no future at all. Placing his hand over the child's heart, he drew the life straight out of him. The child's eyes flickered briefly as his soul left the body he had lived in for less than two hours. The red eyes glowed momentarily as he felt the energy surge into him. The dead baby's body faded away as another piece of magic destroyed all traces of the crime.

The woman knew nothing of any of this, she had not seen him arrive and she would not see him leave. With her husband she would raise this child as their own and die not ever knowing the truth.

'I always keep my promises, Chard,' he whispered softly. 'You shall see your son again. Is it my fault that you shall not recognise him?' For a few seconds more, he pondered the scene before putting on his glasses and retreating out of the door and down the corridor.

He walked slowly and smiled as a man came half running, half walking towards him clutching flowers and a large teddy bear. The man skidded on a piece of wet tile and lost his hold on the presents.

'Damn it!' he said in a startled tone as he managed to stop himself from falling.

'Allow me,' said the stranger pleasantly and picked up the flowers before returning them to the new father.

'Thanks. Thanks a lot.'

'When's it due?' he asked politely.

The man grimaced. 'Already had it, mate. Got caught up and missed the birth. Don't suppose this lot will get me out of the fire,' and he gestured at the gifts sheepishly. He held out his hand as best he could, which was duly shaken. 'Name's Jack Monroe.'

'Pleased to meet you. But you should go to your family; I expect your wife is waiting for you.'

Jack Monroe grinned with boyish enthusiasm before hurrying past and towards the room where his wife was waiting with his child.

'I've got a son!' he yelled back.

The stranger raised his hand and waved. A smile made its way across his face, a genuine smile which a passing nurse returned.

'Good news is it, sir?' she asked politely.

The Devil's grin widened.

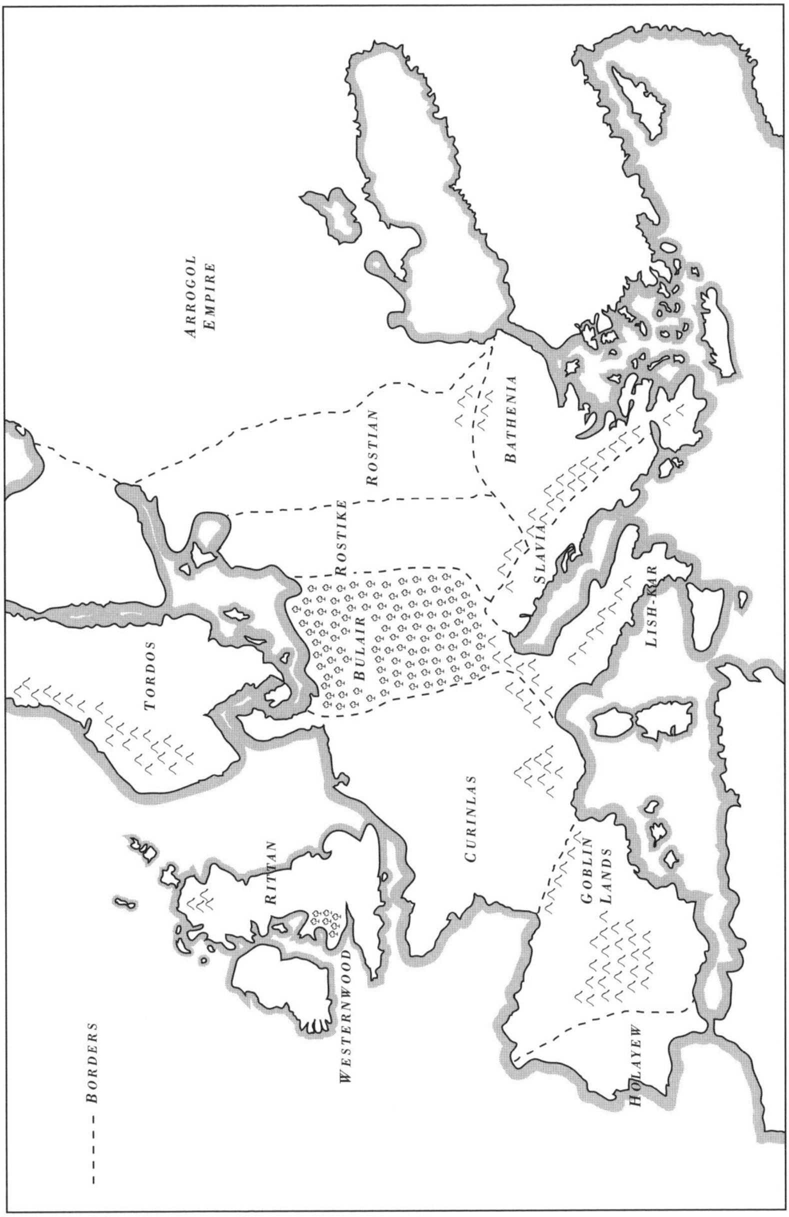
ARROGOL
EMPIRE
ROSTIAN
ROSTIKE
BATHENIA
SLAVIA
BULAIR
TORDOS
LISH-KAR
CURINLAS
RITTAN
WESTERNWOOD
GOBLIN
LANDS
HOLAYEW
BORDERS